# A FEW KISSES AGO

A Novel

By

Alexandra Y. Caluen

A FEW KISSES AGO


Cover design by RK Young

Cover image by Amir Esrafili @amirvisuals *unsplash.com*

This is a work of fiction. Characters, main events, and many of the named businesses, including the Underground Cabaret and its productions, are fictional. Any resemblance to real persons, events, or businesses is strictly coincidental.

# A FEW KISSES AGO

**The Playlist:**

If It Kills Me - Jason Mraz

Crazy for You - Madonna

For Your Love - Ed Townsend

Un Beso - Quintango

Close Your Eyes - Dolores Gray

I Don't Want to Miss a Thing - Aerosmith

La Vie en Rose - Lady Gaga

In Perfect Dreams – k.d. lang

Let's Fall in Love - Diana Krall

Would You? - Scarlett Strallen

At Last - Etta James

*I remember you*
*you're the one who made my dreams come true*
*A few kisses ago.*

- *Victor Schertzinger / Johnny Mercer*

A FEW KISSES AGO

## Chapter 1
December 2017

The every-other-Friday thing had been pretty steady for a long time, but since Sandy's promotion he'd been a lot less reliable. Tasha laughed to herself as she read the text: *I swear I'm about to flip this desk, why am I still running two offices??*

She wrote back *And why are you still there at 6:30 again? All this time I thought your hours were 9-5:30 then you tell me it's 8-5 and you know they owe you a meal break JUST GTFO*

*I keep thinking I'm almost done here*

*I have a table at CPK and they're about to take my order, should I get anything for you?*

*I don't know if I'm going to make it :-(*

*You need fettucine*

*OMG I love fettucine*

*Mmmm fettucine*

*Stop it LOL I'm a hungry man*

*OK I'm going ahead without you but keep me posted*

*Will do oh FML here comes this idiot again*

Tasha was shaking her head when the server got to her table. "Everything all right?"

"Oh, my friend got held up at the office. On my own tonight, I guess." She ordered the fettucine just in case. She had her dinner, storing up snarky observations about the entitled tool at the next table, bitching out his parents because he hadn't gotten into

Loyola, like it was somehow their fault. She could tell Sandy about him later. She'd begun to think she'd better ask for a to-go box when Sandy texted again: *fuck this fucking fucker*

*OMG sweetie what?* She could hardly type, she was laughing so hard. The people at the next table were giving her the side-eye.

*That asshat in SF has been editing a different version of this fucking document and he just now drops it like oh hey I'm in v3 which one are you in I want to punch him in the throat*

Tasha leaned her head on her hand for a moment, giggling helplessly because the thought of Sandy actually punching somebody was so ridiculous. *Sandy stop already it is almost 7:30 and whatever that is the firm will not implode without it*

*I know I know gaaaahh*

*You are a masochist. In fifteen more minutes I'm going to a movie*

Two blocks away and thirty stories up, Sandesh suddenly hit the wall. "This is stupid," he said out loud to the empty office. "No one cares if I do this now." The office did not disagree. He typed *What movie?*

*LOL get over here!*

*Everything on the plate, let them fucking chop me. See you ASAP*

She was actually surprised. He had never given in before. It must have been a really shitty day. *Really long day too*, she thought. When the server came back, looking as if she would seriously like to turn this table, Tasha said unrepentantly, "Sorry, my friend just got free. Since I ate most of this, can I get another order for him? And two glasses of the merlot, please." The server looked slightly irritated, but was pacified by the wine order.

She was checking in with her ex-husband Matthew to make sure he'd picked up their son Theo (he had) and that everything was fine (it was) when the server came back with the new plate of pasta. The wine was already on the table. Tasha looked up and Sandy was there. He said, looking not at the departing server but at Tasha, "Thank you," and leaned down. She thought he was going to kiss her cheek – they'd been doing that for years – but he kissed her mouth. Lightly, quickly, but definitely with feeling. She knew her eyes were wide when he stepped back. He smiled at her, looking a little taken aback himself, and sat down across from her. "You're a lifesaver," he said, and picked up his glass. "Why do I do that?"

She knew he meant stay late, not kiss Tasha. She wasn't ready to think about that quite yet. "Because they keep telling you you're indispensable?"

"Could be. Sorry, I am so starved," and he started eating. Tasha sat and watched, holding her glass, sipping the wine. She had forgotten about her intention of going to a movie. He ate quickly but neatly, as always.

"You look thin," she said after he'd had a chance to put half of the fettucine away. "Are you skipping lunches?"

"Not on purpose." He set down his fork, took a breath, had some more wine. "God that's good. Don't let her take this plate."

Tasha laughed. "It's all yours, baby." He gazed at her then, those dark dreamy eyes serious, studying her face as if he hadn't seen her for years, instead of the four – or was it six? – weeks it had been. She cast about for something to say that wasn't 'why did you kiss me.' "Your hair is looking a little wild."

"It's a wonder I haven't torn it all out. You're going to miss your movie," he said, conscious of a tiny, but growing, sense of possibility because she was still there.

It wasn't what she'd thought he might say, but she went along with it. "I don't care. I've got all weekend." Only after the words left her mouth did she think about the possible implications.

Sandesh thought *all weekend to do what?* His mind was racing. "Matthew has Theo again?"

"Yeah."

"So you don't have to go straight home?"

This was different too. They often ended up hanging out for two or three hours, talking and laughing and bitching about work, but it was always based on 'let's get together for a drink,' and they rarely discussed who had to be where, or when. One or the other of them simply wrapped up the evening at some point. Tasha had always assumed that Sandy went on to some kind of date most of the time; she couldn't imagine that he wasn't cutting a swath through the single ladies of West L.A. There were lots of good-looking men in Los Angeles, but not many were as much fun as he was. "No," Tasha said slowly. "I don't." They stared at each other for a moment without speaking. Then she finished her wine while he finished his fettucine.

Sandesh was thinking *What do I do now*? Because after all these years he'd finally kissed her, almost without meaning to, and all he wanted to do was kiss her again, and again. Well, that wasn't quite all he wanted to do.

And she hadn't slapped his face, hadn't protested, hadn't gotten up and left. She had looked at him like 'oh,' like she'd never thought of that. Hadn't she? Had she really thought the age difference put her (or him) in some kind of box marked 'not for you'? *Have I not made myself plain*, he thought, almost laughing, because of course he hadn't. He'd talked about his brother, a year younger, who'd followed him out here for a tech job, who'd already married, who already had a child. He'd talked about his friends, and their dating disasters. He'd talked about his own dating disasters. He'd never once said 'can I please take you on a date.'

There had been that one moment, on her last day at the firm where they'd met. He was so close to risking it and saying something then, because he was so afraid he'd never see her again. Then she said "I'll email you," and he could breathe, and he thought he'd wait. She was in the middle of her divorce then. He was only twenty-four, and terrified she wouldn't take him seriously, that she would laugh. What if this was the moment? He finished his wine. The server came back as if she'd been monitoring their progress; she probably had. "We're ready for the check," Sandesh said, and when she brought it he took it before Tasha could get it, saying, "Oh no you don't." She laughed, and waited without speaking until the receipt came back, until he signed it (tipping lavishly), and until he looked back up at her again. "Can we go for a walk?"

This was usually the point of the evening when they would go their separate ways, but Tasha nodded. "Sure." The mall was a great place to go for a walk with someone. On a date, or not. She wasn't sure what this was now. There would be shop windows to look in, people to watch, music to listen to. If they wanted another drink, or coffee, or after a while some dessert, they had options. There was even the movie theater. *What am I doing*, she thought. *What are we doing?* Sandy put his hand lightly on her back as they left the restaurant. He'd done that before and she hadn't thought anything of it. Now she felt it all the way to her core. When they were outside and he wasn't touching her anymore, she felt bereft. She was aware of him, his height, his physicality, in a way she never had been before. *Or maybe I was stifling it*, she realized.

They walked without speaking for a few minutes, down the north side of the mall, then turned left. Tasha wasn't thinking much about where they were going; she went where he went, which was up the escalator to the landing overlooking Santa Monica Boulevard. There was no one else around. It was unexpectedly quiet, almost secluded. Sandy stopped at the railing; she stopped beside him. He put his hand on her back again and she looked up at his face, unspeakably handsome in the strange half-light from the building's nighttime fixtures and the streetlights below. "Tasha," he said.

"Sandy?"

She was so beautiful in that moment, it terrified him; but he knew he had to say something, not let the moment pass. There was never going to be a better moment. "Did you know I've been in love with you for nine years?" he said in a rush. Her eyes went wide again, and her lips parted as if she were about to speak. *Don't speak*, he thought, afraid she might be about to say something about how that wasn't what she wanted, never had been, never would be. To prevent that from happening, and because he'd always wanted to, he kissed her.

Tasha didn't pull away. His mouth on hers felt good. It felt right. It told her that what they'd had all this time wasn't just 'co-workers who get along,' it wasn't even 'besties,' it definitely wasn't 'oh this cute kid at the office who charms all the ladies,' though all of those things were true. She closed her eyes and opened her mouth, heard the low sound he made as he deepened the kiss. He tasted like wine. She felt his hand slide across her back as his arm wrapped around her and his other hand came to the side of her face. She leaned into him, feeling her breasts compress against his body as hers flooded with desire. *I've wanted this*, she thought, in a hazy sort of revelation, *this is what I've wanted all along*.

What seemed like forever later, her forehead was pressed to his shoulder and her hands were on his ribs. His hands were on her shoulders, those long fingers cupping her neck as if it were the stem of the Holy Grail. She knew his head was still tipped back, had been since she'd had her mouth on his throat and her hands in his shoulder-length mane of coal-black hair. She'd seen his eyes were closed. They were both breathing fast. "There's this one thing," she said, and heard him swallow. *He's afraid I'm going to say he's too young*. "You have to stop smoking."

He huffed out a laugh, his whole body relaxing. Well, almost his whole body. She pressed even closer and he made that low sound again, wrapping his arms around her, holding her tight. He shivered as if he were imagining something more, and a fresh wave of desire washed through her because she definitely was. She felt rather than heard him say, "Can I take you out to dinner tomorrow?"

Tasha moved her head, pressing her mouth to his throat again, suddenly hungry for him as she hadn't been hungry for a man in years, *decades*, and said, "How about you take me out to breakfast instead." Then her head was in his hands and he was kissing her again, and it was probably a good thing that they both heard the giggles from the four teenagers who came down from the rooftop restaurant and passed them. Sandy's heart was pounding beneath her hand, and she felt light-headed. She took a deep breath. "We'd better get out of here."

His eyes looked sleepy and his face was slightly flushed. He had to clear his throat before he could speak. "Can I walk you to your car?"

*My God, what does he look like when he comes*, Tasha thought, and had to take another deep breath because she really wanted to find out. "Where are you parked?"

"I'm still at my building, it was faster to walk. Are you still at yours?"

"Yeah." They moved slightly apart. She gazed up at him again, thinking, *Why didn't I know*. "Let me give you my address." He looked like he didn't want to make any assumptions. She probably shouldn't either. "Can you come over tonight?" His breath went out and he moved his head sharply, closing his eyes. He breathed in, out, in again, and looked back at her. He wanted to say something but he was afraid his voice would betray him, so he nodded, and got his phone out so he could input the information. Then she said quietly, "Can you stop at a drugstore or should I?" She didn't think she needed to spell out why. Nine years of judgement-free oversharing had surely already covered it.

Sandesh knew what she meant. *Oh my God,* he thought, *is this really going to happen?* "I will." They didn't say anything else. He walked her to her building, kissing her cheek before she went inside, without otherwise touching her because if he had he wouldn't have been able to let go, then jogged up the street to his. It seemed to take forever to get inside, to get down to the parking garage, to get his car out. She lived in the Miracle Mile district, on the opposite side of Century City from him. He'd been over there plenty of times, going to the museums, and knew where to find street parking. He walked to her building with his messenger bag hanging from his shoulder, grateful for this intermission. If it had been possible to take her to bed immediately everything would be over by now, and instead he still had that to look forward to. If she meant what she'd said about breakfast, he might even have the whole night. He kept losing his breath at the thought of it. He punched her number on the security keypad.

"Hello?"

"Tasha. It's Sandesh."

"Come up." The panel buzzed, the front door clicked. He reached for it and went inside, waiting to make sure the door latched behind him. In his own building, it often needed some help. There was a small foyer, with mailboxes to the left and an elevator to the right. He went up, got off at her floor, and walked down to her door. It was standing ajar.

He stepped inside slowly, into an entryway that looked through to a living room. He closed the door behind him and flipped the deadbolt. "Tasha?"

"In the kitchen. I made some coffee." He walked in further. There was a dining area to one side. He set his messenger bag on a chair and turned the other way, toward the kitchen. She was standing there, leaning against the counter, already undressed, wearing a pink chenille robe and fuzzy slippers. He smiled. So did she. "I didn't want to be obvious," she said, "but I wanted to get out of those jeans." The crotch had been wet. She was still wet. She knew they needed to talk but she wanted his hands on her. The lighting in her apartment wasn't as magical as it had been at the mall. He still looked good enough to eat.

"You look comfortable," he said softly. She hadn't taken off her makeup though. She didn't wear much, only eyeliner and mascara. Her dark-brown skin was perfect. He couldn't wait to see, and touch, the rest of it.

"You look tall. I forget you're six feet tall. We don't usually stand this close together. Coffee?" He nodded, so she poured two cups, giving him cream and sugar the way she knew he liked it, adding only cream to hers. "Let's go in the living room for a minute." It wasn't yet ten o'clock, not late. Not bedtime. Sandesh understood that they were taking a few minutes to adjust. Letting the change in their relationship start to sink in. "Take off your shoes and stay awhile," she said, glancing at his face, and he almost laughed.

She curled up at one end of the couch; he sat at the other, angled toward her, legs crossed, watching her. He was glad he'd worn a nice pair of socks, and almost laughed again at the thought. The coffee was good. "How's Theo?" he asked after a minute. "He started school this year, right? First grade?"

"Right. He's getting used to it. He's not a fan of the hours." Sandesh laughed under his breath. "Matthew's happy though, the school is a lot easier for him to get to, and he's not having to help pay for that kindergarten anymore." Tasha watched his face as she said this. An eight-year age difference might be nothing much, but an ex-husband and a child were significant.

"That was a Montessori school, wasn't it? Probably a lot different from a public school."

"Yeah, I think so." *He remembers everything, doesn't he.* For the longest time Tasha had thought Sandy's attention to detail was simply how he was, but now she thought he might have reserved a little more brain space for her. It was a pleasing thought. "What kind of school did you go to?"

"Public," he said, shrugging. "In South Carolina. It was all right. There were other nerds. I had some good teachers." School hadn't been what he hated about South Carolina. It was everything outside of school. "How about you?"

"Public too, here in SoCal." There wasn't much more to say about that. "I was in a foster home for a little under two years, toward the end of high school."

"What happened?"

"My mother wasn't married to my father, we didn't even know who he was. My brother got in trouble. I told you about that before." He nodded. "While he was away, my mom overdosed. So CPS put me in a group home, but there was a family willing to take me because I didn't have any of the obvious problems, and actually they were really great. When Terry got out they let him live with all of us for a while."

"And then you went to community college?"

"Yeah, got a job, went to college, took some dance lessons, made some friends. Landed my first job in an office after I graduated, paid off my little loans. Got a promotion or two. Met Matthew."

They'd talked about her marriage a lot, but never about the *why* of it. "There were a lot of guys at the office who came on to me," she said.

"You're beautiful," he said, because it was obvious. "And you're kind, and smart, and hard-working." Those things weren't as obvious, but he'd seen them right away. He wouldn't have fallen in love with her - or stayed in love with her - if she had been just a pretty face. "Plus you're well-spoken." That was not a minor thing for him.

"I took speech classes in college. I didn't want to end up stuck behind a cash register because I sounded ghetto."

Sandesh nodded; he'd worked hard not to acquire a Southern accent, or to unconsciously mimic his parents' Indian accent. "But back to Matthew." Matthew the white guy, the head of IT. A guy who made good money but didn't flaunt it, a guy with no discernible sense of humor who – he knew, because she'd told him, indiscreet in her distress – had cheated on Tasha while she was pregnant.

"He was so practical," she said. "He didn't really flirt with me, or act how guys act when they just want to get with you. He offered to pick me up a coffee once in a while. Then one day he came up to the reception desk and said, could I take you out to dinner sometime, and that's how it started. He seemed steady. He wanted a baby. I never would have thought he would cheat on me."

"Did he ever tell you why?"

"I never asked," she admitted. "I mean, it didn't really matter, did it? I confronted him with it, he admitted it, he didn't explain. He didn't look like he felt guilty. You know what he's like. I was pretty far along then and I couldn't deal with it. So I didn't deal with it. But it happened again when Theo was about a year old, and that's when I said I wanted a divorce."

"I can't imagine being unfaithful to you. Not if I were married to you."

She smiled a little. "Does that mean you've been unfaithful to me?"

He laughed under his breath. "You know I was. I tried to get over you. I tried and tried. So many dates. That girlfriend. A couple of one-night stands. Nothing worked."

She finished her coffee and set the cup down on the side table. "Are you sure you want to do this?" she asked abruptly. "I've got a lot of baggage."

Sandesh set his empty cup down too. "I've wanted to do this since the day I met you. I never thought I'd get the chance."

"Why did you kiss me tonight?"

"I didn't mean to," he said, smiling a little. "It just happened. You looked up at me and you looked so happy to see me, and I was so happy to see you I went there without even thinking about it."

*I'm glad you did*, she thought but didn't say, standing up. "I'm going to go brush my teeth. There's a powder room behind the kitchen."

"Okay." He watched her go, noting the direction; the master bedroom and bath were on the dining-room side of the living room. He stood up and took the cups into the kitchen, then found the powder room. Theo's room was beside that. Sandesh brushed his own teeth; since he'd been stopping at a drugstore anyway, he'd prepared for that. He hadn't had a cigarette since midafternoon, and was seriously craving one. He applied one of the Nicoderm patches he'd bought. Then he put a couple of condoms in his pocket, and went back through the apartment. Tasha was sitting on the end of the bed. The robe was unbelted now, and her feet were bare. She was wearing a short, silky, pale-pink nightgown.

"Can I see you?" she said. "I want to see you."

"Okay." He took off his shirt. He knew she noticed the patch. He took off his socks, fished the condoms out of his pocket, then shucked off his pants. Undressing for her brought him to full arousal. He handed her the condoms; she took them without looking. He heard her suck in a breath when he peeled off his boxer briefs. He was standing about four feet from her, and wasn't sure what to do next. He waited for a cue.

"Here," she said. He took a step, then another. She set her hands on his hips and leaned forward, pressing her lips to his belly. His whole body reacted. "God, you're gorgeous," she said, and took him in her hand, rubbing her thumb across the tip. He made a muffled, desperate sound. She let go of him and scooted up the bed, setting the condoms on the nightstand, stripping off the robe and throwing it toward a vanity stool in the corner. She pushed the bedcovers back with her feet. He was watching, and when her gaze met his again he moved, getting on the bed and crawling toward her. She took his head between her hands and kissed him, then took one hand away. "Do this," she said, and set a condom in his hand. He ripped open the wrapper and threw it somewhere. She laughed under her breath, still kissing him, her hand on his neck. He rolled on the condom and she slid down beneath him, the nightgown bunching up around her waist. He put his hand on her hip, sliding it between her legs, making a low hungry sound as he discovered her wetness. She gasped, moaned as his fingers dipped in, threw her head back as he slid one inside her. "Jesus, Sandy."

"Now?" he said, bracing himself over her, sliding against her, mouth on her throat. She made a sound that might have been 'yes.' It definitely wasn't 'no' because her hand went to the back of his thigh, pulling. He sank into her slowly, eyes closing for a moment at the glorious heat of her. "Oh *God*," he said. Her leg was hooked over his and she arched up against him with a moan. "Tasha." She came so fast, the pulse of her was so strong he almost couldn't stand it, it almost sent him over, but he fought it. He wanted this to last, needed it to last. His heart was racing and he could hardly see. Her gaze was intent on his face as he worked in her. Then he lowered himself to his elbows, changing his angle, and almost at once her breath hitched. He kissed her mouth, her face, her neck.

Tasha tensed around him, the weight of him a delirious delight, face pressed against his. "Sandy oh God I'm –" and he arched up, holding still deep inside her, for just long enough for her to catch his wave and go with it, coming again with a breathless cry. Then he moved, losing control, crying out against her shoulder as he finished. They lay together for a minute, breathing hard.

He disengaged, got rid of the condom. Lay back down beside her. Looked in her eyes, and said, "I love you." She gazed back at him, realizing that she had never seen him so unguarded. Those soft, dreamy eyes, the long straight lashes … those she had always noticed, almost studied, because they were so beautiful. But he had always, she realized, kept some distance. His friendly professionalism had put her at ease, had kept things light so that she didn't feel pressured. Not that he ever would have pressured her. Now those beautiful eyes were anxious. His mouth, almost always smiling when he'd been looking at her, was serious. She lifted a hand and traced it over the lines of his face, the smooth cheekbones, the long aquiline nose. He needed a shave. He caught her hand and kissed her fingers, glancing at her long oval nails. "You always have such great nail art." They were painted tonight in Hot Wheels blue, with flame decals.

"I did that last night because I knew I would be seeing you. I just now realized, I've been doing that for years. A fresh manicure when we had a date." It suddenly seemed obvious to call it that.

"You have beautiful hands." Smooth, with tapering fingers. "You could be a hand model."

"So could you. I'm so confused," she said. "All this time, I mean basically from the day we met, you've been one of my favorite people in the world. I've enjoyed every minute we've spent together. Including this." He smiled a little then. "Somehow I never thought, what if, you know? When we met I was married. Then I was pregnant. Then I was getting a divorce, and we weren't even working together anymore, but seeing you made me happy. Even when everything else sucked, you made me happy. I was broke, I didn't understand what had happened, I had no time for myself but whenever I managed to see you I was happy."

It wasn't 'I love you' but it was, in its way, 'I care.' Sandesh nodded once. "I was happy too. I knew you didn't have time for me. The fact that you still made time for me gave me hope."

"You did such a good job being my friend."

"Too good a job, maybe. Should I have kissed you long ago?"

She stared at him for a long minute, letting her gaze travel down his body, asking herself if she'd ever imagined what he looked like naked. His skin was lighter than hers, the kind of tawny ivory that tanned easily. She remembered a time he'd come back from vacation, when his skin had been the color of caramel. She had noticed his hands, his wrists, his forearms when he rolled up his sleeves. *How could I not have wondered*, she thought.

He was long and lean where she was not. There was silky black hair on his forearms and shins, at his groin, hardly any elsewhere. She moved her hand again, touching his smooth chest. "I noticed this," she said absently. "When you didn't wear a tie, like today, I could see this." Her fingers moved to the hollow of his throat, then down again. "Your legs are beautiful too. All of you is beautiful."

"I've always thought you're beautiful," he said, his hand flexing on the bedspread as if he wanted to reach for her. She hadn't answered his question. "Will you take that off? So I can see you?"

Tasha sat up, pulled the nightgown over her head, and threw it across the room. If they hadn't already made love, if she hadn't seen and felt how much he wanted her, she would have been self-conscious. She was five foot six, a hundred and sixty pounds on a good day, thirty-seven, a desk worker. She still had an hourglass figure, but it was a full figure. None of her old dance costumes fit anymore. She hadn't danced for years. Suddenly she wanted to again. "Do you like to dance?" she asked.

His eyebrows went up with surprise. "I used to go swing dancing a lot. It was fun. I learned back East. They do it different out here, but it's still fun. Would you like to go?"

"Yes I would. And yes," she said. "You should have kissed me a long time ago." He shifted toward her, wrapping an arm around her, pressing his mouth to her belly. She stayed still, eyes closed, feeling him kiss his way up from belly to breasts to neck. She tipped her head back with a sigh as he moved around behind her, mouth still on her neck, hands full of her breasts. "Did you dream about this?"

"So many times," he said against her skin. "I dreamed of touching you. Tasting you. Kissing you." She turned her head so he could, and he did. Then he moved to sit propped against the headboard, and tugged her with him. She settled back against his chest. "I didn't want to lose what we had. It was so much better than nothing. But I *burned*." Tasha leaned her head back and let her forehead rest against his jaw. She felt him smile. "I should shave. I used to shave before we'd meet."

"So vain."

"I wanted you to see me at my best."

"You got Nicoderm."

"You said I had to stop smoking."

She moved her head again so she could look up at him. "I didn't think you actually would."

"Whatever you ask me to do, I will do," he said, and she could tell he meant it.

"I don't know if I'm ready for that much responsibility." He laughed behind her. She thought she knew why. "It's different with a kid. A kid literally doesn't know what he's doing. You're a grown man, you're smart, you're educated. You know what you're doing."

"Not when it comes to you. All I've been doing, up to tonight, was what seemed to work."

"What you did tonight worked." She sat up and turned around, straddling his legs, and leaned in to kiss him. One hand went to his neck, her thumb brushing along his jaw as her fingers dug into that wild head of hair. She grasped a handful and gently pulled, tipping his head back so she could kiss his neck again, feeling through her lips the vibration of the sound he made. The other hand went down his body, finding him, wrapping around him as he put a hand on her face, bringing her mouth back to his. She was already aroused again; so was he. He murmured something, reaching for the nightstand. He ripped open the condom behind her back, but she didn't let him put it on yet. "Wait."

He closed his eyes, and waited. *It might kill me*, he thought.

"I know," she said as if he'd said that out loud, moving down, "but I can't resist. It's like I knew you were a man, right? But I never thought it through. And now that I see you … ." He lost his breath as she took him in her mouth, briefly, enough for a taste, then moved back up to kiss him again. "Now," she said. He put on the condom. She raised herself up, then sank down slowly, watching his face again. *Everything about him is beautiful*, she thought, hardly moving, just enjoying being full of him for a minute. *How is it possible I never imagined this.* She raked her nails lightly over his thigh and felt him react, saw his eyelids come down halfway. "You want to go hard, don't you," she said. "You want to put me on my back and make me scream, don't you." His breath was shallow, lips parted, eyes hot. She set her hands down behind her and leaned back.

"God!" He couldn't take it. He pushed himself off the headboard and she gasped. He was so deep, he needed to move, but he waited, because he only wanted to give her what she wanted.

"Take it," she said breathlessly. "Do it." She unfolded her legs and wrapped them around his hips as he leaned forward, following her down, lifting her with an arm under her hips to move his legs without disengaging. She was barely sane enough to think *wow he's strong* before he was moving in her, hard and fast the way she wanted it, and before too long she did scream. He had his mouth on hers and drank that scream like it was wine. He made a rough sound a moment later and went still, then almost withdrew, and as she made a sound of protest he plunged deep again. She felt him come, felt the force of it in the way his whole torso contracted, in the cry that he again stifled against her shoulder. *One day I'll make him forget anyone could hear*, she thought, wrapping her arm around his head as his body relaxed. They lay still together for another minute before he slowly, with obvious reluctance, moved away. She turned herself around to get under the covers. "I hate those things," she said when he stretched out beside her again, twining his legs with hers.

"A necessary evil." He kissed the side of her face.

"Only till we get the all clear." He didn't say anything; she couldn't tell what he was thinking. "I haven't been faithful to you either. Is that patch thing working?"

"Something is."

"Sandesh." It was the first time she'd used his real name, instead of the nickname he gave everyone.

"Yes, Tasha."

"Thank you for kissing me tonight." She moved to rest her head on his shoulder, draping an arm across his chest.

He folded his arm over her and kissed her forehead. "Sorry I was late." He felt her smile.

Tasha woke before Sandesh, got quietly out of bed, and put on her robe to go to the bathroom. Then she went to the kitchen to make a fresh pot of coffee. When she returned to the bedroom he was sitting on the side of the bed. She'd heard him go through to the bathroom. His hair was damp, swept back from his face as it usually was when she saw him. "That hair of yours has a mind of its own, doesn't it?" she said. He looked up at her with a trace of a smile. She came close, lifting a hand to touch his face, smoothing the heavy eyebrows and brushing her knuckles over his stubbled jaw. "You're going to be a wolfman when you're older."

He turned his head to kiss her wrist. "Will you mind?" He put a hand on her hip and drew her in to stand between his knees. Being here with her was like the best of all his dreams. In that moment of waking, of realizing where he was, of realizing it hadn't been a dream after all, he'd tipped his head back, staring at the ceiling, willing the tears away.

Tasha stroked both hands through his hair. He leaned forward to rest his head against her midsection. She didn't want to think too far ahead, but all she could say was "No, I won't mind."

## Chapter 2
January 2018

Tasha had a date with her brother Terry and his wife the weekend after New Year's. She had the fullest intention of giving them hell, too, because they'd run off to Las Vegas on New Year's Day and gotten married without her. They'd only been engaged since November, and she'd been talking to Anya about doing a bachelorette party. Then she got that text saying *Sorry Tasha we couldn't wait.* Tasha thought she probably wasn't feeling quite as done-out-of-a-party as Anya's mother, and they'd both get over it, but still: there was some scolding to do.

In the meantime, Matthew had Theo for the weekend, and Tasha was dithering. She hadn't told Terry about Sandesh. That is, she hadn't said anything about the change in their relationship, which was still so new that when she had a child-free weekend all she wanted to do was spend it in bed. Sandesh apparently felt the same way. But at some point, he had to be part of her public life too. He wanted that, and so did she. And of all the people who wouldn't judge, Terry and Anya topped the list. She'd told Sandesh about the date. He hadn't asked if he could come, and at the time she hadn't invited him. She'd been feeling guilty about it ever since. So on the Friday before, during their usual check-in window between three and five p.m., she sent a text: *Hey baby, I've got that thing tomorrow with Terry and Anya. Are you free? Would you like to come with?*

As usual, it took some time to get a reply. He was always busy. But her phone buzzed at a quarter to five: *I'd love to go with you. Anywhere, anytime*

*Great. I know they'll love you. It's at three, what time do you want to get together?*

*6:30 today :-)*

*LOL okay how you want to work the cars?* Tasha's neighborhood had some safe overnight parking, but there was a lot of competition for it. Sandesh's neighborhood was even worse, and neither building had any guest parking.

*Gaaahh stupid cars if I take mine home could you pick me up?*

Tasha thought that probably made the most sense. He didn't live that far away, and Matthew was in the same direction. It would be simple to go get Theo after dropping Sandesh off again on Sunday. *Good call, works all around. I'll be over there as close to 6:30 as possible. Don't let them keep you late*

*Not a chance. XOX*

*XOX.* That was how they usually signed off. He didn't often tell her he loved her. She knew it hurt him to say it and not hear it back. She still wasn't used to the whole thing, still wasn't sure she was ready to say that, though in moments of irritation with herself she wondered why. *Well it's barely been a month*, she thought, but even that was dodging. She'd known him for nine years, after all. The only thing that had changed was … *oh stop kidding yourself.* Sex changed everything. And with that, she decided to give her brother a heads-up. As soon as she shut down her workstation, she picked up her phone again to call him. He was undoubtedly already at the club where he worked, but he always picked up her calls.

"Hey Tasha, what's up?"

"I'll make it quick. No emergency, no change of plans, except I'm bringing someone with me tomorrow."

"Oh yeah? Anybody I know? Theo's with his dad this weekend, right?"

"Right. Not Theo. Sandesh." She waited to see if he would make the connection.

"Sandesh," Terry said slowly. "You mean Sandy? Your drinking buddy?"

"He's not just a drinking buddy anymore."

"Well now that's very interesting." She could hear a smile in his voice. "I've got a minute, if you want to fill me in."

"We got together last month as usual, but things changed. Turns out he's been in love with me all this time." Tasha tried to make that sound light. But this was her brother, who'd only recently found the love of his own life. "And it turns out I was happy to hear that."

"You in love with him too?"

"I think probably I am. Still getting used to it. He's eight years younger than me, remember."

Terry made a dismissive noise. "Has he met Theo yet?"

"I'm going to see if he wants to next weekend. If we'd just met I wouldn't, but I've known him so long. He's known me since before Theo even existed."

"Well, thanks for the news, it seems like this is good news. I'll look forward to meeting him."

"Okay. Go sling some drinks. I love you."

"Love you too, baby." Terry disconnected, dropped his phone in his blazer pocket, and turned his attention back to his job. He wasn't slinging drinks tonight. A new bartender was on duty downstairs, and Terry was running the joint. He didn't have a new title yet, but 'manager' still fit him fine. His boss Tyrone wasn't quite ready to drop the reins entirely. It would be a few months until they knew for sure that the plan they were developing would really work for both of them. Terry surveyed the room. That night they had a blues band. He thought he'd have to ask this Sandesh if he'd ever been to Chrome.

Sandesh wrapped up his day's work and went back to the weekly task list, which was not exactly getting more manageable. The San Francisco office couldn't seem to keep a secretary. Possibly because everyone they got in looked at all the administrative shit they'd have to do, and bailed. The office still didn't have a receptionist, a records clerk, or its own coordinator, a person to oversee all the support functions and make sure the legal staff had its needs met. In practice, that meant covering all deficits. Document production, filings, records, facilities, meetings, messengers. Making sure the billable hours were recorded. Making sure the local attorneys' expenses got reimbursed. Making sure the work got out. Making sure all the equipment was functional and all the supplies were stocked. Sandesh was doing all that from Los Angeles, and he was getting tired of it. It was a huge job and the raise they'd promised him was definitely not going to be enough. If it ever actually came through.

Sometimes he thought they weren't filling the San Francisco job because he made it so easy for them to do without. He was constitutionally incapable of deliberately dropping any of the ten thousand plates he had spinning at any given time, and he wasn't an ultimatum kind of guy, but it had been six months. He was committed to going to San Francisco again next week, he was supposedly interviewing a candidate for that job, and if this one was as useless as the last one he didn't know what to tell his own boss. *Maybe, quit jerking me around*, he thought, irritated all over again at the latest passive-aggressive bullshit from management. He'd been promised the promotion for over a year before it came through, and still no raise. It was always another meeting. One more trip to NorCal, one more interview for the never-filled counterpart position there. The job wasn't really technical. It didn't require the degree they were asking for, or the years of experience. It was mostly common sense, and the willingness to show up on time every day, make decisions based on the available information, and then execute. Sandesh couldn't believe that those qualities were as rare as you'd think, judging by the candidates that came in. If by some miracle this candidate wasn't a complete flake, then he'd have to on-board that person, coordinating everything with IT and HR and facilities and the trainer - who was, of course, himself. As if he didn't have enough to do.

He ran down the task list again, deciding that ninety percent of it was pointless. Five percent was important but time-sensitive, and it was already too late for him to do anything about that stuff because the people who'd really needed to act on it hadn't. The other five percent was still within an actionable period, had some value, but not enough to be worth staying late. It was all stuff that would pop right back onto the list next week. He dumped it, and started shutting down.

"Hey Sandy." It was the last voice he wanted to hear, that of the HR assistant.

He didn't usually brush people off, even people he couldn't stand, but he was completely out of patience. "Hi Jessica. I'm on my way out, what can I do for you in two minutes or less?"

"I heard you're doing a prelim interview for us up in San Francisco next week. Thought I should check in about that." But she didn't actually ask any questions or give him any information.

Sandesh stood up, making an impatient movement with his hands, raising his eyebrows, trying to convey 'spit it out moron' without actually saying that. "What do you need from me?" he said after a moment, when she didn't add anything useful.

"Oh nothing. You've got the resume, right?"

"Yes, thanks. I've got the resume, and the job description, and I know what not to ask." It was an effort to keep his voice pleasant. "I really need to get going, was there anything else?"

"Oh no. I just wanted to stop by. I haven't seen you for a while." She was looking at him kind of sideways, but not like she was questioning the wisdom of talking to him. More like she was hoping he would think she was being cute. *Oh fuck me*, Sandesh thought tiredly. He was so over this whole thing. It'd been a while since she came around with this body language, this whole flirty thing. She'd been with the firm for over a year but it seemed she hadn't gotten the memo that Sandesh was nice to everybody and didn't date inside the firm.

"Come by earlier sometime, we can go down for coffee. I'm sorry, I'm meeting my girlfriend, I have to go. See you around, though, okay?" *There*, he thought, *will that do it?* Not rude, not dismissive, not interested. He switched off his monitors, picked up his messenger bag, and moved toward the door. She didn't budge. "Jessica, I'm sorry, I really do need to go." She was looking at him as if he'd left her at the altar. *Fuck me*, he thought again, a little alarmed. "Can I go?" They were, on the org chart at least, not in the same chain of command. She wasn't his boss, he didn't report to her, she didn't have any claim to his time. She was just … not moving.

Then one of the attorneys came down the hall and glanced in. He must have caught the weird vibe. Or he might have correctly interpreted Sandesh's eye contact, detecting his mental 'mayday.' "Hey Sandesh, heading out? Me too. Hi Jessica. Don't waste your Friday night on this place."

She turned around then and registered the young partner behind her, transferring ninety percent of that inappropriate body language to him. "Hi James. Yeah, I'm heading out too. Have a good weekend."

"Yeah, you too." James stood there and watched as she went down the hall with a coy backward glance. Then he stepped a little closer and said in a low voice, "Was something weird going on there?"

Sandesh let out a breath he hadn't realized he was holding. "Definitely." He sat on the corner of his desk. "She came in supposedly to see if I had what I needed for an interview next week in San Francisco, then she, like, didn't leave. I told her I was meeting my girlfriend and the vibe got kind of 'Fatal Attraction' for a minute there."

"That's what I thought. Write it up for me, would you? Send me a text later. I'll pass the word. She got weird with me once too." James pulled a card case out of his pocket and removed a business card, handing it to Sandesh. "The cell number's on there. You ready to go?"

"And how. Thanks." They walked out together and got on an elevator. "Is it legal for me to put a camera in my office? That actually wasn't the first time this has happened."

James studied him for a few seconds. They were about the same height; Sandesh was a few years younger. They looked nothing alike, aside from both being tall and dark. *And not horrible-looking*, James thought, flashing back for a second to something a friend had once said, the friend who was gone forever. "I wonder if any of the other guys in the firm have gotten this. Yeah, it's legal. I'll clear it for you with the brass, though, make sure they know why you're doing it. They're going to want it documented."

"Yeah, I get it. Thanks again." They'd reached the main elevator lobby. Sandesh had an idea that James often walked over from his condo. This seemed to be the case, because he got out with a wave. Sandesh rode down to his parking level alone, and very thoughtful.

He didn't mention it to Tasha that night, but it came up the following day at Terry and Anya's house, as part of a conversation about workplace romances. Sandesh had told the whole story of how he'd carried the torch for Tasha, keeping it as light as possible because he didn't want to make anyone uncomfortable. She was holding his hand, so there was that. Then he asked how Terry and Anya had met, even though Tasha had told him, because he knew people usually liked to talk about their love stories. That somehow segued into things that went sideways, and he said almost without thinking, "Yeah, there's this weird girl at our office right now. I mean, not a girl, she's at least my age, but I've gotten a really wrong vibe from her a couple of times. Yesterday I was on my way out and she was literally blocking my exit, standing in the door of my office. I was like, dude, I can't push you out of the way, what the fuck."

Tasha was frowning a little. "What happened?"

"This guy came by, James, one of the younger partners. Said something innocuous to her, she left, then he comes in and says was that weird, because that seemed weird. I said yeah, he said she did it to him once too, or something like it. Then I asked if it was legal to put a camera in my office, because this was the second time she'd done something like that and frankly I don't want to end up getting sued over something that never happened and then it turns into he said, she said, ugh." He shook his head. Tasha was still frowning.

"James Levine, right?" Anya said. "He works where you work. We know him. What did he say?"

"He told me yeah it's legal, but to write it up, he'd start a ball rolling. I get the idea he's going to do a little asking around, find out if it's happened to anyone else. We don't look much alike but we're both about six feet, both have dark hair, maybe that's her type? Anyway, there's half a dozen other guys in the office who fit the description." He shrugged. "I'll check in with him in a week or so if I haven't heard anything about setting up a camera. And in the meantime I might go work in a conference room after four."

Terry nodded. "Not a bad idea. Just don't be where she expects you to be."

"Yeah. But anyway. Tasha mentioned she'd like to go out dancing sometime. Any recommendations for us?"

"Well yeah," said Anya. "Socials at Shall We Dance, over in WeHo. I'm teaching there now. What's your style?"

"I used to swing dance a lot, I think Tasha knows more than I do." Sandesh looked at her and smiled. "About basically everything."

"Not everything," Tasha said, shaking her head. "But possibly about dancing. Anyway, it's high time I got back in shape, right? Tell us about what's going on at the studio. I still have this child-care issue to work around."

"Good news for you there. We've got kids all over the place now," said Anya. "So Dmitri and Patrick got hold of this shoebox next door and they're turning it into a private-lessons space plus a room to stash rug rats." Tasha laughed. "It's going to be the only studio on the west side that has a safe place for kids to hang out. Dmitri, that's the boss, he's going to use the office in the main space and put Elena next door since one of the rug rats is hers. She's the studio manager. They're planning to have it open by March."

Tasha thought that was a great idea. "Well definitely keep me posted about that, because that would make all the difference. We probably couldn't manage a series without that. But maybe a social here and there."

"I'll bet we can manage a private lesson here and there, too," said Sandesh. "Get me back up to speed."

After that, because Tasha could tell Anya was ready to move on (conversationally speaking), she asked about non-dancing plans for 2018, which gave her an opportunity to give Anya some crap about dodging the bachelorette party, which made Terry laugh. Sandesh watched and listened, contributing occasionally, getting to know his hosts by observation. Their greyhound Lola was lounging on a loveseat under the window. Over the fireplace was a big picture, ornately framed. He couldn't tell if it was a painting or a photograph. While Tasha was telling a story about Theo, Sandesh stood up and went over to the picture.

"Oh," he said softly when he got close. It was a photograph after all, printed on canvas, of Anya and the greyhound in a glamorous Art Deco room, all gold and shadows. Anya was wearing a 1920s-style formal gown with a real-looking fur draped over her elbows; the dog wore a jeweled collar. The print was signed with silver Sharpie, but he couldn't make it out. He turned around to see Anya watching him. "This is gorgeous."

"Thanks. This TV star we know took that."

Sandesh couldn't tell if she was serious; his eyebrows went up and he glanced over at Terry, who was making a 'true story' face. "What TV star?"

"His name's Andy Martin. He's been doing the posters and shit for the Underground Cabaret for years and he did promo photos for the big show last summer. Then I wanted to get a present for Terry and one of the Cabaret people hooked me up."

"It looks like a movie still. Where did you get that dress?"

"A friend of ours made it when I told her the kind of picture I wanted. Andy got us in to do the shoot at Cicada." Anya shrugged; these things were easier for TV stars.

"I thought it looked familiar! I've only been there once, but … hey, Tasha." She looked over at him inquiringly. "They still do those dance nights at Cicada, right? Maybe after we do a lesson or two and make sure I know what I'm doing, I could take you." She smiled at him. Terry looked like he approved, too.

"So tell me about your boy toy," Anya said on the phone thirteen days later.

Tasha bit her lip and tried not to laugh out loud. "I'm at the office, Anya."

"So?"

Tasha snorted. "I'm out of here in twenty minutes. What are you doing aside from trying to get me fired?"

"They're not going to fire you for answering your fucking phone after four-thirty on a fucking Friday. I am avoiding Hirohito, who is trying to steal me away from Ricky. I'm literally out in my car with the seat reclined so he can't spot me through the studio's back door."

"Well you did say Ricky was kind of busy."

"Yes, he's busy, he's getting married any minute now and he just found his long-lost sister, he's got the attention span of a toddler on crack and oh *fuck* me he's standing by the goddamned car."

Tasha was cracking up as quietly as she could. She knew the last 'he' meant Hiro Miyazaki - Anya's colleague at Shall We Dance – not Ricky Castillo, her longtime salsa partner. The office's main line wasn't ringing and there was nobody near the reception area. She hoped that state of affairs would continue. "Anya, start the car. Get out of there. Meet me at Rock Sugar." She heard a man's voice, muffled; heard the sound of a car seat being adjusted; heard an engine start; heard Anya say 'fuck *off*.' Tasha was still laughing.

"God that was close," Anya said. There was so much background noise she must have put the phone on speaker. “Okay. Rock Sugar. Where *is* the boy toy tonight?”

“He’s doing a thing with his brother. We’re getting together tomorrow.”

“Awesome. I will get you drunk.” The call ended. Tasha promptly sent a text to Sandesh: *Hi baby I’m meeting Anya over at Rock Sugar. Probably won’t be looking at my phone much because she is in a MOOD. Won’t be out late though*

His reply came back surprisingly fast: *Oh yes you will. Uber if she gets you drunk*

*I promise XOX*

*XOX see you tomorrow.* Tasha put her phone to sleep. A few more minutes and then she could get out of here. The quiet Friday afternoon continued to be quiet, and she was over at Rock Sugar ten minutes after quitting time. Anya was already there, sitting on one of the outdoor loveseats and wearing an expression that said ‘any man who comes near me will be killed and eaten.’ “You drive like a maniac,” Tasha said as she sat down.

“It’s three miles. Terry says hi.” They exchanged kisses on the cheek.

“He’s working tonight?” Anya nodded. “So tell me about Hiro and his schemes. Is he trying to get you to do the next Cabaret show?” Another nod, with hunched shoulders. “Why don’t you want to do it? Ricky’s not around for that one, is he?”

“I’ve already told him to fuck off about a dozen times. Hiro, not Ricky. I don’t want Ricky to feel like I’m already scouting a replacement. He’s getting married in March, therefore he is not my partner for the Cabaret in March, but it does not follow that he is not my partner. I can take a fucking month off from performance, my business isn't going to dry up. Anyway, Hiro's mostly after me for June. And he's up my ass continuously about my students."

"What's the problem with your students?"

"There *is* no fucking problem with my students. They're happy, nobody gropes me, we're all going to the Emerald Ball. Hiro's trying to give me *more* students."

"Which would make it a little tough for you to do stuff with Ricky."

"Exactly. Ricky won't always be twitterpated."

"Bless his heart. I know you'd rather do performances than all this pro-am ballroom stuff."

"I don't mind the ballroom stuff," Anya said. Then a server arrived. They'd both been there so many times they could give their order without even referring to the menu. "Okay. Now that drinks are on the way. I really don't mind the ballroom stuff, and I actually like Hiro a lot though I will never admit it to his face. But frankly if I'm going to do Cabaret stuff I want to do it with Ricky. We have a good thing. If and when he says he's done, then maybe Miyazaki gets a chance at me. There are all the regular Cabaret things and the pro show. If Ricky doesn't want to do the pro show, and Hiro does, then maybe that."

"Is it set yet?"

"They're doing a first-look later this month. Anyway. Plans for Valentine's Day?"

"Not plans *per se.* I'm feeling slightly awkward about it."

"Why? Problem?"

Tasha could always trust Anya to cut right to the heart of things. "I don't know if this is a problem. The thing is, he loves me. He says he loves me. I know he loves me."

"You don't love him?"

"I don't feel ready to say it yet. I'm still having these little freakout moments." Tasha was hoping Anya would understand. Terry'd been in the same place as Sandesh once, in love with Anya, hoping someday they would both say so. Except Terry and Anya had already been sleeping together. He didn't have to wait years to make that connection. "When did you know?"

Anya might have wished she already had her drink. She had her stoniest stone face on, but she answered. "I still freak out about it sometimes. I didn't expect it, I wasn't looking for it, I hardly even recognized it. It wasn't until I saw that fucking cop standing behind him that I thought, Jesus Christ, don't you fucking *dare* take him from me. And then he said it first and I was like, Goddammit, I guess that's what this is."

Tasha patted her arm. "That was some scary shit. I'll bet that cop still has nightmares."

"I hope he does, the stupid motherfucker."

"Okay, well. That was a very indirect way to get to, I expect Sandesh to do something sweet, and I will try to also do something sweet, and I'm hoping he'll continue to be patient while I figure my shit out."

Anya gave her a withering look. "I don't think that guy has much to prove about patience, do you?"

"No, not really." Then the drinks arrived, and somehow they ended up talking about that bachelorette party Tasha never got to throw for Anya. When Tasha finally went back to her car her throat was sore from laughing. She sent Sandesh another text: *Baby I hope you had as much fun tonight as I did. I'm exhausted. Not even slightly drunk. Tell you all about it tomorrow XOX.* And she did tell him almost all about it.

March 2018

The next time they saw Terry and Anya, there was more dancing news. "I saw you at the studio," Anya said. "You do not suck." She addressed that to Sandesh, who cracked up.

"No, he doesn't," said Tasha, smiling.

"Did you know Vince is doing a swing workshop next month? Two hours, a Sunday afternoon." Anya dug out her phone. "What did he post about that. There was a thing." She pulled up the studio's calendar, clicked on the link, and read it. "Oh yeah. They're going to be taping the whole workshop and doing preliminary registration for a casting call. This movie that's happening this summer. Which is not swing dancing," she added, looking at Tasha. "It's Argentine tango."

"Ooohh I always wanted to learn that." Tasha looked at Sandesh. He could tell she was thinking that summer was a long time away, and would they still be together.

*How can you doubt me.* "The workshop sounds great," he said, "and I'd like to learn tango too."

"Since when?" said Anya skeptically. She hadn't missed that exchange. Terry was laughing under his breath, so he probably hadn't either.

Sandesh didn't answer, though he gave her an amused glance. Instead he said, "Are you doing this movie thing?"

"Probably." Anya shrugged. "Have to make sure my partner wants to. It's not, like, the whole movie. From what Vince said, it's a few big dance scenes like flash mobs, and some smaller combos. But they're going to need a lot of bodies for these group things."

Tasha asked, "Is it choreography, or improv?"

"Not sure yet. I only know what Vince and Dmitri told me, and they only know what Andy told them. That's Andy Martin the TV star, the photography guy," she added, again directing it to Sandesh. "He and his husband are definitely in on this movie."

"Oh my. Victor's in it?" Tasha turned to Sandesh. "Victor Garcia was one of the stars of that play I did back in twenty twelve. He and Andy are on 'L.A. Vice.'" She turned back to Anya. "Is it the same director as the play?"

"No idea. Anyway, keep your eye on the schedule, but if you want in to this workshop I'll tell Vince to put you on the list now, because it's going to fill up pretty fast."

"Yes please," said Sandesh. "Should I watch that TV show?"

Anya glanced at Terry, who looked as though he wanted to laugh. Then she glanced at Tasha, who actually was laughing. Finally she looked back at Sandesh. "There is a reason for women to watch that show, and that reason is called Victor Garcia. I don't know why the fuck else anybody would watch it." Terry was fully laughing now.

"Oh, but Andy," Tasha protested. "Their story is so sweet. And he's fun to look at too."

"Yes, okay. However." Anya had the narrow-eyed look that said she was trying really hard not to laugh. "The man himself told me 'I hate that fucking show,' and when I asked him why he said 'don't get me started' and then proceeded to rant about this Scarface fantasy he had. I laughed till I fucking cried and then I had to fix my makeup and we almost got thrown out of Cicada before we even finished the fucking photo shoot. So when I see him on that show, I think of that and not about how cute he is with Victor."

Sandesh had been watching Tasha laugh through that entire speech. *God, I love you.* "I really think I should watch it now," he said. "You wouldn't mind helping me get caught up, would you?"

"It won't take long," she said, sobering up. "We can skip through everything that isn't Andy and Victor."

"Life is too short to watch the whole thing," said Terry. "Do like she says."

Valentine's Day hadn't been weird. They were definitely dating, after all, so when Sandesh sent a dozen red roses to her at the office, Tasha thought *oh how nice*. She sent him a text that said *Every woman in the office is green with envy. Thanks honey.* She sent him a card – sent it to his office - on the funny-and-suggestive end of the spectrum. He sent back a text that said *Thanks for sending me something I can keep in my office*. The note that came with the flowers was a hand-drawn heart with XOX underneath. She'd signed her card the same way.

She thought it might invite complications, though, going with Sandesh to a wedding. She did know how he felt about her, after all. But he'd been right there when Terry mentioned it. They were sitting at the bar at Chrome after the Underground Cabaret's February show, which they'd come to see because Anya and Ricky were doing a number in it. Terry was busy for a few minutes at the other end of the bar, but he was getting their drink order when the dancers came out from backstage. "Hey Ricky," Terry said, "looking forward to your party next month. He's getting married," he added, turning to Sandesh. "To Luis."

Tasha said, "Sandesh hasn't met Luis yet."

"You should come," Ricky said, leaning in to kiss her cheek. "Bring Theo. My sister will be there with her family." He glanced sideways at Sandesh and raised his eyebrows a little, then collected his shot of tequila from Terry. "Gracias amigo."

Terry was looking at Tasha as if he also thought she should say a little something to Sandesh, but she didn't. Even though it had been fairly clear that Ricky's 'you should come' was intended to include him. *What is wrong with me*, Tasha thought.

Two weeks before the wedding date, she knew she had to say something. He'd come over on a Sunday morning to take her and Theo to the Natural History Museum. He hadn't mentioned the wedding, like he hadn't mentioned that first dinner with Terry and Anya. Tasha didn't know whether to be grateful for the fact that he never pushed, or annoyed by it. Sometimes she didn't want to have to *offer*. They were halfway to downtown when Sandesh said, "So are you going to Ricky's wedding?"

"Yeah, planning to." *Don't be a bitch*, she thought, and added, "You want to come?"

"Do you want me to come?" That was unexpected. She didn't answer right away. He checked the rear-view mirror to confirm that Theo was engrossed in a handheld game, and spoke very quietly. "I always want to be with you. Take that as a given. But I don't want you to feel like, you know, you have to take me everywhere. Especially to a wedding."

"I don't think they're throwing a bouquet," she said after a moment. "Nobody's going to put us on the spot." She turned to look at him; he had his eyes on the road. "I only didn't ask you before because sometimes when a girl asks a guy to be her date at a wedding, he thinks that means she wants him to, you know. I keep forgetting how good you are at not making assumptions."

He was good at that. He was also good at drawing conclusions, one of which was that however Tasha felt about him, she wasn't ready for a proposal or anything like it. *Good to know*, Sandesh thought. "I'd enjoy it, if you'd enjoy having me with you. I haven't been to a wedding for a long time. But if it would make you uncomfortable, then don't worry about it."

"I enjoy everything more when you're with me," she said. "I always have. That's the whole reason we're here." She patted his thigh. "I would like to have you with me. I know Theo would too."

He glanced at her quickly, smiling. "Shoot me the address and let me know what time to pick you up." Then, because he'd detected a slight whiff of fatigue, he said, "I'd like to come over next weekend, too, if you're not tired of me yet."

She huffed out a laugh, shaking her head. Matthew would have Theo the following weekend. She'd asked Sandesh over every single child-free weekend since that first night in December. This was the first time he'd asked. "I like it when you ask," she confessed, all at once understanding why she'd felt resistant. "It makes me feel like I have the power. Sick, right?"

"Oh," he said, sounding surprised. "I never thought of that. Okay, brace yourself." She laughed out loud.

At the reception, after the wedding, she looked around and wondered why she'd ever hesitated. They'd all walked down the street from the little neighborhood church to the modest stucco house where Luis' parents lived. Everyone gathered in the backyard, for drinks served out of a cooler and tacos assembled on a folding table. Music was playing, everyone was talking in English and Spanish, and Theo was stalking the family's chickens. Tasha watched Sandesh from across the yard, so easy with everybody, clearly with her yet not possessive, not overbearing. There to make her day better, the way he always did.

It was second nature to her now to keep half an eye on her child, but she realized that Sandesh was doing the same thing. When Theo actually cornered a chicken, Sandesh was right there to make a suggestion. Tasha had little doubt that whatever he said resulted in a much more positive chicken-child interaction than might otherwise have been the case. Once he'd touched the bird, Theo lost interest, and went to find another of the kids. Even though Theo didn't speak Spanish they were all getting along fine. Sandesh looked up, caught Tasha's eye, and came over to her. "Where'd you learn to be a chicken whisperer?" she said.

"Our neighbors had some, when I was growing up. They've got a lot of personality, when you give them a chance. Theo hasn't been around animals much, has he?"

"None to speak of. Adding a pet to the mix seemed like a little more than I could handle. Maybe now that he's old enough to take some responsibility, we could think about getting one. A little one," she added, which made him laugh.

"A hamster maybe," he said. "Does your building allow pets?"

"I don't remember. It probably says something in the lease but it's a long time since I looked at it."

"My building allows cats and small dogs, but there's a pet deposit, and I don't know why they call it a deposit because I'm pretty sure they've never returned it. Every time somebody leaves who has a pet, they're always bitching about not getting their deposit back."

"Maybe the pets always ruined something," she pointed out. "You talk to your neighbors, huh. I hardly know any of mine."

"Well, you have someone to talk to at home," he said. He was smiling, but it struck her suddenly, what it meant to live alone. And she couldn't help thinking *he's been alone because of me.* She knew he hadn't meant anything in the way of blame. They'd talked enough over the years. She'd heard about all those dates, the girlfriend, everything. Until December, she assumed there were more women that she never heard of, but he said no, and she believed him. In a way, the fact that he'd been with other women made his emotional fidelity even more astounding. Tasha didn't feel that she was all that special. It amazed her that someone like Sandesh – not that there was anyone else like Sandesh – found her uniquely desirable.

His hand was on her shoulder, his thumb caressing her neck. He didn't seem to realize it. She looked up and said, "You ready to go home?" His gaze met hers, then went to her mouth, and he bent to kiss her. "That was very G rated," she said when he straightened up again. He laughed. "Let's go home and get Theo squared away, maybe you can do better." They collected the child, congratulated the newlyweds again, said their goodbyes, and headed out. All the way home Tasha was telling herself, *you need to tell him how you feel.*

A few weeks later, they went to the swing workshop at Shall We Dance and had a blast. "You're really good," Tasha told Sandesh at the halfway point, when the whole class took a break. "How much did you actually dance since moving out here? And why didn't I ever hear about this before?"

"A lot," he admitted. "And I don't know why I never mentioned it." But he did. It was in the category of things he would have liked to ask Tasha to do, and was afraid to. Just as he had never invited her to dinner (or rather, suggested meeting her for dinner) anywhere that wasn't work-adjacent. "There were plenty of weekends when I wasn't doing anything else, but staying at home was so depressing. It was good to have a thing to do that wasn't a straight-up date. I found a couple places, got on their mailing lists. So, can I take you out dancing once in a while?"

"Definitely." *Why is it so much easier to be asked*, she thought. "Thanks for asking. You know I'm usually going to say yes."

He smiled, leaning over to kiss her. "Okay. First, Cicada. Let's start on a high note. Any prior commitments I need to work around?"

"Nope. If the best night is when I have Theo, I can get a sitter." The instructor was waving everybody back out on the floor. "Ready for round two?"

"Oh yeah. Swing me, baby." Sandesh put his arm around her waist and they joined the rest of the class.

## Chapter 3
April 2018

"You look amazing," Sandesh told Tasha when he picked her up for their date at Cicada. "You look like Josephine Baker only prettier." She laughed. She was wearing a 1920s-style flapper dress with appropriately vintage-styled shoes, and had her hair done in a bob. It would bounce right out of it as soon as it got wet, but for tonight it was perfect.

Sandesh was glad he'd gone out and gotten a dance suit at Matsumoto Dancewear, charcoal gray with a pinstripe. Their instructor Vince had suggested it, at the end of the swing workshop when they both signed up for the Argentine tango boot camp. He had also gotten his hair cut at an actual salon, instead of letting his brother's wife cut it for him again, and was wearing his grandfather's ring.

Tasha looked him over with appreciation. He'd generally dressed well at the office, but the combination of the suit and the haircut was impressive. "You're pretty swanky yourself. The haircut's really different." He looked almost austere.

"I look older, huh?"

"Yeah, you do. You look like a bad guy in a James Bond movie, actually." He laughed. "Did you keep it long so you'd look more approachable?"

"Nothing that calculated. It grows so fast that to keep it this length I'd spend all my time getting it cut. Not a bad problem to have."

She was still admiring his profile. "Yeah, a lot of guys would kill for that problem. But as someone who would rather do about a hundred other things than go to the hairdresser, I get you."

"You went this week though."

"Well, I wanted to look right. I'm really excited about tonight, by the way. I tried to be all cool about it while I was getting ready, but it's been a long time since I had a date like this."

"If it's fun, we can do it again." He glanced at her, then looked back at the road. They were going straight down Wilshire. "I used to come this way when we worked downtown."

"I was coming from the Valley then. Lord, life is better on the west side." He laughed. Tasha was grinning. "Not to be a snob, but it's so much hotter and smoggier over there." She touched his right hand. "That's pretty fabulous."

"It was my grandfather's. It's not too much?" The ring had a wide, smooth gold band supporting a square bezel set with a flat, carved green stone.

"It should be but it's not. If you had stumpy little fingers it would be too much." Sandesh laughed again. Tasha touched the ring. "You have such beautiful hands. Is that an emerald?"

"Yeah. For the longest time we thought it was something else. Then when Dad gave it to me, I had it appraised, and they were like, uh, you know what you have here, right? I had to get a rider on my insurance policy." He glanced over at her again. "You told me you were wearing green. Did you know there's a whole thing about gemstones having spiritual properties?"

"Like chakra-balancing stuff?"

"Yeah."

"What's emerald good for?"

After a moment, he said, "It supposedly promotes healing. Balance. Unconditional love."

"Those are all good things," Tasha said. She knew he hadn't brought that up to prompt some kind of declaration. That wasn't the way he operated. *I should be wearing the damn thing.* She had still not said 'I love you' and was still irritated with herself about it. Her hesitation made no sense at all. Sandesh wasn't just the best lover she'd ever had, he was the best friend she'd ever had. Theo loved him. Terry's dog Lola loved him. Everybody who'd ever met him, as far as she knew, loved him. *Including me*, she admitted. *Say it.* But she didn't in that moment, and the moment passed.

It wasn't until later that night, after an excellent dinner, during some satisfactory dancing on the tiny floor in front of the bandstand, that Tasha realized *now is the time.* This was pretty much her dream date, and it was past time to acknowledge that Sandesh was her dream guy. He deserved to hear it. The band was playing a slow swing version of 'All of You.' She'd seen 'Silk Stockings' enough times to remember the lyrics, and was humming along with the band. As the band wound up the tune, Sandesh gave her a spin in their little corner of the floor, then held her around the waist to let her do a thing they both liked, an upper-body sway and roll. She knew it showed off her throat and cleavage really well. When she straightened up, he was looking down at her with the dreamy expression that always turned her on. She slid her left hand up from his shoulder to his cheek. Her head was still tipped back. It was such a blatant invitation that he bent his head and kissed her, briefly, smiling.

Then he started to move them off the floor. "Sandesh." His arm was still around her back and her right hand was still in his left. He stopped for a moment. "Do you know that song?" He shook his head. She indicated he should bend his head toward her again, and sang the last line very softly to him, "'I love all of you.'" He looked at her, clearly startled. "I really do," she said. "I love you."

He lifted his head, closed his eyes, took a deep breath. "Can we step outside for a minute?"

"Sure," she said. She had an idea what was about to happen. She wasn't wrong. The door had hardly closed behind them before he was kissing her, deep and slow, both hands cupping her head.

"I love you so much," he said after a while. "You don't know what it feels like to hear you say that. I can't even describe it."

She reached up and ran her thumb under his wet eyes. "I love you," she said again. "Kiss me one more time. Then we have to go in to see the show." He kissed her again and took her back inside.

Sandesh barely saw the first couple of numbers in the show, a dance revue with eight leggy women. He was dwelling on those wonderful words. Tasha kept squeaking with delight over the people she recognized. Between the second and third numbers she leaned over and said, "Two of those girls did the play with me, and another one was in this group that did some stuff at Chrome that same year. Oh, I miss that."

"Do you think they recognize you too?" She nodded, and when he paid more attention to the next number he could see that the dancers were clearly performing to Tasha. It wasn't so much that they weren't playing to the whole crowd, it was just a quick glance, or a wink, or a lift of the chin. He stored that away, because he was starting to get the idea that Tasha really did want to perform again. If it wasn't with a group like this then she'd need a partner, and he wasn't about to let that be anyone but him.

After the show all three women who knew Tasha came over to their table. There was a lot of squealing and chatter, and Tasha introduced them to Sandesh. He managed to retain their names, if not which name went with each woman, and offered to take a picture of the four of them together. "You should have been in the show," one of them said to Tasha, looking at her dress as they were posing. He thought it was Rita; the one he was absolutely sure of was Sherry, the Japanese girl.

His foolproof method for remembering a name was to have someone write it down, so he pulled out a business card and a pen. "If you'll write your names and numbers here, I'll text you the picture," he said, offering the blank side of the card.

"Text me a picture of the two of you, too," said the one he was least sure of, writing her name on the card. *Okay, that's Annette*, he thought. *Got it now*. "Because you are about ten times better-looking than that other guy."

Tasha laughed. "He is, isn't he?"

"I want to hear all about it someday." Annette gave Tasha a hug. "I have to get out of this thing before it kills me. Never wear a corset," she told Sandesh. "It's so good to see you! Call me!" She kissed Tasha's cheek and headed for the back of the restaurant. Sherry and Rita also made the costume excuse, which seemed perfectly legitimate to Sandesh; he could see how the fishnet tights were practically embedded in their thighs.

"Oh mercy that was fun," Tasha sighed, sitting down again. "I wonder what happened to Maria. That was the fourth showgirl," she clarified. "I'll ask Sherry."

He was smiling at her. "Do you have a video of this show? I'd love to see it."

"Yeah, I do. We all got a copy of the dress-rehearsal video. We could watch it tomorrow, if you don't have to be anywhere."

"I do have to be somewhere. I have to be with you." She looked up from her phone; she was adding her long-lost friends' information to her contacts. She leaned toward him, gaze on his mouth, and he kissed her again. "We'd better go before they tell us to get a room." She laughed, and finished her data entry. He took the card and slipped it into his pocket, stood up and offered a hand. "Shall we?"

"We shall. You beautiful, beautiful man."

They were back at Tasha's by eleven. Sandesh dropped her off first, then went to find parking. When he made his way to the apartment and was buzzed up, she was saying good night to the sitter. Theo was standing by her side. "Should you still be up?" Sandesh asked. Theo shrugged.

Tasha did too. "He was asleep when I got here, but, well."

"I took your mom out dancing tonight, Theo. Doesn't she look fabulous?" Theo looked like he wasn't quite convinced. "She was the most beautiful woman in the whole place, I promise you. Do you like dancing?"

Theo said, "I don't know."

"Have you ever seen your mom dance?"

"No."

"Tasha! You haven't shown him?" Sandesh sounded scandalized. Theo giggled. "Your mom told me she would show me a video of a play she was in. Do you want to see it?" He glanced at Tasha and stage-whispered, "You have your clothes on, right?" Tasha snorted, and Theo giggled again. "You want to see it?" Theo nodded. "We'll watch it tomorrow. Now you should go to bed."

"Okay." Theo turned and headed for his bathroom. He shut the door behind him. Sandesh looked at Tasha.

"He's a big boy now," she said. "He told me so himself. He puts himself to bed. Then I go in after a while and pretend I don't know he's still awake waiting for me."

"He's so cute." He came over to her and set a hand lightly on her shoulder, caressing her neck with his thumb. "You want to go and get ready for bed? I'll take my turn when you go tuck him in."

"Okay." She tipped her head back, inviting a kiss again. Sandesh accepted the invitation, as he always did, still overcome almost on a daily basis with the profound alteration in their relationship. He couldn't get over it. He didn't want to get used to it. This sleepover while Theo was home was a first. Being trusted to stay alone with Theo while Tasha ran errands was slightly less new, but no less valued. He watched Tasha go, thinking about the conversation they'd had the week before. She told him that Matthew had asked about him, that Theo had mentioned him. It wouldn't be a problem, she said. Matthew had girlfriends over all the time. Sandesh had realized that he didn't like being in that category. He didn't like being 'the boyfriend,' even though it was what he'd craved for years.

*Not just a boyfriend*, he thought. Now that he knew what it was like to really be with Tasha, he wanted so much more. He told himself to be grateful for what he had. As of tonight, it was almost everything.

It was tempting to start something when they were together in bed. He still couldn't help feeling that he shouldn't miss a single opportunity, that she might change her mind, that this could end. But it really wasn't all about sex. It never had been. So he kissed her, and she murmured sleepily and laid her head on his shoulder, and he realized it was okay to let that be the end of the evening. After a few minutes, his body settled down. Pretty soon her breathing let him know that she was asleep. *The woman I love is asleep in my arms*, he thought, *and her adorable child is sleeping two rooms away, and this is heaven.*

When he woke up the room was still dark, and it took a second to orient himself. A faint light came through the window, the hazy non-blackness of Los Angeles at night. "Oh," he said out loud, and heard her laugh softly. Her mouth was on his chest and her hands were everywhere.

"I'm sorry," she said. "I got up to go pee and then I checked on Theo and he's out cold, and I came back here and it looked like you might be dreaming of me. I couldn't resist. Were you?"

"Probably," he said, a bit breathless. "I can't remember. Oh God." She was on the move, her body sliding against his, stretching out on top of him, kissing his throat and his face and his mouth. "Mmmm." He rolled them over and she raised her knees around him, sighing with pleasure and relief as he entered her.

"I have to tell you something," she said after a few minutes. Sandesh was still inside her, taking his time, pushing them both to the point of climax and then backing off. He didn't say anything aside from a distracted, querying sound. "I used to go out with Sherry. We were kind of a couple for a while."

"Mmm. She's pretty."

Tasha laughed under her breath, and bit his neck gently. He growled a little, and she shivered. "We were both sick of men. It started out almost as a joke, while we were in the group together and doing that play. Revenge, I guess. It was fun while it lasted. Oh God." He rolled them over again, sat up with his arm tight around her. "Oh my *God*." He moved them both, lifting her so that she stayed in place while he folded his legs underneath him. She wrapped both arms around his neck. "How do you even do that." She adjusted, folding her legs around his hips. He was kissing her, hands roaming over her body, so deep and so hard, so tight against her that all it took was a subtle shift of her hips to push all her buttons. She moaned into his mouth and heard him laugh as she pulsed around him, and then he pushed up and bent forward. She let go of his neck and lay back, watching the shape of him as he drove into her. "Oh God," she said again faintly as he threw his head back, biting his lip, stifling a cry. A moment later he fell forward, catching himself with one hand, eyes closing. She used her legs to pull him all the way down onto her. It seemed like his orgasm just kept going. It made her feel powerful.

It took Sandesh a while to catch his breath and remember what they'd been talking about. More accurately, what Tasha had been talking about while he was inside her. "You know a man doesn't always listen too well in these situations," he said lazily, propping himself on one elbow. "But you seemed to be saying something about having a girlfriend."

"Yeah, I was. It was an experiment."

"Worked okay for a while?"

"For a while. At a certain point we both had to concede that while in many respects a female lover is ideal, in our case there was something missing."

"And that something would be?" He thought he knew what she was about to say.

"Dick." They both laughed. "A vibrator really is not the same."

"Well, I've never used one, but it seems like it could be awkward." Tasha giggled. Sandesh kissed her. "I mean, I like to have both hands free." He considered something for a minute. "Why didn't you ever tell me that before? You told me so many other things."

"I don't know," she said. "Maybe I felt like it put me in the wrong. Like, just because Matthew had cheated, that was no excuse for me to cheat." She stared up at him. "I could have told you, couldn't I. You wouldn't have blamed me."

"He changed the deal on you. You needed someone. If it couldn't be me, I'm glad it was Sherry." He had another thought. "Did he know?"

"Yeah. I didn't hide it."

"And he didn't give you shit about it?"

"He wasn't exactly in a position of moral authority there."

"Probably wanted to watch." Tasha laughed again. "It's getting light out. Time to put on our PJs. When does Theo usually wake up?"

"Any minute now." She kissed him and he rolled away, so they could get up and get respectable.

Two weeks later, Sandesh got a text from James: *FYI they're letting Jessica go today.* It was a relief, such a relief. The past few months he'd been walking on eggshells around the office, aware that an investigation was ongoing. The firm's risk management counsel had spoken with him. The camera had been approved early on, and he'd noticed similar cameras in a few other offices, including that of James himself. He couldn't believe that Jessica was unaware of them, but then she seemed so oblivious to other things. On the rare occasions they met, her behavior was just as off as ever. She was flirty, but not in a fun way. It was in a proprietary way, a way that said *I know you're playing hard to get.* It was creepy, the way she watched him at company events was creepy.

He didn't know how they actually did it. He'd never been fired. Did they escort someone off the premises? Did they take their key card and say, don't let the door hit you in the ass on your way out? He put the questions out of his mind and got back to work.

He didn't see or hear anything out of the ordinary until he was done for the day and in the parking garage. He was almost at his car when he heard her.

"Sandy." He turned around slowly, one hand on his messenger bag and the other holding his keys. She was standing about six feet away.

"Jessica?"

Upstairs at the security console, a guard had half an eye on his bank of monitors. He frowned when it cycled through the garage cameras, and picked up his walkie. "What the … José, something's off on P3 over by the southeast corner. You want to head over there and check it out?"

"Roger. I'll let you know."

Down on P3, Sandesh was trying to keep eye contact with Jessica. The knife in her hand was awfully distracting. "They fired me, Sandy. They said there were complaints. Did you complain?" He didn't say anything. "You did, didn't you. James did. Anthony did. All I wanted was … ." She didn't finish the sentence. Maybe she didn't even know what she wanted. She took a step forward, he took a step back. And again, and again. He was out of room, and she was a lot closer than he wanted her to be. His back was to his car; he was wishing he had his phone in his hand instead of his keys, so he could dial 911. *If the call would even go through from down here.* He was also wondering if he'd actually be able to hit her if he had to. He'd never struck another human being in his life.

"Jessica, what are you doing," he said.

"I need to make a point." She looked at the knife. His gaze followed hers. "Get it? A point?" *Fuck me, she is actually insane*, Sandesh thought, *I am going to die. Tasha.*

"Everything okay over here?"

Sandesh didn't even look to see who said it, just said, "No!" Jessica moved to see who had spoken, her entire body turning. Sandesh saw the knife coming as if in slow motion, past his face in a descending arc that ended with a streak of fire across his upper arm, an inch above his elbow. Then it clattered to the cement floor. Jessica had dropped it. His keys landed beside it.

She turned back to look at him, her eyes huge and horrified. "I didn't mean to do that!" Sandesh looked at his arm. He couldn't even see a cut through the black fabric of his shirt. He couldn't really feel it now. He stared with a sort of distant fascination at the stream of blood, an actual pulsing stream, not drops. A man shouted. He heard Jessica scream and leaned back against his car. There was something he was supposed to do, but he couldn't remember what it was. After a minute he thought he should look for Jessica again, but his line of sight was off, he was looking at the painted arrow pointing toward the elevator, and that was on the floor. It was really close, too. *I'm on my knees*, he thought hazily, *how'd that happen*. He was feeling dizzy, and put a hand down for balance, but it landed on something wet and slid away. The floor felt cold under his cheek. He heard a man's voice again, words he didn't quite grasp, more screaming, and then the lights went out.

James couldn't understand what the guard was saying at first, he was talking so fast and sounded so agitated. Finally the gist of it sank in. He said, "I'm on my way," hung up the office phone, slid his access card into his back pocket, and grabbed his cell phone. He ran for the elevator. *Fuck this thing is slow*, he thought, heart racing, *go faster*. When it finally got to the lobby level, he squeezed out before the door was even open and dived across the bay, past the other guard, and through the door of the garage elevator that the guy was holding open while listening to his walkie. *Faster*, he thought again in the elevator. At P3 he got out and headed for the screaming.

He saw Jessica first, the source of the screaming, being restrained by a third guard. That guy spotted James over Jessica's head and yelled "Over here!" James was there a few seconds later, stopped short, and felt himself go pale. Almost without thinking he used the phone in his hand to take a picture of the scene. Then he shoved it in his pocket and went to his knees beside Sandesh. *Check for pulse.* There was a carotid pulse. *Check the airway.* That was fine. Heart still pumping, lungs still working.

"Sandesh, are you in there?" No response. It took a few more seconds to locate the source of the blood, *so much blood*, a gash above the elbow. James wrapped both hands around the upper arm, over the wound, and compressed them. He noted, almost absently, a reflex response from the right hand. *That's good.* He tried to control his own breathing, tried not to be aware of the blood soaking into his jeans, and tried not to count the seconds.

Tasha didn't know what to think. Sandesh had texted before he left the office, as usual. They didn't have a date that night, but he always called after he got home. She'd sent a follow-up text after a while. Could be he'd gone out with some friends from work and lost track of time. But it was midnight before a reply came, and then it wasn't from Sandesh: *Ms Jefferson this is Lochan, Sandesh's brother. He is in the hospital. He will be all right. You can see him in the morning, please text back for details*

Tasha was glad she was already sitting down. She glanced over at Theo; he was asleep at the other end of the couch. She hadn't wanted to wake him up. Hadn't wanted to be alone in the room. She had never imagined that Sandesh might be in some kind of trouble. She was ashamed to think that she'd assumed he had forgotten about her. *As if he ever would*, she thought, and wrote back to Lochan: *Thank you for letting me know, I was worried when he didn't call. Which hospital?*

Lochan wrote back with all the details, except what she really wanted to know, which was: what happened?

She found out the next day. She and Theo arrived at the hospital at the beginning of the time window she'd been given. The receptionist checked the visitors list and put a check by her name. "Mr. Prasad is in room six-twenty. Down that way."

"Thank you." Tasha went down the hall, holding Theo's hand. It wasn't quiet, exactly, but the ambient noise was hushed. Theo was hanging back, reluctant. "You're not going to the doctor, sweetie. We're going to see Sandesh."

"Why is he here?"

"I don't know. We'll find out." She found the room, tapped lightly on the half-open door, and went in. "Sandesh?"

He turned his head. He looked tired, pale, and very happy to see her. "Tasha. Lochan told me he got in touch with you. Hey Theo. Taking care of your mom?"

"Yes."

"Good boy. Come over here, will you?" He nodded toward the IV in his left hand. "I'm a little tied up."

Tasha lifted Theo up onto the bed. "Good gracious you're getting big, I can hardly do that anymore." She sat down beside him, and leaned over to kiss Sandesh. "I've been so worried. What happened?"

He made a 'closer' gesture and she put her head right next to his so he could murmur in her ear. "They fired Jessica yesterday. She didn't take it well. There was a knife. I was lucky. I'll tell you more later." He kissed the side of her face. She sat up, cold with horror.

She looked at his right arm now, with a bandage showing under the sleeve of his hospital gown. She pushed up the sleeve to see better. "You had surgery?"

"A few stitches." *A lot of stitches*. He could tell her later that some of them were in his actual artery. That they'd given him three units of blood, and warned him he'd need physical therapy.

"When will they let you go?"

"Well, they don't want me to go home alone. But they're discharging me tomorrow unless, well." He didn't finish the sentence because Theo might have been paying more attention than he seemed to be. He was looking around at all the equipment in the room. Sandesh was glad the only thing hooked up was the IV. Some of the things that had been there at four in the morning had been a lot scarier. "Lochan said he would take me to his house."

After a moment Tasha said, "Is that what you want?"

"No. But I'm going to be a little bit disabled for a while."

"I don't care. I want you with me. Will they let you go home with me?"

"Oh, they'll let me go wherever I want as long as it's not alone. I'd rather be with you," he said. "Is that okay, Theo?"

"What?"

"If I stay with you and your mom for a few days, is that okay?"

Theo leaned forward to he could see past Tasha, and studied him for a moment. "Sure."

"Thanks, buddy. I'm going to be mighty boring for the rest of the day, though, so maybe you should see if your mom will take you somewhere more fun."

"Yeah." Theo jumped down and went to the door, looking back at Tasha. She shrugged ruefully and leaned over to kiss Sandesh again.

"I love you," he said, looking exhausted.

"I love you too. Have you got phone privileges now?"

"Yeah, but I can't reach it." He moved his left hand a little to point, wincing. The bruise around the IV spanned the back of his hand.

"Oh, for … ." Thinking that was awfully dumb of somebody, she slid off the bed and moved the phone from the little table by the window to the bed next to Sandesh's hand. The charging cord was plenty long enough. "When do you get to lose the IV?"

"Later. Then I'll be practicing texting with my left hand, I guess. Better go catch that boy."

"Theo?" He was out of sight. "I'll go now. Sandesh, I love you. Please be okay."

"I'm going to be okay. I love you. Kiss me one more time." She did. "Thanks. Go get him."

She went to the door. She didn't want to leave, but there wasn't any choice. He mustered up a smile for her before she left the room. Then he let his head fall back on the pillows, glad Theo had been there so he wasn't tempted to tell her what the doctor had told him, and what the police had told him when they'd come to take his statement, about just how lucky he'd been.

He was hoping to hear from her again that afternoon, and got a text within the hour. *This boy of mine was interrogating the receptionist. He knows that's my job too. It was good though, I think he'll be less scared of the doctor's office now. How are you doing? I love you*

His answer took a good bit longer than she would have expected, but it made her laugh. *I love you too and this is a lot harder with one hand you will not be getting much punctuation*

*Good spelling though*

*Took me like six tries iv out already yay lochan is coming in an hour or so*

*Don't forget to tell him I want you*

*Oh yeah nope wont forget*

*Going to wait till Theo is asleep to have a little meltdown. Terrifying to think I could have lost you*

*It was scary i wont lie*

*It's good you didn't give me too many details. By the time I get those you're going to be fine. Heading into the grocery store now, any requests?*

*Dulce de leche ice cream plz*

*LOL you got it. Remember I love you*

*I love you too.* Sandesh kept hold of the phone for a while in case she texted again, but she was definitely on mom duty now, so eventually he set it down. The TV was on, with the sound very low, and it was set to a sports channel. He couldn't have been less interested, but he couldn't change the channel because the remote was all the way across the room. He closed his eyes, telling himself it was only for a second, and the next thing he knew his brother was back. By the time they were finished arguing about where Sandesh should go after he was discharged, he was exhausted again. At least Lochan put the TV remote on the bed before he left. But then there was a nurse to take his vitals again, and then an orderly with some food, and then a trip to the bathroom, and by the time Sandesh was left alone he was thinking *am I even going to be able to leave tomorrow* because he felt like roadkill. Not quite lousy enough to take the pills the nurse left, though. He disliked the brain fog even more than the pain.

The nursing staff left him alone overnight, the call button next to his hand by the phone in case he needed it. He didn't use it. He slept seven hours and woke up feeling ready to go. He got up, wondering when he could start moving his right arm - it was prohibitively sore - and tending to himself awkwardly with his left hand again. *Too right dominant*, he thought, *if I ever have a stroke I'm fucked*, which shouldn't have been as funny as it seemed at that moment. Lochan had insisted he would come to help transfer Sandesh when he was discharged. It occurred to Sandesh that he had better make sure his brother brought him some clothes, too. He picked up the phone and sent a text. The phone was still in his hand when it buzzed with an incoming.

He was hoping it would be Tasha, but it was James. *Hi Sandesh hope you're doing okay. What's the news?*

*Mildly disabled currently one handed going to stay with my gf when they let me outta here which should be today*

*Glad to hear it. Let me know if there's anything you need*

*Wtf happened with jessica*

*In jail, all I can tell you*

*Thats enough thx*

*How much blood did you lose? The EMTs wouldn't estimate*

*They gave me three units*

*It was a hell of a mess*

*Wait were you there*

*Building management knew what office you belonged to, called in a panic, I was still upstairs. Damned glad the damage wasn't worse*

*Me too oops gotta go my bro is here with clothes*

*That must mean freedom is imminent. I'll be in touch and seriously call if you need anything*

*Will do thx.* There was another round of argument with Lochan, but Sandesh won again. The only concession he made was letting his brother drive him to Tasha's place, park in the red zone with the hazards on, and make sure he got to the door safely. "I'm really okay," Sandesh said gently. "I'll be good as new in a couple of weeks." He wasn't about to admit how fatigued he was from a simple car ride across town.

"Call me if you need anything," Lochan said. "We're glad you're all right." He set down the overnight bag he'd packed at Sandesh's apartment. "Your keys are in there. I put all the stuff in from your messenger bag."

Sandesh didn't ask what had happened to that. He'd already figured out that it must have been saturated with blood. Fortunately it had a waterproof lining. "Thanks for everything. Hug me now, watch the arm, great. Give Paige a kiss for me."

"I will not, she says you're cuter than me."

"Yeah, sorry about that." Lochan grinned and got in the car, watching until Sandesh had called up to Tasha and was through the front door.

In a condo in Century City, James was aware that his wife Silvia was staring at him. He shoved his laptop out of the way and muted his phone. "What?"

"You didn't tell him you're the reason he didn't bleed out down there."

"Not what he needed to hear right now. He'll get the whole story later." The story of the three guards trying to manage everything they had to, which had made James think the building and firm managements both needed to re-write some procedures. The guy who was supposed to be stationed at the main console, holding the garage elevator while directing the emergency responders. The guy downstairs trying to handle Jessica, who'd gone into some kind of frenzy. The other guy on duty in the control room, on the phone to 911 and on another line to the office, because that was part of the emergency protocol, but they always did drills as if it were a fire or an earthquake, not a knife attack.

The firm's receptionist had already gone for the day and it had taken the guard several tries to get an actual human on the phone. The EMTs arrived only a few minutes after James, but they told him his action might have saved Sandesh's life. James got home very late, having called Silvia to let her know what was up, and scared her badly by walking in with his jeans brown with blood from the knees down. He reassured her, then stripped and showered, scrubbing his hands, taking off his wedding ring for the first time since Silvia had put it on his finger, so that he could be sure the blood underneath it had washed away. "Good thing I wasn't wearing a suit yesterday, huh? The cleaners would have called the cops."

She shuddered. "God, don't even joke about it."

"Yeah, too soon. I won't show you the pictures I took down there either."

"Jesus no. Why did you even take any?"

"Well, the firm needed the evidence, I couldn't just let the cops do it and then have to chase them around. That call earlier, that was the managing partner. He's shitting himself because he thinks Sandesh is going to sue." It had been a long call, with multiple partners cycling on and off conference. James had been tired, and profoundly angry, by the time the call was over.

"He probably should," Silvia said. "They should have unloaded that nutcase the minute you told them what was going on."

"But then *she* could have sued. That's what they thought. They weren't thinking she would get violent. None of us were. Obviously we should have. They should have gotten an LAPD termination escort."

"I didn't even know that existed." Silvia went to the kitchen on the other side of their main living space, glad all over again that they hadn't moved out of the condo. It was good they could be in the same room. She started setting up a fresh pot of coffee.

"Well, neither did I. Now we know." He rolled his eyes, shrugged. He'd pushed for that to be immediately added to the termination-for-cause procedure. Too late to prevent what had happened to Sandesh, but not too late to avoid something similar in the future.

"Are they at least on top of rehab and whatever?"

"He'll get whatever he needs, yeah. Maybe this will finally light a fire under them to staff San Francisco, too." That office had been open for almost two years, and was still running with a skeleton crew.

Silvia couldn't believe it. "They haven't done that yet?"

"Nope. He's too damn good at the job. I'm going to nudge him to take the maximum allowed leave. These guys need a swift kick in the ass, and the last thing he needs is to come back to the same situation. They'll be lucky if he comes back at all." James looked up as Silvia nudged his arm; she was holding a mug of coffee. He took it. "Thanks sweetheart."

"How are you doing?"

He didn't ask what she meant. "It's … I'm all right. I'm glad I was there, glad we took that Red Cross class, glad there was something I could do. There wasn't anything I could have done for Ray. There wasn't anything anyone could have done." She bent down to hug him, face pressed against his. "I'm all right," he said again, and turned his head to kiss her.

## Chapter 4
May 2018

Sandesh was using his unexpected free time to think about his future with the firm. Tasha hooked him up with a labor attorney from her office to help him figure out his best play. Ultimately he decided to take medical leave until he was discharged from physical therapy. He had some nerve damage and wanted to get it as rehabbed as possible before going back to work, especially if he was going back to what amounted to two jobs.

Tasha also hooked him up with a full week of what almost seemed like play dates. She stayed home with him on Monday, and every day after that he had visitors bringing him lunch or stopping by to keep him company. On Tuesday it was his sister-in-law, on Wednesday it was Terry, on Thursday it was James' wife Silvia, and on Friday it was Rory, a new friend from the dance studio. She told him, "You know, you could get a wicked tattoo around that scar." The dressing had come off on Monday, and he'd be going in to get the stitches removed in a few more days.

"Yeah," he said. It wasn't a surprising observation given that her own arms were completely covered with tattooed feathers. "I never thought about getting a tattoo."

"It is sometimes, nay often, fun for a harmless-looking person to freak people out with some ink." He laughed. Rory slanted a smile at him. "Anyway, so you guys were signed up for the Argentine tango boot camp, right? Still going to go?" It was scheduled for the coming Sunday.

"Hell yeah we're going to go," he said. "Sling or no sling."

"That's the spirit. It's good you got on the list, the studio's going to be packed. Listen, do you mind if I stretch?"

"No, of course not. I should too, I haven't yet today." He got down on the floor with her. "I can't do my whole yoga thing till this stupid arm is healed, but at least I can keep my back from locking up, right?" They did stuff on the floor for a while in companionable silence. "Tasha was wondering if there was any more info on this whole movie project, do you know?"

"It just so happens that I do." Rory mirrored the stretch Sandesh was doing. "You have some long-ass legs. Our pal Andy, who is exec producing this thing as well as co-starring in it, he's had a more or less final script for about a month."

"I heard a little bit about Andy. Tasha's brother Terry, you know him, right?" Rory nodded. Terry had been bartending at Chrome for a long time before his promotion; he was usually on hand for the Underground Cabaret rehearsals and shows. "Anyway Terry is married to Anya Ivanova, and she did a photo session with Andy late last fall. She told us some stuff. I've been catching up with his show."

"It stinks, right?" Rory said cheerfully. "He and Victor are great, the rest of it reeks. It got kind of good for a minute after they started writing the Romeo and Juliet storyline, but I guess they ran out of ideas. That shit would be off the air if not for those two. Anyway, yeah, I found out about all this a few months ago. Andy and Tanith were sneaking around with it for a year and a half, which I still have a grudge about."

"Who is Tanith?"

"The director. Tanith Salazar. She has a camera guy, he's engaged to another film type person who has committed to run a second camera, and they've got a third guy who's been doing video for our Cabaret stuff for years. I guess for some of the scenes, like these dance mobs they're talking about, they're planning to have five cameras running. Three mobile and two fixed."

Sandesh was way out of his depth. "I don't know anything about making movies. Is that a lot?"

"It might be? Andy said Tanith said it's mostly so they can do things faster. Run five cameras and you only have to play the scene once or twice, versus five or ten times to get all the angles or whatever. Faster means cheaper."

"Oh okay, I get it." He was thinking he ought to do a little Googling after Rory went home. The process sounded interesting, but it also seemed increasingly likely he and Tasha would be on the fringes of this. So many of the people involved were people she knew. It was exciting to think they might be able to do some kind of project together so soon. Since he was off work for a while, this might be the perfect moment.

"So they have a script, a way to film it, money to film it, and a cast. I haven't actually seen this alleged script myself, we're set to do a table read in a week. Sometime soon Dana and I will meet with the camera guys to go over the scene chart. That's mostly to mark out who's doing what with the cameras. We're doing stuff at the theaters where they're going to film this play within the movie, and all the, eh, it's complicated. Anyway there's tons of dance numbers."

"What is the movie about, exactly?"

"Five guys obsessed with tango because they're doing a play about Carlos Gardel. Ever heard of him?"

"Nope." He made a mental note to Google that guy, too.

Rory laughed. "You'll either get obsessed with it yourself, or so sick of it you never want to hear tango music again. Filming starts in July."

"Wow, that's coming right up."

"Yeah, we're all about to get really busy."

Sandesh passed on the updates to Tasha when she got home. She looked excited. "That director, I mean I've never directed a stage play myself, but it seemed like she really knew what she was doing. Are you sure you're okay to do this boot camp on Sunday?"

"Absolutely. I haven't gotten this much rest in years. The arm feels more functional." The sling was off when he wasn't moving around. He did another cautious, partial straighten-and-flex operation. The doctor had recommended mobilizing it as soon as possible. Since Sandesh hadn't filled the prescription for painkillers, the injury itself told him when to stop. It was clearly not healed, but also clearly improving. "These two fingers still don't want to wake up. The therapist will start on those next week."

"So what's going on there, exactly." Tasha took his right hand and fiddled with it for a minute. "They're warm. That's good, right?" He nodded. "You can move them. You can grip. But it's not full strength, huh. And there's no sensation?"

"Off and on. Kind of ranges from totally numb to feeling like they're stuck in a power socket."

"Oh. That's not right." She wrapped her fingers around his and squeezed, then slid her hand up to his wrist to feel the reassuringly strong pulse there. "Hungry?"

"Amazingly, considering I've been a couch potato for five days, yes." He leaned over to kiss her. "I can help, you know."

"Take advantage of it," she advised. "This won't go on forever." He laughed, and kissed her again. She touched his face. "I have to admit I kind of like this beard."

"Not too wolfman? It's just I haven't quite mastered writing with my left hand yet, and brushing my teeth has been an adventure. Shaving seems like asking for trouble." Sandesh had been increasingly annoyed by his persistent inability to use his right hand. He'd never really noticed how the small actions of fingers and wrist referred up the arm before. Now that biceps-adjacent injury was telling him all about it. *Count your blessings*, he reminded himself. It could have been so very much worse.

Tasha was laughing under her breath. She could see in his face how frustrated he was. "Yeah, let's not do that particular test for a while. It's fine." She patted his leg and got up to go fix dinner.

Later that night, Sandesh asked Tasha to play the video of 'What Went Down' again. "And could you, like, do commentary on it? Tell me what was happening on the production side?"

"Why? I mean sure, yeah, but why?"

"Rory was telling me about this movie. She and her wife are going to be stage managers, I guess the idea is to film the thing at a couple different theaters. We talked about it pretty much the whole time she was here."

"Interesting?"

"Oh yeah. Well I thought, if we get picked to be extras, that's going to be a fun thing to do together. But you know me, I like to know the context of what I'm doing."

"I do know that. You realize that's the whole reason you've been working two jobs all this time." Sandesh rolled his eyes. Tasha laughed. "You'll probably find some way to make yourself useful."

"I don't know how useful I could be. But I know you get a kick out of the showbiz stuff. So that seems like something I should learn about." Tasha regarded him for a moment. He wondered what she was thinking. "When we were at Cicada I was watching your friends and thinking about how they did what they were doing. I'm getting interested in the nuts and bolts, that's all." He'd spent two solid hours reading internet articles about film and theater production and hadn't been the least bit bored.

When he put it like that, it made perfect sense. "Okay. Probably a good strategy for putting Theo to sleep, too." She loaded the DVD and they all sat together on the couch. Sandesh stayed awake till the end, enjoying Tasha's song-and-dance performances with the other showgirls all over again. Now that she was pointing out the lighting, scenery, or other technical details, he could see how each little part helped establish the mood or the tone of a scene.

Theo crashed halfway through. When Tasha turned off the screen she looked to her right. Her son was sound asleep on Sandesh's lap. They'd both fallen asleep on the couch the night before. She'd left them there, cuddled together, instead of waking them up to make them go to bed. Sandesh noticed her staring at him; he'd been looking at Theo, with an expression that took her breath away. "What?" He spoke softly.

"It occurred to me that the most precious things in my life were both right there, and I'm so glad you love him, and he loves you too, and I just love you both so much." She blinked back tears. Sandesh smiled at her, doing a little 'come here' thing with his head. She leaned in so he could kiss her.

"If I could have had a child with you," he said very quietly, "that child couldn't have been more important to me than Theo is. He is your heart, and you are my heart, and I am grateful every day to have you both in my life."

"Oh God," she said, "can you please stay? Like, forever? I don't want you to leave." *And I'm so glad I didn't lose you.* She was crying. She leaned against his shoulder; he put his good arm around her and kissed her forehead.

He wanted to ask her to marry him. He wasn't sure about the timing. It hadn't been that long since she admitted she loved him. But like that night at the mall, there might not be a better moment. And why shouldn't she know what he wanted? "Tasha. If you want us to live together, you should know I want to marry you. The one isn't contingent on the other," he added, because she had gone still. "I'll be happy, I'll be *thrilled* to come live with you regardless. But I want you to be my wife. I want to be your husband.

You need to know. Over the past nine and a half years there have been a lot of days when knowing I would see you was the thing that made everything else bearable." She remained silent. "Say something please."

She looked up at him. "I really didn't know," she said slowly. All that lightness, all that humor, all that *fun* for all those years. And all the while he'd been so seriously in love. Once again she wondered how she'd never seen it before. "I can't believe I didn't know."

"I was fronting pretty hard," he reminded her, and she laughed, a little shakily. "That's enough, anyway. Enough for tonight. Yes, I'll be delighted to stay. Thank you for the invitation. Now I must ask you to help me shift this tadpole because bedtime, bathroom, et cetera."

"Yes." She put her arms around Theo, gently tugging him over to her own lap, and got herself situated to stand up with him. "Oof. This child is growing."

"Yes he is. You okay there?"

"I'm not going to be able to do this much longer, but I'm fine. Go do your thing." She waited till Sandesh was on his feet and moving, then carried Theo to his room. When she got to the bedroom Sandesh was stretched out in bed, but still awake. "Not sleepy now?"

"I was thinking of kissing you, so no, not sleepy now. Kind of the opposite of sleepy." He couldn't help smiling. He was so hoping for more than a simple good-night kiss.

So was Tasha. "Well, you did say you were advised to exercise. But didn't they specify non-strenuous exercise?" She stretched out beside him, leaned over to kiss him, and ran a hand under the sheet and down his naked body. "Oh wow, yeah, not sleepy."

He laughed under his breath. "I've been doing some yoga. Going for walks. Nothing wrong with my heart."

"Nothing wrong with anything except that arm, as far as I can tell. Why don't you let me take care of this." She was naked too. She shifted close, pressing her body against his, and kissed him again. Her hand was still on him. His left arm went around her, urging her on top of him, which seemed like a good idea. They hadn't made love for almost two weeks. *There was a time I wouldn't have thought that was very long*, she thought. The kisses got deeper, hotter, hungrier. Tasha had her elbows planted beside his head, both hands in his hair. He had both hands on her body, left hand stroking down her back. She wanted more.

She shifted, resting her knees on the bed alongside his hips, and felt him react. "God, Tasha. Please." She was wet, he was hard, they were both breathing fast. She slid against him, feeling his whole length against her wetness. Her mouth was open against his but she was concentrating on that delicious friction. On the way his breath got shallow each time she almost took him in. She knew once she did it would be over so fast, and she didn't want it to be over. She tortured them both for long minutes until he couldn't stand it anymore. He put both hands on her hips and changed her angle, centered himself, and sank deep with a rough, ecstatic sound. She reared back, moving with him, watching his face in the dim light from the street outside. She could see when he started to go, she could feel it, and she wanted it.

When he pressed his head back against the pillow and arched up into her, the pulse of him sent her over too.

"Your face," she gasped, still upright, still gazing at him while she throbbed around him. "How could I not have imagined that."

"Yours too," he said, and reached his left hand up to pull her down, bringing her mouth back to his. "But I did imagine that. I guess I had better fantasies than you did."

She laughed softly, settling beside him. "You sure did." He fell asleep almost immediately, but Tasha lay awake for a while, thinking about what he'd said.

Sandesh knew she couldn't have any more kids. It was one of the many things they'd talked about over the years. Her pregnancy with Theo had been normal up to twenty weeks, and then she'd been diagnosed with preeclampsia. Ultimately her OB told her, "We don't usually advise women your age to close up shop. In your case, it could be dangerous to try to have more children. Think it over and let me know what you want to do." She chose the option of a tubal ligation after delivery. Tasha wondered how many thirty-year-old men knew as much about pregnancy complications as Sandesh must; his sister-in-law had had trouble, too.

*What about marriage*, she thought then, still wide awake. Six months ago she would have said Never Again. But that was before, before he kissed her, before she knew how much he cared. And before she knew how much that mattered. She thought she'd give it a little more time. See how it was when they had actually lived together for a while. Maybe six more months. They had a lot of ground to cover still. *If I'm not sure by then, I never will be*, she thought, and slid quietly out of bed. She pulled on her robe to walk out to the kitchen, found a pad of sticky notes and a pen, and wrote a message: ASK ME IN DECEMBER. She stuck it on the refrigerator and went back to bed.

Sandesh found the message in the morning, when he went out to make coffee, something he could do one-handed. Tasha was in Theo's room. He could hear them talking about what they should do on this fine sunny Saturday. He started the coffee, then found the pen and added his own block-printed message to Tasha's: IT'S A DATE.

Tasha invited Sandesh to go with her and Theo to the park, but he had an appointment with James. "I'll walk you as far as Marie Callender's," he said. "What kind of pie should I bring home?"

Unsurprisingly, Theo said, "Chocolate!"

"All righty then." They walked out together. Since they were well ahead of the time Sandesh was meeting James, he went with them halfway before turning back toward the restaurant, where he was seated in the bar area.

About five minutes later, James slid into the booth across from him. "Hey. How's everything?"

"Well, the stitches come out next week, physical therapy starts next week, I have no idea where my car is, and Tasha invited me to move in with her." He was smiling, because most of that was in the 'good' column.

James smiled back. "Your car is still in the garage at the office. You can pick it up anytime. Silvia told me you were already bitching about not being able to do all your yoga."

"Yeah. She told me a few things too."

"I know. She warned me." More accurately, Silvia had told James she outed him as the provider of lifesaving emergency response.

"Thanks." It seemed like an inadequate thing to say.

"You're welcome." A server came to take their order. James waited until she was gone. "I've been asked to be your liaison during your leave. What can you tell me?"

"My lawyer says I should take maximum allowable leave. And frankly I'm not sure I want to go back at all."

James nodded. He fished a business card out of his shirt pocket and slid it across the table. "This is the therapist I saw for a while last year after a friend of mine was killed in a car accident. If your doctor hasn't already referred you, this person was good for me."

"Thanks," Sandesh said again, looking at the card and then slipping it into his own pocket. "We haven't had that conversation. I've only seen her once since last Saturday. Can I tell you what she said?"

"You can tell me whatever you want about your health status, and I won't share it with the firm unless I have your written authorization to do so. About your employment status, you need to tell me if I shouldn't share anything, otherwise I'll assume I can. And off the record, they want me to bring you back, they don't want you to sue, and they are shitting bricks."

Sandesh snorted. "Any idea what they're doing about my job? Or jobs, I guess."

"Running around like no one has any idea how to do anything. Who trained you?"

"Nobody who's still there. That's the story of my life at the firm, nobody stays but me, I end up with all their work but I'm still making what I made two years ago." Sandesh studied James for a minute while the server brought their food and some coffee. "I've got nerve damage. The median nerve and the biceps tendon got nicked along with the brachial artery. That's what the PT is for. These two fingers have data failures." He indicated the two outermost digits on his right hand. "Loss of sensation, loss of grip strength, range of motion, dexterity. I haven't tried typing yet. Obviously haven't done anything weight-bearing yet."

James wasn't taking notes but Sandesh had the idea he was getting all this just fine. He did a 'rewind' thing with his hand. "Are you telling me you never got a pay increase after the last promotion?"

"I got a small one with the previous promotion, was promised something significant with the latest. That was ten months ago. I haven't taken any time off in over a year."

"Because they never staffed San Francisco. I can't believe these guys."

"Are they acting on that now?" James made a full-body gesture conveying 'who knows.' Sandesh laughed under his breath. "If I don't go back, they are so fucked." James laughed out loud. "I'm not going back unless that job is staffed," Sandesh decided. "Hired, on-boarded, and trained. You can tell them that."

"What about your raise?"

It was strangely liberating to say, "I'm not going back unless that's in place."

James nodded, like he thought that was the right answer. "What did your lawyer say?"

"She said that, plus she said I should ask for it to be retroactive to the date my new title went live."

"I agree with her."

"So, should I have her write that up?"

"I would. And make sure she pushes to have your disability claim submitted." James wouldn't have thought any push was necessary, but if they'd stalled a pay increase for ten months, there was more – or less – going on in the administrator's office than he'd thought. "So, what kind of pie should I take home to Silvia?"

"Theo said chocolate. Personally, I like rhubarb."

"Yeah, me too. I guess the person who's buying gets the deciding vote, right?"

"Well, it depends on the kind of reception you want," Sandesh said, and James laughed again. When the server came back to freshen up their coffee, they both put in pie orders. "So we're going to this Argentine tango boot camp tomorrow. Tasha kind of thinks we shouldn't, because of this, but she's so excited." *And dammit, I want to go.*

James may also have thought a tango boot camp was premature, but he didn't say so. "Is this for that movie thing? We're going too. My pal Danny and his wife found out about it, they did this dance show a couple of years ago and decided it would be fun to be extras. Danny badgered me into it. Well, he and Silvia and Kate all did."

"You don't dance?"

"I *try*," James said ruefully. "With a greater or lesser degree of success, depending on the music and the partner. Fortunately Silvia is forgiving." After a moment of watching Sandesh stifle laughter, he said,

"You'd better strap up that arm pretty good. People will be careful if they know you're injured."

"Yeah, I'll put this corner brace thing on so I can't move it too much. Listen, this might be a good day for me to get my car out of the dungeon. I've got my keys and stuff. Could you drop me by the office?"

"Sure." James took the bill when the server came back with their pies. He drove them over to Century City, offered his left hand for Sandesh to shake, and watched to make sure he and his pie made it into the building. Then he went home to get on his laptop and start drafting a sharply-worded email to the management committee and the office administrator. He closed with:

> You do not want to fuck with Solange Dasher. The last time a client of hers went to court, the firm she was suing got picked clean and then set on fire. Let's meet Wednesday to discuss.

It was the first time he'd really inserted himself into management. There was a good chance some of the others would get bent about it. James realized he was kind of looking forward to that.

Sandesh went down to the garage and found his car right where he'd left it. It looked as though it had been washed, and there was no sign of the previous week's events. Well, there wouldn't be; the building management wouldn't want people to see a pool of blood. He drove out of the garage and went to his apartment, glad he had an automatic transmission; getting from 'park' to 'drive' (or vice versa) was awkward, but manageable. *Could always work for Uber*, he thought, less troubled than he would have expected at the thought of potentially jettisoning his law-firm career.

His apartment was stuffy. He opened the windows before sending a text to Tasha: *Hello my lovely, James gave me a lift to the office so I could get my car out. Over at my apartment now. What a boring shoebox.*

*Hi sweetheart, we just got home. Don't carry anything!*

*LOL I won't. Well, except some more clothes. I'll drop last week's at the cleaners after I get back there*

*Call it home*

*OK after I get home. :-) Wow that felt good*

*Yes it did. Is Theo going to be happy?*

*If he still wants chocolate pie, yes*

*He always wants chocolate pie. Did you have a piece of rhubarb?*

*Yes! LOL*

*See you soon baby XOX*

*I love you*

*I love you too*

The studio was packed the next day, as Rory had promised, with over a hundred dancers. Most appeared to be couples. Sandesh and Tasha recognized only about a quarter of the people there, but those included Terry and Anya, Ricky and Luis, James and Silvia, and Rory, who was there with her wife Dana.

Their swing instructor Vince was leading the workshop, with his wife Kelli as his partner. Sandesh and Tasha left Theo in the studio's new child corral, under the eye of the manager, and found space in the main teaching room. Vince called the room to attention right on time.

"Hi everybody, thanks for joining us today. As you all should know, this workshop is for the express purpose of casting at least two large-scale dance scenes for an independent film being produced here in Los Angeles. These dance mobs will be shot outdoors, in modern dress, in the afternoon and evening of weekend days in July. There will be featured dancers. There will be no choreography, but there will be direction." He paused for a second to let that sink in. "All of you here should have some dance experience. What you do here today will determine whether you are used in the scenes, and if so where you will be used. Any questions so far?" A couple of hands had gone up but as Vince continued to speak they came down. "Okay, looks like I already answered a few. We're going to work on milonga-style tango basics for an hour and then we'll take a break and see if there's anything else we need to talk about before we start again. First, a demonstration." He took a step toward the music system and then turned back to survey the room. It was a remarkably effective maneuver; everyone was looking at him attentively. "Oh by the way. The tall guy over there is Tomás Calderón, one of the co-stars. He's making the decisions here. So if you catch him watching you, dance good." A few people laughed. Vince cued up a track and went to the middle of the floor, holding out his hand for Kelli. She joined him and he went immediately into the eight-count basic taught in almost every beginning Argentine tango class.

Sandesh was watching intently. He hadn't told Tasha, but he'd spent big chunks of the previous week studying Argentine tango online. As far as he could tell, it had a lot in common with social swing on the leading side, but the dance hold was so different he wasn't sure how he would do. She was leaning against him. He bent to murmur in her ear, "I'm not going to be able to really hold you, so apologies in advance."

"I'll stay close," she murmured back. "Don't you worry." Vince and Kelli finished their demonstration. Tasha slid her left arm up under Sandesh's right, resting her hand on his shoulder blade. "How's this?"

Sandesh took her right hand in his left and made a few experimental moves. Tasha went exactly where he meant her to. "That's genius," he said. "Now if we can manage not to get squashed like bugs in this crowd." She laughed under her breath. He had his arm in its sling, with extra padding around the injury. A few people had given them an 'are you crazy' kind of look when they arrived, but before long everyone was too busy to pay any attention to anyone besides their instructor.

Sandesh was vaguely aware of the tall guy - Tomás - as well as Kelli, moving through the room to give suggestions or make corrections as Vince demonstrated and talked through various figures. After about forty minutes, Vince went to the front of the room, his back to the wall of mirrors, watching everyone practice. "He looks a little judgemental," Sandesh said softly to Tasha. She snorted, leaning her head on his shoulder to hide the laugh. "Oh crap I think Kelli heard me." Kelli was looking over at them, saying something to Vince. Then she beckoned them over. "Oh *shit.*" Tasha laughed again, this time covering her mouth with her hand. They went up to the front of the room.

"Don't look so scared," Vince said. "Hey everybody. Have your attention for a minute?" He used Sandesh and Tasha to demonstrate body connection. "For these dance mobs, we're looking for a very quiet style. This is not the place to be doing showy hand leads, right? The fact that this guy can't even use his right hand but his partner is still receiving his lead, that's from body connection. Almost all of you are couples, so be thinking of that."

Vince turned to Kelli. "The kind of extreme version of this is hands-free." They stood very close together, her left ribs and hipbone contacting his right, close enough that when Vince stepped forward, his body moved hers and she stepped back. They did forward and backward walks, rock steps, and a box step without ever taking hold of each other. When they eventually stood apart again, the class applauded. "It's good practice," said Vince, smiling. "Anyway, time for a little break." As people started milling around, he turned back to Sandesh and Tasha. "Nicely done. How's the arm?"

"It's not bad," said Sandesh. "By July it should be fully functional."

"Glad to hear it. Kelli thinks you look like Pablo Verón." Sandesh clearly didn't know who that was, so Vince added, "Star of 'The Tango Lesson.' Dmitri has a copy here, I'll check it out to you if you'd like to see it. Great movie."

"Sure," said Tasha. "Thanks."

"You're doing really well," Vince said. "I remember you from the swing workshop. And weren't you in some stuff with the Underground

Cabaret, back in the day?" He was looking at Tasha. "The first time they did the 'Torch' theme, weren't you in a group?"

"That was six years ago! How can you remember that?" She was pleased.

"We watch the old DVDs sometimes. Your group was always great. Anyway, glad you came today. Go get some water or whatever before we get started again."

"I can't believe he recognized me from that," Tasha said to Sandesh after they got a drink. "That was right after Theo was born, I was working like crazy to get back in shape. The group had done some stuff before but it wasn't until the Cabaret opened up their auditions that we got so many chances. If I hadn't been so mad at Matthew about the whole cheating thing I would have been really happy with him because he did all the babysitting so I could do that." She huffed out a laugh. "Of course then he doubled down and cheated *while* he was babysitting."

"I hate to say I'm glad he did," said Sandesh, "but I'm glad he did." Tasha laughed. Then Vince called the class to order again.

"Okay, I am tired," Tasha said over pizza, after they got home. "How was your afternoon, Theo? We didn't see you at all, did they have stuff for you to do?"

"They had games and stuff," he said, shrugging. "There were some little kids there. Little kids are kind of boring." Tasha stifled a laugh. Theo went back to his pizza. "They're tiring too," he said after a minute's thought.

“I remember,” she said, and looked over at Sandesh. “You held up pretty well.”

“It’s sore though,” he said. He’d taken off the sling as soon as they got home and his injured arm was now stretched out and resting on the back of the couch. “Too much time in the sling, a little too much trying to do things. My brain kept sending messages and my arm was like, yeah, not happening. It’ll be fine tomorrow, I think.”

“I can give you some massage around the shoulder later. It probably all tightened up on you, huh.” She figured it had only been stubbornness that kept him going for the full length of the boot camp. Straightening his arm once the sling came off had not been a rapid or thoughtless process.

“Yeah. That would be nice. Is this movie R-rated? He leaned over to check the case, lying on the side table. “Oh no, it’s PG. Is it okay if we watch this dance movie, Theo?”

“Sure.”

Sandesh helped Tasha carry the leftovers to the kitchen, then called out to Theo. “Hey buddy, you want a little of this pie?”

“Yeah!”

“Thought so.” He watched Tasha cut three small pieces and then took the plates out, the first one going to Theo. “Here you go. Drink your water.” He watched the child eat while he waited for Tasha to come back out. He heard the coffeemaker gurgling. *I love this life*, he thought. *I’m glad I’m not missing this.* When she brought the mugs to the living room and set one down on the side table, he stretched up a hand and tugged her down for a kiss. “I love you.”

"I love you too. And I love you, too," she said to Theo, rumpling his hair. "Ready for this movie?" She fed the disc into the player, then sat down beside Sandesh on the couch.

Meanwhile, over in West Hollywood, James and Silvia were having dinner with friends who had all come to the boot camp. "You did good, honey," Silvia was telling James. "I think we may have found your dance."

His friend Danny said, "It's about time. I remember that night at Chrome, with the salsa, and wow."

James made a face at him. "We haven't all been music experts since we were twelve, so blow me." Across the table, Vince laughed. "Do you agree with my wife?"

Vince nodded thoughtfully. "I do. I also agree with Danny." Danny's wife Kate laughed.

"Jeez, give a guy a break! So how many people is Tomás taking out of that horde?"

"Well, counting Danny and Kate there were sixteen couples who were already on the list. Including you, because you get the friends and family pass." James rolled his eyes. Silvia patted him consolingly. Vince added, "Definitely taking your friend from work. Even though my wife is being completely inappropriate about him."

"Sandesh Prasad," Kelli said with relish as Kate and Silvia laughed. "Woo! He's like a walking Kama Sutra. I can't wait to see what he does with two arms, after a few more lessons."

Vince shook his head, smiling. "He and Tasha are a good couple. Anyway, Tanith wanted thirty couples, we had more than fifty to choose from, so we can have a few alternates in case somebody can't do the actual dates. Tomás is going to go through the tape tonight." Each leader at the boot camp had worn a number, as if they were in a competition. Vince had made that call after he saw the event was fully booked; there were too many people coming that he didn't already know. Kelli had matched up the few singles who'd come. "Tanith specified maximum diversity, and he's got plenty to work with."

"We even have a redhead," Kelli said. "Nick's wife."

Vince nodded. "It's going to look like Los Angeles out there, which is the whole point. So what's the story with Sandesh and that arm?"

James said, "Call it a workplace accident. He's on medical leave for a couple of months and he's probably going to be bored off his nut by the end of next week. I don't suppose there's anything he could do for you on this thing? He's used to basically running two offices."

"I don't know about for me," Vince said thoughtfully. "All I've got is choreography, which is what I do all the time anyway. But maybe Tanith. She's going to have interns from each of the guilds. From what I've read they're going to have their own agendas. Someone who's there only to work for her might be welcome."

"Could you ask her? If she's interested, you could pass it along."

"Sure."

Kate changed the subject. "That closing demo you and Kelli did was so lovely. I remember that from 'Gaucho.' It reminded everyone why they came, I think."

"So much," Silvia agreed. "After three hours of basics it was like, God, I'll never get this. So it was great to get another look at what's possible when you actually know what you're doing."

Vince smiled. "There were some good milonga dancers there. We were just showing off."

"Speak for yourself," said Kelli. "I love 'Palomita Blanca.' I'll do it any chance we get." She looked at her watch. "We'd probably better wrap this up. Rosa is going to want to unload the bambinos pretty soon." She and Vince had arranged to leave their twins at the studio's baby corral. Vince's mother Esmeralda, their usual babysitter, had come with a friend to the boot camp and gone straight on to a milonga. "Gabriel won't be bringing Esme home till late, right?"

"Right. If Thing One and Thing Two actually go to sleep like normal people, you and I can have a few minutes to ourselves," Vince said. Kelli looked like she thought that would be nice. Then Vince signaled for the check and changed the subject again, glancing at Silvia. "Speaking of bambinos."

"What?" Silvia said. "Oh crap, did he tell you we started trying?" She glared at her husband.

"Might have mentioned it," James said, looking guilty. Kate and Kelli both laughed. "Well, we were talking about our moms."

"Ah." Silvia understood this. "And Ruth wants nothing more in life than a grandbaby. You're lucky," she told Kate. "Danny's brother has that covered."

"Oh don't act like you're doing it for Ruth," Danny said, then frowned. "That sounded really wrong." Everyone agreed, and then someone mentioned what time it was. Vince and Kelli threw some money at the table and made their excuses, and before long everyone else was headed out.

Back at home, Silvia said, "I don't really mind that you blew the whistle on us."

"I know." James was grinning.

"I meant to ask how that meeting went, on Wednesday. You seemed a little grim when you got home." Silvia hadn't asked about it then, because James often wanted a day to process when there was some kind of conflict. And the next couple of days she'd been swamped with stuff for her own practice. "Everything okay?"

"No," he said. "Darlene is a, well, I don't like to use that word."

"Use any word."

"She's a cunt." Silvia laughed. James smiled, gave an apologetic shrug, and said, "She said Sandesh had to exhaust all his accumulated vacation and sick time before he was eligible for disability. That's what it says in the handbook, she said. Carver and the others were sitting there going yep, okay. I said, with what instrument would you like to get fucked up the ass, and someone's head exploded." Silvia was cracking up. "I said, this is a worker's comp issue, and a liability issue, and we are in no position to make him jump through any of these ridiculous hoops. If you want to stay in business, put that claim through immediately. He could sue tomorrow. I'm pretty sure Solange has the complaint ready to go." He hadn't yet spoken to Sandesh's attorney himself, but her reputation preceded her.

"What did they say?"

“Oh, there was some huffing and puffing. I said, how many settlements have I negotiated for this firm. Nobody knew, so I told them. They were like oh, really? That was you?” James didn’t even try to hide his exasperation. “I said, I know what a loser looks like. Put that claim through.”

“So did she?”

“Yeah, she did. There was some whining about how going outside the firm’s written policies opened us up to all kinds of bullshit later on, people would take advantage, blah blah blah. I was like, nobody is going to intentionally get stabbed in the parking deck in order to get extra time off work.”

Silvia put her arms around him and squeezed. “He’s lucky to have you on his side. If Solange handed you a cherry bomb you’d drop it right in the gas tank, wouldn’t you?” James laughed.

## Chapter 5
May 2018

The week after the boot camp was almost as busy as a week in the office. Sandesh had to go and talk to the police again about the whole Jessica situation. At the end of the interview, the cop who seemed to be in charge of things said, “The arraignment was last week. A no contest plea was entered. The sentencing hearing is in two weeks.”

“Does that mean this is over?”

“For the criminal charges, basically, yeah. If you want to file a civil suit, no. Do you have an attorney?”

“I never even thought of that.” *A civil suit?!* Sandesh couldn’t remember ever hearing of one like that, except for the OJ Simpson thing.

“You should talk to a lawyer.”

“I’ll work something out. Thanks.” As soon as he got out to his car, Sandesh called James. He got voice mail, so he left a message. “Hey James, quick question, the cops say I could file a civil suit on this thing, I mean the Jessica thing. Is there any point in doing that? Or is answering that question a conflict? If you could just text me yes or no or give me a name, that would be great. Thanks.”

By the time he got home he had a reply via text. *Hi Sandesh, I can’t really answer that but I can refer you to a friend at PPH Law. I’ve sent her all the relevant information and she will call you shortly.*

Sandesh sent back an acknowledgement and in due course talked to the other lawyer. A civil suit for assault sounded like enormous hassle with very little likelihood of accomplishing anything. His decision was to forget all about it and move on to more enjoyable things. He'd done the same thing with the referral James gave him. He didn't throw away that business card, but with everybody he was already talking to, adding one more person seemed like a waste of time. He shut down the tiny internal voice saying *but you're not talking about what happened.* It happened, it was over, he was okay. That seemed like enough for now.

He and Tasha filled out paperwork to add him as a tenant (and to get him a parking space), he put in his notice at his old apartment, and they took the awkward but necessary step of having dinner with Matthew and Theo. Tasha was nervous about it, but Theo was still Matthew's son and things would be a lot easier if they all got along. On the way home she said, "Well, that seemed to go okay. He's hard for me to read sometimes."

"He was civil. That's all we need him to be. And he's great with Theo."

"Yeah, he is." She glanced in the rear-view mirror; Theo was asleep in the back seat. Her next words were quiet. "I've wondered, for a long time, if Matthew wanted a child more than he wanted a wife. He doesn't have any brothers or sisters. His parents were only children too. I wonder if he needed that feeling of leaving something behind for the world."

"Well, he couldn't have gotten a much nicer kid. Better-looking, either."

"It's a good thing Theo's got you now. You can teach him how to be good-looking without being an entitled prick."

Sandesh stifled a laugh. "I'll do my best. So when I went to the bathroom, did Matthew say anything to you? I thought there might be something he wanted to say."

"He said, I hope it works out for you. I was never so surprised in my life."

"Wow. Yeah." He thought about that for a minute. "Maybe he can tell I'm not just in it for, you know."

"I wouldn't have asked you to move in if you were." Tasha glanced at him again, then back at the road. "I'm sure he can tell you care about Theo. That you'll be a good third parent."

"I'll do my best at that, too."

"I know you will, baby." She drove the rest of the way home in silence, hyper-aware of Sandesh's injured arm, out of its sling because it was so confining with the seatbelt. He didn't look uncomfortable. But he was wearing a short-sleeved shirt, and the stitches had come out that day, and the bandage they'd put on at the doctor's office was a stark reminder of how close she - and Theo - had come to losing him. As if he could read her mind, he reached out with his left hand and patted her shoulder. *One of these days we need to talk about that*, she thought.

On top of the domestic rearrangements, Sandesh got a totally unexpected call from Vince, the tango instructor. He picked up the unknown-number call out of boredom. "Sandesh Prasad, who's calling?"

"Hi Sandesh, this is Vince Connor. I had dinner with James Levine the other night and he said you're out on leave from your regular job for a while. Is that because of the injury?"

"Yes," Sandesh said, a bit cautiously. "Is that a problem for the whole movie thing?"

"No no no. Sorry. Bad way to introduce the subject. I'm sure you're going to be fine by the time they film those scenes. Tomás will be in touch with everyone who's been selected, probably by the end of this week, but you and Tasha are on the list. Anyway what I was wondering was, if you have some time on your hands, or hand," Vince paused because Sandesh was laughing, "would you have any interest in helping out on the production side? Rumor has it you are the one guy in Los Angeles who actually can herd cats."

Sandesh said, "That's not a bad way of describing it. I'm used to managing a lot of moving parts, yeah. What exactly would I be doing?"

"Well, I don't actually know. We thought I could see if you have a greater-than-zero interest level, and then get in touch with the director, Tanith. I don't know how much you know about movie-making."

"Next to nothing." He was interested, though.

Maybe Vince could tell. "Me too. And this is her first time, but she's directed a bunch of theater things. Anyway, if she happened to be in the market for open-ended, undefined, unpaid assistance, would you want to be put in touch?" Vince was smiling, knowing how ridiculous this would seem to most people.

Sandesh could hear the smile in his voice. "Was this James' idea? Like, give him a job so he doesn't go back to work too early?"

"Something like that. The words 'bored off his nut' were spoken."

Sandesh laughed. “I’ll be honest, I’d love something to do. I have therapy and stuff, but otherwise, you know, there’s only so much TV a person can watch. I’m used to being busy. And I’d like to learn something new.”

“That I would have bet on, given the whole swing and tango thing. Okay, so I’ll call Tanith, and give her your number. Did you watch that movie?”

“Yeah, we did. I loved it. Read a bunch of reviews, all these people being snotty about Sally Potter. I liked Roger Ebert’s review the best. He’s like, why shouldn’t she make a movie about learning how to be good at something, and why shouldn’t she be in it herself, if it were a man everybody would be all oh look how brave.”

“My wife says that snotty shit is what people say when they’re not good at anything themselves.”

“Oh snap! She’s right.” Sandesh smiled, listening to Vince laugh. “So yeah, thanks for getting in touch. I hope it works out. Otherwise I’m going to have to go and volunteer for a dig at the tar pits or something.”

“Do not do that,” said Vince. “We’ll find some way to keep you occupied. Talk to you soon.” He disconnected. Sandesh saved the contact information, then went back online to read some more about movie production. He was realizing he’d never really had a hobby, never really done anything except go to school and go to work. Dancing was fun, but not something to do alone. So he might as well read up on this stuff.

He wasn’t really expecting the director to call – how helpful could he be, knowing basically nothing about making movies – but she did, the next day. He’d come in from a walk and was staring into the refrigerator. He wanted to cook something, and they had produce, but it required the use of a knife. His right arm was still not up to that kind of activity, and trying to do it with his left hand seemed idiotically risky, so he was frustrated. When the phone rang he picked it up even though it was another unknown number. "Sandesh Prasad."

"Nice way to answer, it lets people know they dialed the right number. This is Tanith Salazar. I understand you got a call from my choreographer yesterday."

"Hi! Yeah, Vince called me. Did you decide you can use a complete movie novice in some way shape or form?"

"I am at the point in the project where I need someone to organize me so I can fucking think. Is that in your wheelhouse?"

He bit back a laugh. She sounded serious and single-minded, and he didn't want to give offense. "Yes ma'am."

"Ugh," she said, and he almost laughed again. "When and where could we meet? Vince said you're injured, can you drive?"

"Yes, I can drive. I can write and type, though at speeds that are not up to my usual standard. Where are you located?"

"In the Valley. I don't suppose you're out here." She sounded like it was a very faint hope.

"No, I live near LACMA. I don't mind coming to you. Is there anything near you with good curry?"

"Yeah, actually."

"Could we meet for lunch? I'm dying for a good curry and I usually cook my own but the use of knives is contraindicated."

"Are you allergic to cats?"

It was such a complete non sequitur that he could only come up with, "Uh … no."

"How about I order the menu and you meet me at the home office, it's easier for me than hauling all my crap."

"Uh … okay."

"Don't be nervous, it's only one cat. I'll text you the address. Meet up in about an hour?"

"Sure. Why not. I'll see you in a bit." She disconnected without saying anything else, and Sandesh stared at the phone for a second before adding the contact information. The text came in before he even set down the phone, so he added the address to his navigation app and then sent a message to Tasha: *Hi sweetheart, I am going to meet the director of this movie about possibly helping her with some organizational stuff. Will text if it looks like I'll be home after you OK? Love you.*

He didn't expect a response because Tasha usually had her phone muted while she was on duty, and only picked it up if it was something about Theo. He went to take a quick shower and get dressed, wondering what a movie director's unpaid assistant was even supposed to look like.

The address was a small block of condos on the border between Sherman Oaks and Van Nuys. The complex wasn't gated, and there was ample parking on the wide street. It was hot out in the Valley; Sandesh was glad for the median planted with mature shade trees. He walked in to the complex, found the right door, and rang the bell. When a short, dark-skinned, pretty young woman answered he thought he'd gotten the number wrong.

"You must be Sandesh," she said, and stood back. "Vince said six-foot-tall Pablo Verón with his arm in a sling." He nodded, and walked in past her, then turned to look at her. His expression must have said something because she said, "What?"

"I didn't expect you to be so young."

"Come in here, you angelic creature." She closed the door and showed him through to a living-dining room. A strange-looking cat was on the couch; it stared at him with suspicious green eyes, then rearranged itself so it couldn't see him. "How old did you think I'd be?"

"Well, Vince said you'd directed a lot of theater things. I meant to Google you yesterday but I went down this rabbit hole of moviemaking stuff."

"I'm forty-one. My mother is Filipina."

"Oh yeah, that explains it." He shrugged, smiling a little. "My girlfriend worked for you once."

Tanith was immediately interested. She'd worked *with* a lot of people. Not many people had worked *for* her. "Yeah? Who is she?"

"Tasha Jefferson. She was one of the showgirls in that play you did with Victor Garcia. He's in this movie, too, right?"

"Yes he is, he and his husband. I remember Tasha. So I'm guessing you're hungry. Let's eat, and then I'll tell you what I've got going on, and you can tell me if you want to help out."

Sandesh happily ate mass quantities of excellent curry, was not allowed to help tidy up, and then got an hour-long introduction to the project and all its moving parts. "Are you using a shared calendar?" he asked when Tanith seemed to run out of steam. She shook her head. "That's the first thing I'd do. It eliminates so much of the 'who goes where and when' guesswork. If anybody has to reschedule something, everybody can see. Would that save you some time?"

"Time and aggravation. We're heading into rehearsals and things could get ugly. How hard is that to set up?"

"Everybody participating has to get the app, but aside from that it's totally easy. I'll bet you're used to working alone."

"You could say that. So what's the second thing?"

"A Gantt chart. It's kind of like a calendar too," he said, when she looked blank. "Only instead of people it's projects. It's a way to keep track of the status of specific action items, with their various delivery dates marked along the way. Like say you have music to be recorded for this thing. You have a date by which you need to book the recording studio, and a date by which your musicians and singers have to be rehearsed and ready to go, and a date by which you need to have your musicians booked. Whatever the variables are. The chart gets updated as each item is delivered and it's graphic, so you can just look at it and it tells you, we're set up to this point, and here's what's next."

"Where do you learn about something like that?"

"It's the heart of project management. My degree is in business economics, but I took extension courses in project management after I graduated, because I was working in administration."

"My degrees are in theater," Tanith said. "I know my subject matter very well. The business side of a production like this, not so much. My biggest project before this was that play, and the level of complexity was … not this."

"If you have time to run down your various departments and their deliverables, I could throw something together for you pretty fast. I mean, I could get it back to you by this time tomorrow. I have literally nothing else to do," he added, because she looked like she didn't quite believe him. "I'm helping get Theo out the door in the morning, that's Tasha's son, and then unless I have physical therapy I'm staring at the walls." And he had not realized until he was in this conversation just how much he missed his job. Not all the people there, maybe, but the constant challenge of it.

Tanith stared at him for a few seconds. "I'm trying to get my head around your terminology. I'm in the camp that says, is your thing going to be ready when we need it, and they either say yes or no. If it's no, you try to figure out if you can function till you get it." She laughed at his expression. "Yeah, it's not optimal. How do you want to work this? You're right-handed, I'm guessing."

Sandesh rolled his eyes. "This whole situation is so annoying, I can't even tell you. Yes, my manual note-taking speed is somewhere between sad and ludicrous. But I've been practicing with Evernote, it's really low-demand for my arm. Getting pretty speedy there. So if you want to?"

"Yeah. Um. Take ten or so. Bathroom's down the hall. I have to get in touch with my other half, and look at all the shit that's landed on my phone." She got right to it while Sandesh acted on her suggestion. When he came out, he went to introduce himself to the cat. Tanith was still busy with her phone, but she said, "His name is Edgar. Sid pulled him out of a dumpster downtown."

Sandesh assumed Sid was the good-looking guy in the framed photo on a bookshelf, the guy wearing an LAPD dress uniform. "Hi Edgar, nice to meet you." The cat accepted a head rub, having apparently forgotten his suspicions. Then Sandesh went back to the table and sat down, pulled out his phone, and waited for instructions.

"Be right back," Tanith said, and set her phone down. She went down the hall. Sandesh looked around the room, thinking *she is really trusting*, and considered all the different pieces she was trying to pull together. It wasn't all that different from the law office, really. Only instead of the departments he was used to, it was props, and set design, and lighting, and costumes. Casting, and choreography, and rehearsals. The music variables alone could drive a person to gin.

He figured if nothing else, he would learn so much about the process that he'd have a whole new appreciation for a good movie. He'd always enjoyed the behind-the-scenes features, and making-of stuff. When Tanith came back into the room, he asked her, "What do you do when you're not making a movie?"

"I'm a voice artist for ABC/Disney." She shrugged. "It's a living. In show business, that's a thing not to complain about. Ready?"

"I'm ready." They spent another hour together, Tanith going through her notebook and her phone and her laptop to identify each piece of the whole sprawling project. It seemed to Sandesh that she was in pretty good shape, and he said so.

"Thanks. I've been holding it together. But now with casting the dancers, and getting the rehearsals started, and I need to cast some other people, and then there's the set construction and the musicians." She sighed. "A lot of stuff is about to get added in, is what I'm saying. What's this calendar thing, can we set that up right now?"

"Sure." He walked her through activating the app and then notifying everyone she wanted to include. "If you're paying these people, you should tell them it's not optional. Because if there's still that one person you have to chase down, it kind of torpedoes the whole thing."

"Yes, I can see that. I'll lower the boom. Listen, if you want to get back over the hill before rush hour, you'd better get moving. Thanks for this, it was really helpful to go through it all, even if you decide you can't do it."

"Hey, I'm happy to. I'll get you that chart by noon tomorrow. If you like it and you think it will be helpful, then you can call me and tell me what's the next thing you need. Okay?"

She studied him for half a minute as if she couldn't believe he was real. "Okay. Hang tight for a second." She stood up, and used her phone to take a photo of the table covered with scribbled notes, proposals, script pages, and electronics. "That goes on the Kickstarter project page."

"Kickstarter. Right." Sandesh didn't know anything about that, either. *God, this is fun already.* "You need to tell me what your target dates are for that."

"I'll send it to you later. Seriously, you need to hit the road or you are going to be hating life." They exchanged thank-yous and then Sandesh did get on the road, arriving back at the apartment before four. After making sure things were tidy and reasonably prepped for dinner (knife work aside), he went to his computer and did research on all of Tanith's variables. He knew nothing about recording a cast album. How a movie put together costumes for the cast, or how digital set design was accomplished, were questions that had never crossed his mind. *This is fun*, he thought again, before getting sucked down another wormhole.

He told Tasha about the short-term project over dinner. She said, "You're getting a kick out of it, aren't you? Is it really different from the office-coordinator gig?"

"No, that's what's tripping me out, it's the same. I mean, the same approach works, it's just a really different set of requirements. She remembers you, by the way." He smiled at her. "She remembers you, Vince remembered you. We'll have you back on stage in no time."

Tasha laughed. "I don't know if I could take that much excitement. I'm all dizzy about doing those tango mobs. At least I can fit back in my costumes now." Something about replacing snacking with sex. She hadn't even thought about it until she put on her Friday jeans and they were loose.

"Oh you can, huh? Going to model something for me?" Sandesh wouldn't at all mind seeing Tasha in one of those showgirl costumes from the play. *Nobody would*, he thought.

"Maybe later," she said, glancing at Theo, who was scowling at a sheet of homework. "I can't believe they give homework in the first grade."

"School's out pretty soon, though, right?"

"On the seventh. Then it's back to daycare." She turned to her son. "Whatcha got going there, honey?"

"It's addition."

"Want to show me?"

He sighed. "Yes please." Tasha bent over the sheet with her son. Sandesh cleared the table, tidied up the kitchen, and then brought his laptop over to the table to work on Tanith's chart. He was still at it when Theo went to bed, and hadn't reached a good stopping place when Tasha had to call it a night.

"Don't stay up all night," she said. "Don't turn this into another way to overwork yourself. I can tell your arm is sore."

"Yeah. You're right. I need to remember to stay balanced. I can do this in the morning." He saved his work and shut down the computer. Tasha leaned down to kiss him, then tugged him to his feet. "I keep forgetting it's only been however many days."

"I know you do. Go get washed up." When Sandesh joined her in bed, Tasha was waiting. She made him lie down on his front with a pillow under his right shoulder. He hissed a little as he stretched the injured arm out to the side. "I'm going to get you loosened up now. Relax." She wasn't a trained masseuse, but she'd learned how to get his tight spots to release. "Do your yoga in the morning before you get started on that again, you hear me?"

"Yes ma'am." He sounded like he was smiling. After a while, Tasha lay down beside him, her arm draped over his back. He was sound asleep.

Sandesh finished his project a little before noon the next day, and emailed it to Tanith with the subject line Gantt Chart Mark One. He had a reply before three o'clock with the subject line YOU'RE HIRED. The body of the email read:

> That is so much better at-a-glance than a list. OMFG. Can you come to a table read this weekend? Sunday at Chrome. The cast and chief technical contractors will all be there. They should meet you. You might regret this. Anyway if you can come to the thing text me a yes and I'll send you time & address. TYVM.
>
> Abrazos - Tanith

Sandesh promptly texted *YES* and got the promised data more or less instantly. He was back at his laptop reading something else about moviemaking when Tasha got home with Theo. "Hey baby," she said, "did you get your thing done?"

"Yes I did and she liked it. So I think I'll be learning how to make movies this summer. Crazy, right?" He set down the laptop and went to join her in the kitchen. "Have I mentioned I really like this life? I know it'll be different when I'm back at work full time, but … I love being here with you and Theo. Is he all right? He kind of made a beeline for his room."

"He's tired. They're trying to pack an awful lot in before the end of the year. I told him he can go and have some me time." She leaned against the counter and looked him over. "You look like you didn't overdo it today. Well done you." He laughed. "Have you heard from the firm about Solange's letter?"

"Not a peep. I may ping James and see if he's heard anything. But not tonight. I have this table read to go to on the weekend. Is there something I can help you with, or something you'd like to do?"

Tasha patted his good shoulder. "I'm still recovering from that boot camp. I thought I'd take Theo to the park, if he wants to go. He may want to hang out at home."

"Then we'll hang out at home. Anything I can help you with in here?"

She took a moment to study him. "Honey, you don't need to be doing things for me, or looking for things to do, all the time. If I want something, I'll ask. I'm happy you're here. Okay?" He nodded. She reached up to touch his face. "It's really okay," she said gently. "We haven't hit a rhythm yet. It's going to take some time. Just relax."

He wrapped his good arm around her; she leaned close. "How long did it take you and Matthew to be comfortable living together?"

"Oh baby, don't go comparing this to that. You guys are nothing alike." She tipped her head back and he kissed her. "I love you. Now get out of my kitchen so I can fix dinner." He laughed, kissed her again, and left her to it.

Sandesh still wasn't shaving. Tasha gave him a trim after dinner. Neither of them expected it to be so erotic. Toward the end of that enterprise, she leaned close and said, "Next time I'm waiting till Theo is in bed before I do this."

"Good idea," he said. "Could you sit on my lap for a minute? Without your pants?" She laughed, kissed him, and backed away. They had an episode of Planet Earth to watch with Theo. It seemed like much more time than it actually was, until they were finally in bed together. "I'm so tired of this fucked-up arm," he said. "I can't hold you properly, I can't do anything."

"You're doing fine," she said. "It hasn't even been two weeks. What did you expect?" She was lying on top of him, and he was inside her, and it felt great. He knew she liked being on top, and he certainly wasn't going to complain, or not out loud. "Mmm," she said, and closed her eyes, changing her angle a bit. Then she straightened her legs, squeezing them together, and he forgot all about his defective arm.

"God, I love you," he said softly, a few minutes later. He kissed the side of her face, and she made a low contented sound.

Tasha kind of wished she could be a fly on the wall for that table read. She had only the vaguest idea what the story of this movie was meant to be. Since she hadn't been invited and was too shy to ask, she'd decided to see if Annette was free to come to the park with her and Theo. "Hey girl," she said when they connected. "It was so good to see you at Cicada, and then I did the same damn thing I always do, which is get busy and think oh I'll see her later. But this is late enough."

Annette was laughing. "Don't feel bad, I've done the same thing with all the other girls. If Rita and Sherry hadn't hooked me in, I'm pretty sure I'd still be doing my little solo thing with tap classes, wondering why I never see anybody. What are you up to?"

"Well, Sandesh has a thing on Sunday. I have a date with my boy at the park. If you're not busy, would you like to join us? We could get some lunch.

He'll be running around, we'd have time to get caught up."

"That would be great! I am not busy! Where and when?" They settled on their rendezvous and signed off.

Tasha told Sandesh about the plan later. "That's great," he said. "Maybe you'll decide you want to do a thing with those girls again. I'd love to see that."

"So would I," she admitted. "And now I don't have to be sitting on the bench going damn, my man is hanging out with movie stars."

"You'll be hanging out with movie stars any minute now," he said, and kissed her.

She left before Sandesh on Sunday, telling him to have fun and fully expecting to have fun herself. Annette had promised her a ton of being-an-extra stories.

"And one of those things gave me my favorite tap routine of all time," Annette said later. "I was at this thing in the Marina for a rum commercial. We were all going out on the Flyer, and there was going to be dancing. The background coordinator put me with this guy named Dexter Parker."

"No she did not."

"You know him? About six feet, looks like if you mashed together that guy who plays the Falcon with the guy who plays Black Panther?"

"I am having this six-degrees freakout. I was in a play six years ago that he was in. A musical, and it was a big old mess because this girl in the cast killed somebody." Tasha had lowered her voice because she didn't want the other parents at the park listening in.

"I will be damned." Annette stared at her for a second. "Okay. That's Hollywood for you." Tasha laughed. “Well so he was cool, and we kind of clicked, and we spent the whole time bullshitting about dancing because he does tap too. And we ended up putting together a number.”

“Is it online? Can I see it?”

“Yeah!” Annette got her phone out and pulled up the link. They leaned their heads together to watch.

“Girl! That is the *bomb*!” Tasha was fully envious. She didn’t know tap; her skill set didn’t go far beyond basic theater-arts jazz. *At least I can swing,* she thought. *And tango is happening*. “Did you work with him after that?”

“Not really,” Annette said regretfully. “He got cast on ‘10-31’ after one of their actors was killed in a car accident. Not to replace the guy, but to fill in a story that made sense out of that, because it was right in the middle of the season. This was only last winter, early twenty seventeen. And right after that he got a Netflix movie, and then it was that show ‘Going Down.’ So, you know. I was like, dammit.” Tasha laughed. “But when we did this number, Rita and Sherry were at the same showcase. They did ‘Hot Honey Rag,’ they were so good. I got in touch with them through the studio, and they were starting to work with that group that did Cicada.”

“That is awesome. All I’m doing right now is tango.” They talked about that for a while. Annette got excited about the whole movie story, and bitched for a while about not knowing any tango, which made Tasha laugh. “Thanks for that,” she said. “I was thinking I needed a better skill set, but we can’t all do everything, can we?”

“No we can’t. Where’s Theo?” Annette was looking around. “Oh there he is. Oh look at that little cutie." Theo was playing catch with a younger girl. "What a sweet boy."

"He is a sweet boy. He loves Sandesh."

"That's good. How's that going?"

"He moved in with me. There was this thing." Now Tasha told her friend all about the knife incident. They were still talking about it when Theo wandered over, looking hungry. "Is it time to feed you, honey?"

"Yes please."

Sandesh was strongly tempted to leave the sling off for the table read. He knew if Tasha saw it at home she would read him the riot act, so he resentfully fastened it on and got himself ready to go. *At least I'm getting more adept with the left hand*, he thought. He drove up to Hollywood without incident, waved to Terry on his way into Chrome, and spent the next few hours having his vision of the movie project expanded by an order of magnitude. Tanith had sent him a copy of the script the day before, and he'd read the whole thing, but there was something special about seeing the actual actors read it.

After the dancers were dismissed, he listened to the production contractors talking to Tanith about their pieces of the puzzle. He was taking notes all the way through, and he could tell that the next few weeks were going to be really busy. Set design, preliminary construction, costume design and assembly, music contracting and arrangements were all happening already. The most out-there piece of the production design was a scale model of an Art Deco ballroom being created by a local miniatures artist. The model would be photographed and the images projected to create a virtual full-scale ballroom on stage at the

Million Dollar Theater. Real, 'practical' set dressing would enhance the effect. Sandesh couldn't quite picture it, but the professionals seemed confident that it would work.

Tanith's music producer Valerie was also the arranger, and would be the sound recordist during production. They were using music made famous by Carlos Gardel, in their own arrangements, performed by the cast and by local musicians but in several different versions. Sandesh had thought there were only a dozen or so songs, but with all the dances it was more like thirty. All of the actors' solos, plus a quintet, would be recorded for the cast album. Some of those tracks would be used for filmed scenes. The actors and musicians would also be recorded live on set for the film. And then there were some incidental recordings to be done, and live music for some of the dance numbers. *I need a whole chart just for this.* He knew he'd have to review it with Tanith later.

At the end of the meeting, Tanith took a few minutes to speak with the co-stars. Then they left, and she talked to Terry about the arrangements for filming at Chrome. Sandesh updated his notes. He finished before she did, but sat there for a while, staring at the empty stage, trying to imagine how it would look once Tanith's contractors got done with it. It didn't look like much now, but he'd been to that one Underground Cabaret show with Tasha. The Cabaret used hardly any physical sets, mostly lighting, so he had an idea what was possible. The designs under construction for the movie would make a huge difference.

When he walked out with Tanith, she gave him a sideways look and said, "Any burning questions?"

"One comes to mind. Who goes to rehearsals?"

"Vince is running the dance rehearsals. Valerie is rehearsing the musicians, except for my actor-musicians. The guys are in charge of rehearsing their own songs. They've all gotten their arrangements. Andy is setting up rehearsals for the dialogue scenes. I'm not going to try to get to everything. Why, do you want to go?"

He didn't answer directly. "Where would you most want to be? The dialogue scenes, I'm guessing." She nodded. "Your day players, they're coming in cold?" She nodded again. "And that's because you already know them and you know they can ad-lib if necessary." Those names had been added to the master chart a couple of days earlier.

"You're getting the lingo down, aren't you? Yeah, they have the sides already, with enough background to know what they're playing."

"They're for those historical scenes you'll be shooting here, right, where Francisco and Edmundo are singing for the milonga crowd. All on the same day. And," he thought about it for a few seconds, "I'm guessing you'll rehearse them once they're costumed and on set? Okay. So nothing to add to the calendar there. And the extras for your ballroom scenes don't speak or dance, they only have to stand around looking classy, so they also just show up, right?" Tanith was nodding. "If it's okay with you, I feel like I should do the rounds of your contractors a few times. Actually physically see what they're doing and what the status is. And then work around that to get to some of the dance rehearsals. Is that helpful?"

"That's helpful. You can feed me updates and I can concentrate on working with the actors. This is Vicky's first speaking part. You could probably tell she's good with words, but her role is a little weird."

Tanith's phone buzzed in her pocket. She closed her eyes and sighed. "I'd better get back over the hill. Send me your notes on music and let's get that clusterfuck sorted out."

"Yes ma'am." He waited until she was in her car before getting into his. Then he texted Tasha to see if she wanted him to pick something up for dinner, which she did. He called in an order before heading out.

Chapter 6
June 2018

Sandesh did his first round of contractor visits a couple of days later, starting with executive producer Andy Martin, who lived nearby. They had a brief, enlightening conversation before Sandesh had to move on. Almost everybody else was out in the Valley, and Tanith asked him to swing by when he was done because she'd have Valerie with her again talking about music. "That's perfect," he told her. "I've got a mark one chart for the whole music clusterfuck."

"Or cluster bomb, potentially," Tanith said. "What the hell was I thinking. Anyway, ping us when you're on your way over and I'll order some food because this could go for a while."

"Okay." Sandesh sent a text to Tasha again, this time to tell her he wouldn't be home for dinner. *Sorry honey this round of visits is ending with a music meeting I shouldn't miss :-(*

Tasha wrote back within a half hour, which surprised him. *No worries, I'll pick up Theo and we'll go someplace kid-friendly for dinner. Are you making yourself indispensable again? I warned you about that :-)*

*You sure did. This is only till the end of July though, then it's back to real life I guess*

*That office of yours is not real life, it's the fourth circle of hell*

*LOL kind of yeah*

*See you later baby, love you*

*Love you too!*

Tasha had news for Sandesh when he got home. She waited until he'd unloaded his gear, taken off his sling, and joined her on the couch. He stretched out the injured arm and then leaned over to kiss her. "Where'd you go for dinner?"

"Poquito Más. I brought you home a burrito for breakfast."

"Thanks, honey." He kissed her again. "You look like something's up. What's up? Something good?"

"Yeah, something good." She leaned forward. "I'm so excited. Vince called me today and asked me to be in the cabaret routine in the movie!"

"That's fantastic! Wow!"

"That's what I said. I was like, really? Are you sure? Did you mean to call somebody else, and Vince laughed and said yes we're sure, it's going to be filmed on a weekend and we'll be doing most of the rehearsals at the studio in the evening or on weekends, so can you do it. And I said yes without even looking at my calendar."

Sandesh laughed. "That's too fun, though. We can work around whatever else. Your rehearsals will pop into the shared calendar, so I'll know when you need coverage for Theo."

Tasha had some news about that, too. "Actually, Matthew had a request. He sent an email today. He was looking at the second-grade curriculum and thought like we did, damn, and wondered if I thought Theo would like to get out of town this summer. He wants to take our boy on a road trip, national parks, historic sites, stuff like that. Like a month to six weeks depending on how much time his boss will give him. I thought it was a great idea. It would sure beat the daycare. What do you think?" She looked like she really wanted his opinion.

Sandesh also thought it was a great idea, and said so. "We know he'll take good care of Theo. Is anyone else going with them? He might not know it now, but he's going to want some backup at some point."

"Yeah, I mentioned that. He said he's got a friend, which means girlfriend, who's a script supervisor and between jobs at the moment. I asked Theo if he knew this person and he said he did, and she's okay." They both knew that in Theo-speak, 'okay' meant anything from 'tolerable' to 'my best friend.' They both also knew that Matthew wouldn't propose sharing this responsibility with someone he didn't trust at least as much as Tasha trusted Sandesh.

"Then yeah, I mean it's not my place to decide, but I think it would be good for Theo. It would sure give him a lot to work with when they get into the history and science stuff."

"That's what I thought." Tasha patted his knee. "I'm going to tell him yes, then. And I'll get Theo a DokiWatch so he can call us whenever he wants to." Sandesh had never heard of it, but assumed Tasha had done some research as soon as the road-trip idea had been floated. Then he realized this meant they would be child-free for several weeks over the summer. He loved Theo, but the idea of being really alone with Tasha for so much time was mind-blowing. Judging from the look on her face, she was looking forward to it too.

They went to dinner with Terry and Anya the next weekend, meeting up at Hollywood & Highland. Terry was in charge at Chrome all summer; his boss

Tyrone was out of the country. Anya told Tasha that Terry was still not used to being away from the club on the weekends. "His second in command is fine," she said. "Regina's been there for over a year now and she knows her shit. But you know what it's like to step away when something's been your job for a long time."

"Actually I'm about to get a taste of that," Tasha said. She told Anya and Terry about the road trip. "I don't know what I'm going to do with myself."

Sandesh said, "I do," and Terry laughed. Sandesh shot him a sideways smile like 'yeah that,' and said, "She's going to be in the movie, did she tell you?"

"She did not," Terry said with disapproval. "And why not?"

"Because I knew we'd be seeing you this weekend. I'm still inclined to squeal about it." Anya snorted. Tasha shot her a sideways look. "We're doing those mobs, but they called me for that cabaret number. Vince told me you're in that too. Did you know he cast me?"

"Yeah, I knew. I didn't tell your brother because I thought you'd like to do that." Anya shrugged, eyes narrowed with amusement.

"Thanks, sweetie. So I get to do three big dance things in a bona fide movie, and I'm so full of squee." Tasha and Anya talked about the dances for the movie for a while. Sandesh and Terry watched and listened while they ate their dinner.

Once they'd moved on to the dessert and coffee portion of the evening, Sandesh said, "Maybe you could tell me this, Terry. We supposedly start shooting at Chrome on July twenty-three. When does the set go up?"

"The weekend before. That Friday is the last night we're open. Tanith's dude Red, he's up in Canada doing this adventure movie, but he said he'll fly back in that weekend to put the thing together. I'll be there, and we're getting a couple other guys who know their way around a pair of pliers. The piano's getting delivered the twenty-second."

Sandesh had his phone out to make a note. "Are you opening right back up again when we're done?"

Terry shook his head. "No, we're keeping it dark for a week so we can get some updates done, and some deep-cleaning. It's a bunch of years since the build-out and things are a little beat up. We barely got the drywall patched after installing the monitor in the green room."

"Yeah, about that," said Anya, with an expression that said this had been discussed previously. "Literally years ago," she told Tasha. Terry waved a hand, laughing.

When they started down to the garage, the women went ahead. Terry hung back to talk to Sandesh. "So I'd ask how things are going," he said, "but it looks like the answer would be pretty good. My sister looks happy."

"I hope she is. I love her so much. Did she tell you I want to marry her?"

"Might have mentioned it."

"She told me to ask her in December." Sandesh knew there was impatience in his voice.

"Damn, she's making you work for it." They both laughed. "Anya did too. When she finally let me know she wouldn't object to the notion, it was all I could do not to ask her that same night."

"You waited though. Tasha told me you did kind of a big thing, on stage at Chrome. Weren't you nervous?"

"Hell yeah I was nervous. But it turned out great."

Sandesh made sure the women were out of earshot. "Do you think Tasha would like something like that? She told me Matthew took her to a jewelry store, stopped in front of the rings, and said pick the one you want."

Terry laughed again. Tasha and Anya looked around. "Oh damn, they're slowing up. Yeah, don't do like he did. You'll know what to do. You're a smart motherfucker."

"Thanks," Sandesh said.

"Thanks for what?" Tasha said as they caught up.

"Told him he was a smart motherfucker," said Terry, like it was obvious.

"Maybe too smart," Tasha said when she stopped laughing. "He went around to some rehearsals this week and that tall guy, Tomás? They were talking about the rehab and Tomás said did you ever play the piano, and Sandesh said no, and Tomás said you should try it. So now on top of everything else, Sandesh is getting piano lessons. If I were trying to learn that much new stuff in one summer I think my head would explode. He doesn't even look tired."

"All this stuff is fun, though." *And I'd be going stir crazy without it*, he thought. Maybe by the end of all this, he'd have learned some ways to be about more than just the job. They were parked on different levels, so they said their goodbyes. Sandesh and Tasha went to her car. "Sling gets retired next week, finally," he said. "I could drive tonight if you want me to."

“I’m fine,” she said. “I know you think it’s been forever. Three weeks is not that long. And you’ve been driving all over this week. What did your physical therapist say about that?”

“I didn’t tell her.” Tasha laughed again. Sandesh was smiling. “I’ll tell her about the piano lessons next time I see her. Then I’m counting down till she and the doctor say I’m cleared for weight-bearing exercise.” She glanced over at him. He was looking at her in a way that said ‘I have plans for you.’

“I might be counting down to that too,” she said.

June 2018

It was the latest in a series of unproductive meetings, and James couldn’t believe what he was hearing. “Are you seriously trying to make this all out to be Sandesh’s fault? Because it isn’t. You have all these complaints. You have all this footage. You have *her* confronting *him* with a knife. He never laid a hand on her. His personnel file is solid gold.” He looked around the room, seriously pissed. There were a lot of uncomfortable expressions. Darlene, the office administrator – still and always the source of most of the obstruction - wouldn’t make eye contact. “We are not talking about someone who broke an ankle rollerblading at Venice Beach. We are talking about this.” He flipped a switch and the conference-room wall screen came to life, showing the one photo he’d taken downstairs before he got his hands on Sandesh, in that moment when he’d thought *Jesus Christ am I too late*. He’d cued it up on his laptop because when they called another meeting he’d decided to take all necessary measures.

Everyone around the table flinched away from the image of their employee lying on the garage floor in a pool of his own blood. Grimly satisfied, James let the reaction sit for a few seconds before saying, "That is *our fucking fault*, people. As is the fact that the San Francisco office was never adequately staffed. As is the fact that someone kept blocking the raise this man was promised and has more than earned. If he takes us to court, if you make him do that, we will lose." He looked around again. "Now what, exactly, about his attorney's letter do you find unreasonable? And it had better not amount to, this is inconvenient *for me*."

"You sound like you're on his side," one of his partners said, sounding grouchy but resigned.

"I am! We all should be! He's a dynamite employee and we need him back here. If he has to sue to get what I frankly do agree he is owed, he will not come back. And listen to me: he is going to win." *One more dose of shame, you unbelievable shitheads.* "Our planning has been poor, our execution has been worse, and this resistance to doing the right goddamned thing is disgusting." He stood up, out of patience, and disconnected his laptop from the USB hub.

"We're not done here, Mr. Levine," Darlene said huffily.

She wasn't his boss, and he wouldn't have cared if she were. "I am done here." He left the room without another word, went back to his office, and texted Silvia: *Honey I may have to quit this job*

She must not have been busy because he got a response immediately: *I've been expecting you to say that for years. What's new? The Sandesh thing?*

*If these fuckers make him sue them, I may join PPH Law and take his case pro bono*

*They would plotz*

It made him smile. *PPH or these assholes?*

*Both. What's the rest of your day like?*

*I'm packing up and coming home. Got some stuff to do but I don't want to talk to anybody here*

*See you in a few. Besos*

*Y abrazos.* He packed his briefcase with material for his work-in-progress, slid his laptop into the side pocket, and left his office. He stopped by his assistant's desk, halfway down the hall. "Hey Janice. I'm going to work from home the rest of the day. You can forward client calls, but I don't want to talk to anybody in the office except you."

She looked him over, assessing conditions. They'd worked together for a long time. "Okay," she said slowly. "So if the managing partner wants you, what do I tell him?"

"Tell him to go fuck himself." She laughed. James smiled. "I know, you can't say that. Tell him to leave a voice mail and I'll call him back."

"Will you?"

"Probably not." She snorted, shaking her head, and he went down the hall to the elevator and freedom. When he got home, Silvia took him straight to bed, which improved his day immensely. Then she took charge of his cell phone so he could get some work done uninterrupted. "You're the best," he told her gratefully. "This whole mess has been so distracting. Don't let it interfere with your work though."

"I'm good. Rescheduled an appointment or two, no worries." She patted his shoulder and went to her side of the den they both used as a home office. She had his phone muted but she could see when a text came in from his secretary, about six o'clock. Her eyebrows shot up. They'd both been working for almost three hours; she glanced over at James. He had the look that said 'clearing out in-box,' so she said, "This is interesting." He looked up inquiringly. She handed him the phone. Janice's text read *They fired Darlene!!!*

"Holy shit," James said blankly. "That was not what I expected." He called Janice on her cell; she picked up right away. He put her on speaker so Silvia could hear. "For real?"

"Management committee never even left that conference room," she said in a hushed voice. "The risk-management guy was back here about an hour after you left. I don't know exactly what happened, but you know I can see reception from here. An hour ago they walked Darlene down to her office and, I swear to God, they just escorted her out. I about fell off my chair."

James snorted. "I guess the risk guy made an impression. I know he had the same thoughts about the situation that I did."

"So now we have no human-resources staff at all," Janice said, still *sotto voce*. "It is a wonder to me that this business survives."

"Me too. Thanks for the update. I'll see you tomorrow."

"Call in sick," she said. "That should really scare the crap out of them."

James laughed, as much at the fact that Janice had made the suggestion as at the gleeful look on his wife's face. "Yeah, not a bad idea. I could go work at Silvia's office. I'm going to call Mr. Prasad now and fill him in on this development. It should be good news for him."

"Yeah, do that. Tell him we miss him."

"I will. Give my regards to your wife." He disconnected, and looked over at Silvia, shaking his head with wonder. "Un-fucking-believable." He scrolled to another number and dialed. "Hey Sandesh, is this a good time?"

Sandesh, who was currently at liberty, said, "Sure. What's up?"

"I've been reliably informed that Darlene got fired today. There was yet another meeting in which she tried yet again to throw you under the bus. I unloaded on everyone and then walked out. They got the risk-management counsel in later, and apparently he told them where the real problem was."

"Wow," Sandesh said, after a few seconds' delay. "So should I do anything?"

"I don't think so. I have a feeling your lawyer's letter is going to get a response really soon. And Janice says hi, said to tell you that you're missed, which is very true. Anyway so how are things going?"

"Tanith is losing her mind but she's such a good actress hardly anybody has noticed. All I'm basically doing is organizing her, but I'm learning so much. I am not sick of Argentine tango yet." James laughed. "Oh, and Tomás is giving me piano lessons. I told him about the physical therapy and he said, have you ever played piano. We're doing a little bit every day, he's got a piano at home so I go there in the morning and then it's out to the Valley. The first few times were a train wreck, but the hand is already improving. My therapist was impressed in this kind of 'damn I wish I'd thought of that' way."

"That's great."

"Tasha and I might get a digital keyboard so I can practice at home. Maybe Theo will want to learn."

"He'll probably want to do anything you're doing," James said, smiling. "That kid is crazy about you."

"He's a sweetheart. Anyway, thanks for letting me know about the latest. I'll wait to hear from my lawyer, I guess. How are you and Silvia?"

"We're good, thanks for asking. We'll see you at class."

"Yeah, looking forward to it. I expect great things from you." He disconnected on James' laughter.

It turned out they saw each other a good bit earlier than anticipated. James did call in sick the day after Darlene was fired, but went back to the office the following day. He'd only been there an hour when the managing partner tapped on his open door. "Got a minute?"

"Hi Carver, sure." James sat back and watched as the older man stepped in, closing the door behind him, and took a seat in one of the guest chairs. He was holding a letter-sized manila envelope. "What's up?"

"So you heard what happened the other day." He looked at James for confirmation. "The management committee has been up my ass continuously since the whole Jessica thing started, about protecting our position and the firm's reputation and all this bullshit. I was pissing and moaning to my wife yesterday during lunch and she said Carver, with all due respect, none of you will have a position to protect if you do not solve this immediately, and by the way the only person who seems to know anything about actually managing that stupid office - her words," he clarified when James snorted, "is this kid who got knifed. So quit acting like a skunk with its head in a tin can and get him back." He waited, with clear and present irritation, while James tried a little too obviously not to laugh. "I take it you agree with her."

"With all due respect, the five of you couldn't manage your way out of a cardboard box." James saw the offended expression forming and held up his hands in the 'stop' position. "That's not what you were trained to do. None of you studied business. None of you ever held an executive position. You're lawyers, and you're good lawyers, but that doesn't mean you know everything. So yes, I agree with Margie. The only person currently employed by this firm who, first, did study business and, second, knows how all of our support departments operate is the guy out on leave."

Carver sighed, looking tired. "I know. We all know. Why do you think Jason and the others have been so bent? It's infuriating to find out you don't know how your own business actually runs. Anyway, I came back to the office yesterday and blew another three nonbillable hours drafting a response to that letter. The others signed off on it this morning." He handed the envelope to James. "Tell me what you think."

James wasn't a hundred percent sure why he was being asked for his opinion, but then he wasn't sure why he'd been roped in to all these meetings in the first place. He put on his negotiation face, opened the envelope, and read the letter. Before giving his opinion, he looked up and said, "Tell me why I've been in on this. It's not only because I was the one with his life in my hands."

Carver winced a little. "No. It's because you are apparently the one person in the firm who will speak truth to power."

"You don't have any power," James said bluntly. "And all of you need to get clear on that. The firm only exists if the clients are happy, the clients are only happy if the work is good, and the work is only good if we have the support we need. Your clients don't give a shit about your power. They only care about your expertise, and whether you can deliver it effectively." Carver wasn't saying anything. James went on. "Everyone working here could walk out and get another job across the street, and you're damned lucky none of them have quit over this whole situation. You're losing the trust of your staff. If you want to do your work in this office, with this team, the entire partnership needs to get on board with a reboot. Anybody who won't needs to get the fuck out."

Carver stared at him for a long silent minute. Then, "That said, how's the letter."

James couldn't quite believe he'd said what he'd said. "It's good. Send it to Dasher, and I'll take the meeting if you want me to. You understand if he accepts both parts, I'm going to advise him to take no prisoners."

"I would expect nothing less." Carver stood up. "Thank you for your time, Mr. Levine." He went out, leaving the office door open. A minute later Janice came to the door and made a 'what happened' face. James did a 'who knows' thing, slid the envelope into his briefcase, and gestured her in.

She closed the door behind her. "What was that? You didn't quit, did you? He didn't ask you to leave, did he?"

"No and no. He asked me to deliver an offer letter to Sandesh. And he sat there while I fired a cannon full of shrapnel at him. I can't even believe some of the shit I just said." He stifled a hysterical giggle. Janice bit her lip, trying not to giggle too. "God I wish I'd had a recorder on, I know I'm going to get it wrong when I tell Silvia later." After a moment he said, sounding amazed, "I told him the management committee couldn't manage its way out of a cardboard box." Janice squeaked and covered her mouth with both hands, eyes wide. "You want some coffee? Let's go get some coffee." James stood up and opened the office door again, made sure he had his wallet and key card, and ushered Janice out. They both managed to get all the way down to the coffee shop before laughing out loud.

James checked in with Sandesh after getting back to the office, arranging to meet him not at the Miracle Mile apartment but at the office of his attorney Solange Dasher, down the street in Century City. He left his own office at four to walk over, a little nervous at being the one handling – almost, it seemed, by default – a significant negotiation on behalf of the firm. Carver had said, when James told him the meeting was set up, "Do your best for us." James chose to interpret that as 'do right by everyone to the extent possible.' He was sure Carver knew that in any serious disagreement, James would come down on Sandesh's side.

Once he was cleared up to reception, he greeted Tasha, who seemed surprised to see him. "Hey there. Sandesh tell you what's going on?" She shook her head. "Trying to wrap this up today. Cross your fingers. If all goes well, I'll buy you dinner later." She smiled, then a new call came in. James paced a little bit, not in the mood to sit and wait for the labor attorney's secretary to come and escort him down to the conference room. She got there in a few minutes. James waved to Tasha again as he went down the hall.

"Hi James," Sandesh said when he entered the conference room. He looked well-rested, James was happy to see. He also looked a bit wary. "So what the what?"

Ms. Dasher gave her client a sideways look, like she thought things should be a little more serious, and said, "Good afternoon, Mr. Levine. Thanks for coming in."

James said, "Hi Solange. I believe you've already gotten this by email." He handed the envelope with the offer letter to the other attorney and sat down. He knew for a fact that Solange had received the letter in advance; the whole review-the-hard-copy thing was part theater, and part confirmation that nothing had been changed. After a few minutes she passed the letter to Sandesh, who read it quickly, looked startled, and then read it again.

"Initial thoughts, Mr. Prasad?"

Sandesh glanced at James, then answered Solange. "Well, part one is basically what we asked for. Part two is … unexpected." Part two of the letter offered Sandesh the office administrator position, with a comprehensive listing of the firm's current staffing and operations deficits. Sandesh had never seen anything like it. He'd seen plenty of offer letters since he started working at the firm, but they never laid out the challenges a candidate might expect to face when they walked in to the first day on the job. "Can I ask a couple of questions?"

"Of course," said James. "I'm here to work this out."

"Why all the detail?"

"Because they know you already know. One of our guys, after going through the outgoing administrator's files, saw how you'd been copying her in on all the department business, the interview reports, the cost reports, the hour and wage reports, all that stuff. Everything the management committee got from her and thought she was handling. It was his suggestion to put all that in this letter." James waited to see if Sandesh had more to say on that. Apparently he didn't.

What he did have was the question James had thought would be first on his mind. "Does this mean I'd have the authority to hire and fire support staff without consulting the management committee?"

"Yes, it does."

Sandesh shook his head like he couldn't believe it, frowning a little. "Did Darlene have that authority?"

"Yes, she did."

"Then why the fuck wasn't she hiring anybody?" James laughed, and Solange looked shocked. Sandesh didn't wait for an answer. "Whatever, moving on. I need to take a day to think this over. I really didn't expect anything like this."

"We understand."

"And it says immediately, or as soon as possible. You know I'm not fully rehabbed yet."

"My suggestion would be that the firm issue you a laptop so you can work from home until you're discharged from physical therapy. As you know, there are some immediate staffing needs. My assistant can be assigned to you pending your return, if you'd agree to come in to handle interviews in person. And if there's something in San Francisco that needs personal attention, one of us will go. We all know a little bit more about things than we did a month ago."

"Are you on the management committee now?"

"Eh." James shrugged. The answer was 'not officially.' "Let's say I've been in a lot of meetings."

"You know that means they're going to send you up there all the time." Sandesh glanced at Solange, who'd made a move indicating that she thought they were straying from the point. "Okay. I need a few minutes with Ms. Dasher, and we'll be in touch within twenty-four hours. Fair enough?"

"Fair enough." James stood up. Sandesh did too, and offered his right hand. "Oh yeah?" James smiled while they shook hands. "Talk to you soon. Thanks, Solange. Give me a call if you have any questions."

"I'll do that. Thanks James." She also stood to shake his hand. As soon as he was gone she indicated Sandesh should sit down again. "Are you happy with the terms?"

"I think I want a couple more things in writing. Like about working from home. I'd like that to be an option going forward, not only a while-I'm-disabled thing. And I'd like some limits on the amount of travel. There is no point wasting days in travel when we have video conferencing, most of this stuff is trivial."

"You might consider," she said slowly, "writing up some of your thoughts on efficiencies. Some of the things we've talked about. Mr. Levine might be able to get some of those things cleared now, while they're motivated."

"Yeah, good idea."

"Do you trust him?"

Sandesh looked at her, surprised. "He's the one who saved my life. Didn't you know?" She clearly hadn't known. "Oh, did you think I would have talked to just anybody like that? No, we're friends. We're taking tango lessons together, we're going to be extras in this movie. Anyway yes, I trust him completely. So I'll write something up and shoot it over to you, and we could talk it over in the morning? And then you can pass it to him, and then like you say, if they're motivated maybe we can wrap all this up by the end of the day tomorrow." Solange agreed, they shook hands, and she escorted him back to reception.

Tasha had already suggested they go over to the mall for dinner after she got off work, so Sandesh was expecting to hang out for a while. She waved him over after Solange went away and said, "How'd it go? James tipped me."

He leaned over to give her a quick kiss since nobody was around. "They're offering me the administrator position." Her eyes got as big as they did that first time he kissed her. "I know, right? Now I have to figure out how to wring the maximum good out of this situation, and also make sure I've got man-traps and catapults set up in case they try to fuck me over once I'm back there."

She was laughing under her breath. "James said if it went well we could all have dinner tonight. You want to?"

"Sure, I can brainstorm with him about how to put the screws to the management. I'll text him. Is Matthew picking up Theo?"

"Yeah. I'll remind him." The phone rang. Tasha rolled her eyes and answered. Sandesh went to sit down, sent a text to James, and then opened Evernote to start listing the many ideas he'd had since he started running both offices. Once again he was thinking, *there may never be a better moment.*

James wasn't surprised, exactly, when he got the email from Sandesh the next morning. They'd spent most of their post-meeting dinner brainstorming ways and means to manage the office better. James had learned a lot since Sandesh had been out on leave. All of the partners had, because there hadn't been anybody between them and their support staff. But even he wasn't quite prepared for the extent of the suggestions.

Above-the-line items, things that Sandesh was requiring in order to accept the full offer, included work-from-home privileges and a firm-issued laptop, maximum travel of two days a month, four weeks of vacation time, and a weekly action meeting with the managing partner. He footnoted this with the comment 'it's up to him whether he actually consults the rest of the committee, but we cannot continue to allow action items to roll over week after week.' James thought that was well within the parameters of 'reasonable.'

He wasn't sure about the biggest thing below the line, though. Sandesh recommended breaking their lease in San Francisco and going to a virtual office, with an e-suite for any necessary meetings. He footnoted that one with 'financials and logistics upon request,' which James interpreted as 'I have it ready but if you're going to knee-jerk a no, why bother giving it to you.' He called Sandesh to see if he was right.

The reply was, "Yes, you're right. I stayed up a little too late doing that, I'm tired and cranky, so when I wrote the email I was like, they'll probably refuse to even consider it, so fuck it. I mean, Solange thought I was insane."

"Can you run it down for me, in five minutes or less? I promise if it makes sense to me, I'll go to bat for it."

"Okay, sure. Hang on." Sandesh set his phone down and opened up the document on his laptop, taking one more look at it to see if it still made sense. *I'd rather be de-conflicting rehearsals right now*, he thought, but this one thing would make such a huge difference in his overall plan that it was worth taking the time. "All right. You ready?" James assented, and Sandesh started making his case. When he got to the end of the short version he paused and said, "Is that enough?"

"Well, you've convinced me," said James. "But I don't have my ego involved with having a physical office up there. Send over the whole thing so I can put it a little more tactfully." Sandesh laughed. "I mean, not that I've been super good at being tactful lately. Anyway, all your must-haves are things I don't think we're going to have any problem with. I'll present all that today, and you should have an answer tomorrow. Now you probably have a piano lesson or something, so I'll talk to you later."

"Bye James." Sandesh hung up and let things settle for a minute. He hadn't mentioned the recent developments to his family, and since nothing was signed he figured he'd wait a little longer. The last thing they'd heard was that he was thinking of leaving the firm altogether. He hadn't even tried to explain the whole movie-intern thing. A switch to 'oh hey I'm staying at the firm but by the way I'm now an administrator about five years ahead of my most optimistic projection and I'm going to be making a fuck-ton more money' needed to be carefully delivered. His parents were both academics and had literally no idea how a law office operated. *Eh*, he thought, *one thing at a time*. He and Tasha were due to have dinner with Lochan and Paige soon; he could run through it with them. For now, he had to herd some cats.

## Chapter 7
June 2018

The cast lists for the dance numbers in Tanith's movie had been delivered the night before. The featured dancers all had some experience with film projects, and either worked or trained at Shall We Dance, with two exceptions. Tanith had cast a couple of amateur dancers who trained with Vince. Sandesh called her up to ask about them. She said, "They're good enough for the scenes where they'll be featured. Vince has had them going out for tango competitions for two years. But they also put a chunk of money into the Kickstarter. So, since they have the right look and they are in fact good enough, we put them down for newsreel and funeral along with our four pro and semi-pro couples."

"Is Vince choreographing those scenes?"

"That's a no. All five couples will freestyle. Diego and Linda are also doing the big outdoor mobs, which are also not choreographed, but when we set those up let's try to have them visible. With thirty couples they could get lost."

"Gotcha. What else do I need to know about these dance scenes? There's an awful lot of them."

He could hear the shrug in Tanith's voice. "It's a movie about tango, you can't not have dance scenes. Can you shoot me one of your chart thingies that's just for the dance scenes? If each one is a project, then the deliverables are music, choreography, set or location, costume, and actual dancers, right?"

"You're getting the hang of this," he said, smiling. "And if it's live music to be recorded during filming, it's musicians too. No worries, I can get you that tomorrow. I'll send a copy to Vince. Between the two of you, you can fill in any blanks and then we'll know where we're at. Is everybody using the calendar?"

"So far we seem to have one hundred percent compliance. It's amazing the power money has." *Pause for laugh*, Tanith thought, appreciating him.

Sandesh was about to sign off when he remembered something. "Hey, did Vince talk to you before casting Tasha in that group? She's so excited she can hardly eat."

"Tell her to eat, it's a few weeks before we film that. Yeah, he mentioned to me that he remembered her from that group she was in, and that he's seen you both working on your stuff at the studio. He could have pulled someone else from the studio but I think he likes her. And I liked her when she worked on my play. Since it was actually Andy who put her name in the hat, I didn't have a problem with it. Vince says she's doing fine with the routine."

The women's cabaret routine was going to be filmed at a historic downtown building, and staged on its staircase. Tomás and Vince had been grousing about how to block it (since the dance studio did not have a staircase) until Sandesh made a suggestion. "We're setting up to do the blocking video over in Century City. Do you want to be kept in the loop on that, or what?"

"As long as we have it in Dropbox by the end of next week and nobody gets arrested, do what you gotta do. Say hi to Tasha for me."

"I'll do that. Talk to you tomorrow." They both disconnected, and Sandesh got to work on the new chart.

He was still studying online when he wasn't working. He'd discovered MasterClass, considered the subscription fee a necessary investment, and devoured segment after segment. After finishing the day's quota of movie-related tasks, he found a new class from filmmaker Werner Herzog. He wrote down a quote and texted it to Tanith: 'Just grab your stuff and make the film.' She sent back a thumbs-up emoji.

Before he shut down for the day, Sandesh looked back at the email exchange about the law office and thought, *I may yet say no*.

He talked to Tanith the next day after she'd had a chance to review the dance chart. First they went through it together to fill in any blanks. Then, because she didn't immediately have a new task for him, he said, "So I know it's partly the novelty and learning so much, but I'm liking this so much more than running the law office. What are the odds I could actually make a living at it?"

"Not good," she said, sounding regretful. "I mean you could, certainly. But one thing that's easy to forget is that a movie is a temp job. This one's being produced by Dream of Tango, LLC, a company I set up. Once the movie is done and - we hope - sold, the company is done. Every person who's employed by the LLC for this movie is unemployed the day after their specific work is done. I might hire all the same people again, for another project, but not until we go into production. It's rough. And the truth is, as terrific as you are, and as essential as I can see you becoming by the end of this project, I couldn't pay you anything close to what you're worth. What do you make at the law office?"

He told her, and then told her the number for the new offer. She made a wheezing sound. Sandesh couldn't help smiling. "I'm guessing that's not in the same ballpark as this."

"Sandesh, that's not even the same sport." He heard the email notification on her laptop go off. "Goddammit. Listen, the only reason I can do this is I've worked for the Mouse for a whole lot of years, and I have a ton of paid time off available, and I had enough money to get the ball rolling. I have a lot of friends in the business who are helping me out. And still, if it were not for Kickstarter it would not be happening, Werner Herzog notwithstanding, because you cannot make this kind of movie by yourself with a cell phone. You need people, and people cost money. As they should."

"Okay," he said. "I get you. Well, I'm having fun anyway. I guess I'll go back to the law office and this will be the story I tell when I'm old."

"Or, you know, I do another one and build you into the budget. You can throw away all your vacation time on me and my madness."

"I would totally do that." At the moment, it sounded like the best-case scenario: work at the law office for eleven months, make a movie for a month.

Tanith laughed. "We haven't even started filming this thing yet. You may change your tune. When do you go back to work, anyway?"

"When I'm released from physical therapy and when I'm satisfied with the deal they're offering. The first thing is probably end of July. The second thing sooner than that."

"End of July works for me." He knew it did; the shooting schedule was locked. Tanith added,

"Seriously though. It's a lot easier to love creative work when you're not living in a garage apartment and eating Top Ramen twice a day."

"I can see that. You have emails to read now, so I'll let you go. Ping me when you think of something else for me to do."

"Count on it." Tanith disconnected, and Sandesh went back to the living room to cue up another video on moviemaking. He was halfway through it when he got a text from James that said *call me.* He didn't really want to, because he didn't want to switch gears, but on the other hand he needed to know if staying with the firm was even an option. Before calling, he went to the bathroom, then got himself a glass of water, confirming it was at least an hour before Tasha would be home with Theo. Plenty of time for negotiation. Then he picked up the phone and dialed.

James expected to spend the day fighting with members of the management committee, but it seemed they had all raised the white flag. Possibly because around noon the support staff quietly staged a walkout. Everyone vanished, ostensibly for lunch, and while they all did eventually come back it was late enough in the day that a number of attorneys were in an absolute panic about getting work out. Miraculously, or perhaps due to well-laid plans (James gave the staff more credit for both ingenuity and nefariousness than most of his partners did, perhaps because he spoke freely with his assistant Janice), all the work did get out. Nobody left anything essential unfinished. Nobody admitted to any collusion, either. Carver called James at four and said, "Make the deal."

"Full power to negotiate?"

"Do what you gotta do. This can't happen again." Carver hung up. James looked over the detailed plan one more time and sent a text asking for a call. He didn't have to wait very long.

"Hey James. Got some news for me?" Sandesh sounded cautious.

"First let me tell you what happened today." James had his office door closed, and gave Sandesh not the short version of 'mini strike, complete capitulation, come back and wreak havoc' but the long, embellished version. Sandesh was laughing before he was a minute into it. "So yeah. Anyway." He waited for Sandesh to compose himself. "Carver told me to make the deal. I'm here to tell you that all your above-the-line items are approved. Below the line, everything is cleared except closing San Francisco. That is not off the table, however. They want the folks up there to come down here and respond to the plan in person. They're afraid those guys might feel this is a way to edge them out, which it isn't."

"No, it isn't," said Sandesh. "It's advantageous to the firm to have our own people up there with connections in the community and at the local courts. It is the opposite of advantageous to be paying for all that infrastructure when they can be functionally supported almost entirely down here." *And I can't wait to fire that fucker in IT up there.*

"I'm with you. So is that satisfactory?"

"Yes it is. Write it up and I'll sign it. And I'll be happy to write up something more detailed about the e-suite option, including which of the facilities up there it could be, once I know their home addresses."

That was information that had only been in Darlene's files. "Then when they get in and we say 'oh hey we're thinking of having you work from home' we can hand them that, and they'll know how much easier their lives are about to get."

"If I couldn't walk to work I might have quit years ago. Anyway, okay. I'll write it up, and I'll try to have it over to Solange before six. If you can get it back to us in the morning that would be great."

"Thanks, James. I really appreciate all the trouble you've gone to over this."

"I'm glad I was here to handle it. We have a lot of people who will be very happy to hear you're coming back. Now there is one big favor I have to ask you."

"What's that?"

"Can you come in to run payroll?"

"Oh my God." Sandesh cracked up all over again. After a minute he said, "That's right, you don't have anybody there to do it. Yeah, how about I hand deliver that thing tomorrow."

"You're a mensch. Talk to you tomorrow." James disconnected, heaved a sigh of relief, and went to tell Janice the good news. Then he got out his cell phone and sent a text to Silvia: *THE DEAL IS MADE*

She wrote back in a few minutes, while he was cleaning out his in-box again: *Glory hallelujah. When's he back on the job?*

*Full-time, end of July. Till then on a part-time, work-from-home basis with support here. Tell you more when I get home. Love you, thanks for all your help*

*Love you too, you're welcome XOX*

By the end of the following day, Sandesh had signed the revised offer (and run payroll). He had a bottle of champagne chilling when Tasha got home, and a chocolate cream pie ready to share with Theo. "I know all this work stuff is over his head right now, but I thought it would be mean for us to celebrate something and not include him," Sandesh told Tasha while they were getting dinner ready.

"You're sweet. And a great role model. You are setting the bar awfully high, though." He snickered. Tasha was giggling. "Seriously, that kind of money at your age? What are you going to do with it?"

"Spend it on you." He actually had no idea. With shared living expenses, his old rate was more than plenty. The new rate was kind of ridiculous. "Give Theo a fat allowance to spend on this trip."

"Oh lord," she said. "He was so excited about the DokiWatch, but I didn't even think of that. He's never had an allowance before."

"Shit, I guess not, huh? I keep forgetting he's only almost seven. He's such a character already." Sandesh hadn't ever lived with a child, not since he and Lochan were kids themselves. "How about we give a chunk to Matthew and say if there's stuff he thinks would be a great resource later on, books or DVDs or whatever, or a really great souvenir of the trip, to use it for that. He could FedEx it back here so they don't have to haul it along."

Tasha gave him a fond look. "Okay, honey. Thank you. Let's get him in here so we can eat." Sandesh gave her a kiss and went to fetch their boy.

The next morning, the firm messengered over a laptop and a cashier's check for the amount owed from backdating the raise due on his previous promotion. Sandesh opened the envelope and said "Holy shit" out loud. Then he had to send Tanith a text: *Going to be a little delayed, have to go give some money to my 401k so the tax man doesn't take all of it*

*@#&% taxes*

*Yeah. Photography for your miniature set today, are you going to be there?*

*The artists very tactfully suggested that it might go faster without me*

*LOL*

*Shut up*

*I'll ping Yoshi and see if I can swing by. Already scheduled to see Lesley about costume. I'll buzz you after I'm done there to see if you need anything else*

*URA rock star TTYL*

Sandesh knew that when Tanith started abbreviating, she was really busy, so he didn't send a reply. He put himself together and headed over to Schwab.

By the end of that day he'd updated the production chart with the status of the miniature set (complete) and the costumes (in progress). Tanith's friend Lesley was handling the wardrobe, and that was a hell of a chart all by itself. She had all the costume construction and rentals ironed out. The only open item on the chart that Sandesh thought needed to be closed immediately was an assistant dresser. The person Lesley had used most recently wasn't available. Sandesh had made himself a note to ask Rory and Dana, the stage managers, if they knew anyone who could fill the role. He was about to make that call when Tasha got home. "Hey sweetheart, how was your day?" He got up to give her a kiss.

"I was halfway to the daycare before I remembered Theo wouldn't be there! I had a moment," she said, and kicked off her shoes. "It was like, oh my God, my baby's out in the big world without me."

"He's with Matthew. He was so excited this morning." Sandesh hugged her. Matthew had been excited too. So much that when Sandesh helped load the car and saw that Matthew's girlfriend Katie was set up to drive the first leg out of town, he'd given her a thumbs-up and a silent 'thank you.' He had a feeling father and son were going to be doing a fair amount of bonding on this trip. *Don't be envious*, he reminded himself. "Theo's going to be fine."

"I know, it's just *wow*. I was talking to one of the women in the cabaret group about it and she said she had a moment like that. A few years ago, her little girl was going away to French camp. Her daughter was totally fine, really excited, but she was freaking out." She shrugged. "I checked my phone after I parked, and there was already a message. He said, hey Mama, we're going to the Grand Canyon, I'll send you a picture."

"He's going to have a great time. So, I had kind of a thing today."

"Did you get something else?"

"They sent over a laptop so I can start digging through email, and they sent a cashier's check for that back pay. I was like, whoa. Had to take it over to Schwab."

"Big check?"

"Scary big. I didn't dare put it in my checking account. The IRS would have taken half of it. And I might have been tempted to spend the rest on a trip to

Argentina." Sandesh hugged Tasha again, because she was laughing.

"Someday. So it's almost go time on this movie, huh?" Tasha moved through into the kitchen, opened the refrigerator, and started pulling out the things he'd prepped for dinner. "When do you even find time to do this?"

"In between emails. Yeah, next week is the first big thing, the date at the recording studio. I'd love to be there but I'd only be in the way. Tanith and her producer Valerie – you remember Valerie, right? – they've got this little orchestra coming and the actors don't even know it yet. They think they're working with backing tracks. I wish I could see their faces."

"And then the week after, it's full speed ahead? Is everything set?"

"Not quite. Lesley, the costume person, she's still looking for an assistant dresser. There's a ton of costume and hair and makeup for some of those scenes." Tasha had read the script by now, and seen the cast list, so she nodded comprehension. Sandesh added, "I guess Lesley worked with someone she liked last summer, but that person just had a baby and is going to Paris in August and it's not happening. I was about to ping Rory and Dana to see if they knew somebody."

Tasha said, "I might know someone. I mean, I don't know if she's available. You remember my showgirls? When I got together with Sherry last week she told me Maria, the missing showgirl, she went into hair and makeup. She's done some TV and movie work. I hadn't called her yet, but I have her contact info. Want me to reach out? Tanith and Lesley know her already, so that might help."

"Yeah, that would be great. Let's get this dinner rolling first though." Thanks to his prep work, that didn't take much time. After they ate, they cleaned up the kitchen together, then went to the living room. Sandesh picked up his laptop, then glanced at Tasha. "I keep looking around for Theo."

"I do too!" Tasha had her phone out, checking for a message. "Nothing yet. I told him to call or text anytime. I might have a little meltdown later." She leaned against his shoulder.

He kissed her forehead. "I might see if I can distract you. I've been looking at you on this couch for months, thinking evil thoughts." She laughed. "And I'm almost fully functional again."

"From my point of view, you always have been. Hey now, I have to make this call." She giggled and squirmed away from his wandering hands. She curled up at the far end of the couch. He opened the laptop, but watched her instead while she dialed Maria's number. "Hi Maria? This is Tasha Jefferson. From – yeah! You remember. Sherry gave me your number. How've you been?" She listened for a while. "Yeah, I had to divorce that guy. I'm with someone better now. He's my boy toy." She laughed. "Sherry told you that? She's naughty. Listen, she told me you're into hair and makeup now, and we're kind of involved with this movie project that Tanith Salazar is doing. Yeah, same lady. It's about tango, and it's starring Victor Garcia, yep that same guy, and I get to dance in it. But so, the costume designer dresser person is Lesley Hayes again, and she needs an assistant. So I wondered, are you on a job right now? This one, they're shooting July ninth through twenty-seventh. Are you available? I'm not sure which of those days they'd need you." She listened for a minute. "So you want us to give your info to Tanith and Lesley? I'm sure they'd get back to you really fast either way. And either way, let's get together real soon. Okay. Will do. You too." She disconnected and nodded at Sandesh. "She'd love for us to put her up for the job. I'll email you her stuff and you can shoot it over to Tanith."

"Thanks." Sandesh opened his email window and waited for the incoming message, then forwarded it to Tanith with a note: *Your former showgirl Maria Pocatello is now hair/makeup pro for TV/film, possible assistant for Lesley?* Then he set the laptop aside, because while he could have spent hours going through work email, there were other things he wanted to do with this first child-free night. "So I'm your boy toy, huh." He scooted across the couch and leaned in to kiss Tasha.

"Yeah. You know, I was reading this thing that said women in their forties should always be with men in their thirties. Something about sexual peak."

"Sexual peak. Okay." He had his mouth on her neck, her legs across his lap, and his almost-fully-functional hand on her breast. "This kind of peak?"

"That might be one of them," she said, breathless. "Mmm. I should have taken my clothes off as soon as I got home."

"No time like the present." He unfastened her jeans and started peeling them off while she wriggled out of her top. "Wow, honey. Were you thinking about me when you chose this underwear?" It was a matched set in purple satin. He ran a finger under the edge of her panties, then further, leaning in to kiss her again. "You're already wet," he said softly. "You know what that does to me?" They shifted, so that

Tasha lay half underneath him. He took his weight on his left arm, right hand free to touch her.

"I can feel what that does to you. Don't you want to take those jeans off?"

"I really do. But I don't want to stop touching you." She took her hand off his neck and unbuttoned, then slowly unzipped his jeans. She slid her hand inside. "Oh God, Tasha." He kissed her while they played with each other for a few minutes. "This is like being a teenager again."

She laughed against his mouth. "It is, isn't it? You're already at third base. You wanna score? Oh yeah, you do." She used her hand and a foot to push his jeans off his hips. "It's so easy when you go commando. Give me that."

"Jesus!" She had him in her hand, rubbing him against her, the panties still there but somehow not in the way. He had his eyes closed, letting her do what she wanted, which was driving him crazy. She put her other hand on the side of his face and brought his mouth down to hers as she raised a knee and positioned him. Then she tipped her hips up and he sank in with a muffled moan.

"Oh. My. God," she said. He was still taking his weight on his left arm, resting on the couch beside her head. His right hand was pressed against the arm of the couch. She had a moment to think *I hope that arm is all right* before he started moving in her and they both lost their minds.

After a while Sandesh lifted himself off of her and rolled to his left side, relaxing. Tasha was still breathing hard, still almost laughing because she'd finally heard what he sounded like when he wasn't trying to be quiet. "What," he said. She could tell he was smiling, even though his face was pressed against her hair.

"You didn't care about the neighbors tonight."

"Nope."

"You want to sleep out here?"

"Not really." He slowly moved, inclined to laugh at the undignified state he was in. "When you're sixteen you don't think about how it looks to be bare-assed on a couch with your jeans dangling off your feet." Tasha snickered. He thought about pulling the jeans up, figured *why bother*, and shucked them the rest of the way off. Then he pulled his tee shirt over his head.

"That arm okay?"

"What arm?"

"Give me your hand." Tasha sat up, and Sandesh gave her his right hand. She manipulated his fingers for a minute, made him flex and straighten and fan them out, made him push back against her hand. "It's really better, huh. Oops." She stood up. "I'm all squishy."

"Worried about the couch? We can always slipcover it."

"That's true. This might happen again, huh."

"God, I hope so." They both laughed softly. Sandesh stood up, wrapping his arms around Tasha. "I love you."

"I love you, too. Mercy you look good naked." He undid her bra. "Thank you." Then he knelt down and peeled off her panties. "Oh." He put his mouth on her. "*Oh!*"

"Mmm. I was just here." He had his hands on her hips. "You are squishy. I had to see what you taste like." He was still there, speaking right into her. She had her hands on his head and was barely breathing, astonished at how quickly she'd heated up again. His touch was light, so light it tantalized instead of overwhelmed, lips and tongue and the tiniest bit of suction. "Mmm, yeah, again baby." She didn't think she would, she never had standing up like this, but then it had never been Sandesh on his knees in a fully-lit room. She felt so gloriously exposed, she felt like a goddess, and when she came with a muted, panting scream he growled into her like a lion. When he stood up he was fully aroused again. She hadn't taken her hands out of his hair; now she tugged his head back down to kiss him, tasting herself, feeling that strong lithe body and wanting more of it, of him. She backed toward the bedroom and he followed, keeping contact. When they got there, she turned around and climbed up on the bed, then stayed on her hands and knees. She looked over her shoulder at him. "Tasha," he said, and set a hand on her back.

"Do it," she said. "In me. More." He knelt on the bed behind her and positioned himself. She pushed back. He slid inside. "God *damn*."

"Jesus, Tasha, you're so hot."

"You make me hot. I want to feel you come again. I want you to come so hard I can taste it." He said something indistinct, moving fast, holding her steady with both hands. She listened, since she couldn't see his face, and she could hear his breathing start to catch. "Touch me now." Without changing his rhythm he did, moving a hand around to press between her legs. She breathed out hard, then sucked in a breath and held it as that pulse started again. "Go *now!*" she said tightly.

"Jesus!" He came hard like she wanted, and they both froze for a moment before he folded onto her back and she slid down. "Holy hell," he said faintly. He shifted to his left side again, lifting his right arm and straightening it for a second.

She rolled over to look at his face, lifted one hand and touched him lightly. "That's what I call a righteous fuck." He closed his eyes, laughing silently, and rolled onto his back. "Every girl wants a boy toy like you." He laughed out loud. She patted his chest. A few minutes later they managed to crawl up and get under the covers.

"I'll get your phone in a minute," he said drowsily.

*No you won't*, she thought, smiling to herself.

"So," Anya said on the phone at the end of June, "I've been deputized to ask how things are going with this whole cohabitation dealio."

Tasha giggled. "Terry didn't want to do it?"

"He was afraid you'd tell him about your sex life. Said, that's still my baby sister." She sounded amused, which didn't surprise Tasha. Anya's face rarely showed it, but she had a lively sense of the ridiculous. "Are you free tonight? Because if you'd like to get together for a drink that works for me."

"That totally works for me. I was about to head out, and I'm child-free at the moment thanks to Matthew. Where can I meet you?"

"Melrose Umbrella Company?"

"Oh yes, honey." She'd heard of it. "I'll send the man a text to let him know where I'm going, and then I'm on my way."

"See you in a bit." Anya disconnected and Tasha composed a text to Sandesh: *Hi honey I'm going to meet up with Anya for some girl talk over on Melrose. If you ever get home ping me so I know you're safe. Love you, see you later XOX*

She was surprised to get a text back before she got on the elevator; preproduction was keeping him beyond busy. *Hi sweetheart thanks for letting me know, say hi to Anya for me. Uh wait are you going to be talking about me?*

*What do you think?*

*Eeek*

*LOL don't worry I only have good things to say about my boy toy*

*OMG I have to look that woman in the eyes you know NOT TO MENTION TERRY*

*Don't worry Anya knows better than to share too many details. But I'm giving her some*

*LOL have fun XOX*

Tasha put away the phone and got on an elevator, smiling. She imagined that she would end up giving Anya some details; they'd had some mighty frank conversations over the past couple of years, and Terry had passed on a few things too. She knew that Anya had never lived with a man before moving in with Terry. She hadn't told him that; Ricky had. She'd acted like it was a convenience thing, right up till she and Ricky went to Las Vegas for a multi-week gig. Things changed after that.

Tasha hadn't lived with anyone since Matthew. It was too much of a complication to contemplate, with a little kid to consider. But Sandesh wasn't a complication. If anything, he made life easier: always cheerful, always helpful. And now more than ever, always right there when she thought of something to tell him. She still found herself storing up the little funny things that happened, so she could share them with him. Still loved that they laughed together. Having him to come home to was the best feeling she could imagine, after hugging her son.

And then there was the sex. Thinking about some of those details, the ones she might or might not share with Anya, got her heart rate up. Tasha had never thought of herself as someone with a strong sex drive, but maybe that was because she'd never been with someone who made her feel so desired. Someone who could be washing dishes with her and give her that sloe-eyed look that said 'just you wait.' Someone who never seemed to miss an opportunity to touch her, or kiss her, or gaze at her as if she were the most beautiful, precious thing in the world.

She was smiling – still, or again – when she went into the bar. Anya was sitting at a table facing the door, legs crossed, eyes narrowed in that way she had. "You look like you're ready for Sum Yun Gai," she said, and Tasha laughed. They'd never been here before but Tasha had looked at the drinks menu online. That was certainly the best-named cocktail.

"I don't know about jalapeño vodka," she said, sitting down across from Anya. "Maybe The Living Daylights," she said to the server who appeared a moment later. "Hey lady. Everything good with you?"

"Melrose Mule for me," Anya said. "And mac 'n' cheese times two. Thanks. Everything is good.

Ricky's playing around with shit for the Cabaret's Milonga and Halloween shows, but he and Hiro were both 'nope' for the pro show. Hiro's going to Paris with the gang for the Gay Games. So at the moment all I really have is these Latin students and the movie stuff. It's like being on vacation. Your brother is settling into being in charge."

"It'll be good for him. When do Tyrone and Indira get back?"

"Sometime in August." The drink order arrived. "Did you see the theme for Halloween, by the way?"

"Yes I did and I thought, that is going to make for an interesting poster." Anya snorted some of her drink. The theme for the Halloween show was 'Vagina Dentata.' After she got done coughing, and Tasha was done giggling, Tasha said, "What song are you using?"

"That crazy man wants to do another apache. He's using 'In the Flesh.' That Blondie song."

"Oh lord, you better be careful. I saw the video of that first one. That was seriously scary."

"Yeah, this one won't be quite like that. He's in a different place now. And speaking of which, let's get the reporting-in portion of the evening out of the way."

Tasha was ready. "Girl, I can't imagine how I knew that man for nine years and never frickin' jumped on him. Every time I see him I'm like, what was I even looking at that I didn't see you? Right in front of me!" She shook her head. "I must have kept seeing him the way I first saw him, and never noticed what he turned into. He's phenomenal."

"Giving you what you want, huh?"

"All of it." They both laughed. "All the time. We've done everything."

"Everything?" Anya looked skeptical, but Tasha nodded. "I tried that, you know, once. Once was enough."

"Yeah, once was enough. We were curious." Anya almost laughed. Tasha did a 'well you know' thing. "He doesn't even mind period sex. He's shockingly perfect. If I'm like, not tonight baby, he's all okay let's cuddle. And that's all he does. He doesn't try to get me going."

"That's the best. When a guy doesn't try to talk you into shit. That's one of the things I like about Terry." Anya swallowed some more of her drink. "I mean, not that he *hasn't* talked me into shit. But if I ever seriously said dude, no, he was always, okay baby." She looked thoughtful. "Trying to remember the last time I said no."

Tasha laughed again. "I haven't said it much either. Sometimes I don't want to do any work, and you know what, Sandesh is fine doing all the work."

Anya pointed at her. "Yes! Exactly! I'm going to just lie here, okay, and you get me off, and then do whatever you want." Tasha was giggling again, aware that this topic of conversation was getting some attention from the adjacent tables. Anya may also have been aware. "How strong is this fucking drink?" She finished it as their mac 'n' cheese arrived. "Wow. No, thank you, water please. I have a student at eight o'clock and why the hell is that anyway."

"Eight o'clock!"

"Eh. This guy wants to do this competition next month in Palm Springs. It doesn't conflict with the filming dates Tanith gave us, so I told him we could enter."

"Has Hiro tried to talk you into a pro event yet?" Hiro was Anya's counterpart at Shall We Dance, an International Latin ballroom specialist.

"He tried to talk me into Embassy. Irvine, Labor Day weekend. I pointed to the calendar. He's only doing one thing for the movie but then he and Kristine are going to Paris. Because her brother's going to compete. Anyway I said are you fucking insane and he just laughed." Anya shook her head, rolled her eyes, and said, "I'm probably going to have to do it eventually. Terry says girl you know you want to."

"You like competition."

Anya couldn't deny it. "Maybe I want one of those trophies to put up there with my salsa shit. Dmitri would like it if I did."

Tasha knew Dmitri by now. The owner of Shall We Dance had a large fan club that definitely included her. "He loves Hiro, huh."

"That guy, I swear. Dmitri's like love first, ask questions later. Yeah." They addressed the mac 'n' cheese for a few minutes. "This is good drinking food," Anya said. "So I guess I can tell Terry that Sandesh is triple A, four stars, whatever."

"All of that," Tasha said, after draining her glass. "And a cherry on top."

## Chapter 8
July 2018

Sandesh and Tasha were invited over to his brother's house for a barbecue on the Fourth of July. It was the second time they'd been over, and the first time since Sandesh started working with Tanith. His sister-in-law Paige wanted to hear all about it. Tasha ended up hanging out with Lochan for a while after they ate, helping supervise their two-year-old daughter Maya. "Has Sandesh told you any of this stuff?" she asked. "Obviously we talk about it all the time at home."

"He's mentioned it. I don't know anything about making movies." Lochan was a systems administrator for a healthcare company. "I never even look at the credits."

"He's going to get a credit. Tanith told him this week she's going to put him in as a line producer. I had to look up what that was." They both laughed. "I've done a few stage things before but this is my first movie, so I don't know anything either. I guess Paige is really into it, huh."

Maya toddled from Tasha to Lochan; she was fretful. He picked her up. "Getting tired, baby? Rest here for a minute." He settled the child on his lap. "Paige came to L.A. to be an actress. I met her at the DMV."

"She told me you met there, not about the actress thing."

"She'd been here two years when we met. She was living in this two-bedroom apartment with three other girls, they all went out for jobs as extras, they all had other jobs. She said it was fun for a while, but an extra day can be ten to twelve hours, with early starts. She got tired. There are so many people who want to be actors. She didn't know how hard it would be, not just to get an audition, but the actual days. After we started dating, she went to fewer auditions. And then she got pregnant, and I asked her to marry me, and here we are." He cuddled Maya.

Tasha said, "Do you think she misses it? I didn't miss dancing very much while Theo was little. Or I didn't realize I missed it. Then after Sandesh and I … well, I kind of woke up to how much I missed it. And I never even tried to make that my job."

Lochan looked across the yard at Paige, still chattering away with Sandesh. "Paige said she was going to look for a job again once Maya can go to preschool. Maybe we should talk about that." He glanced at Tasha. "We're okay for money. She thought if she got a job, we might be able to buy a house. But I'm not sure I want to buy one here. We could never buy one in this neighborhood." They rented half of a duplex in West L.A.

"Ugh, no."

"With this promotion, Sandesh could probably afford a house." Maya was dozing now. Lochan looked over at his brother. "He said he hasn't told our parents yet. I asked him why, he said he was waiting until it was official. But that was last week, right?"

"Right. He needs to call them. He mentioned there might have been a few too many life changes recently, they might be wondering what the heck is going on." After a moment she added, "Are your parents okay about us? I mean, me and Sandesh?"

"I think they want to meet you. I think … I know they wish he would have children. I'm sorry," he said, glancing over at her again, "it's none of my business, and I know he's really happy with you. But it might come up if you go to meet them."

She sighed. "I was afraid of that. If I were them, I'd want him to have kids of his own too. I just, I shouldn't. My doctor said it could kill me, or worse. It's hard to imagine being the mother I'd want to be, if I were permanently disabled."

"That's what Paige said too. Neither of us wanted to stop at one." Maya's head was cradled in his hand, so much like his brother's. Tasha had a moment of missing Theo terribly. Then her phone buzzed and she thought *maybe that's him.*

She sent Lochan an 'excuse me' look. He nodded and she pulled out the phone. It was a text from Theo: *we get fireworks*

*Hey baby, going to a show?*

*Yes*

*Where are you?*

There was a pause. Then she got a text from Matthew: *We're in Kanab. They have this whole thing every year. We're staying at a motel near here.*

*Everything good?*

*Great so far. Thanks again*

*Have a fantastic time :-)* The next message was from Theo again. Tasha texted back and forth a few more times until he signed off with something about tacos. She was laughing under her breath as she put the phone away. Then Sandesh and Paige came across the yard. Paige lifted Maya off Lochan's lap and said, "I'll take her inside now."

Tasha took that as a cue for wrapping up the evening. She followed Paige inside, saying, "I'll help you tidy things up. Thanks so much for having us over."

Sandesh sat down next to Lochan. "Good grilling today."

"Thanks. You need to call our parents."

Sandesh sighed. "I know." Lochan made an impatient gesture, and Sandesh said, "I'm resisting because every conversation lately goes to the relationship. Here I am with this huge career jump, which I really want to tell them about, but all they're worried about is my reproductive plans and it's like I don't want to share the other thing."

"I might have mentioned that to Tasha. To warn her, in case you were planning on going back East sometime soon."

"Well, I'm not, and the more they annoy me about this the longer it's going to be." He sat back, frustrated. "There are one and a half billion Indians and that's only in the mother country. Why do I have to have kids?"

"Because you're their son, their first son. You know this about them."

"They're gonna have to get used to it. I almost lost it last time we talked. Like, the F word was halfway out of my mouth." Lochan laughed. Sandesh shook his head, exasperated but half-laughing too. "I clawed it back somehow, I forget what I turned it into. Whatever. You know it takes a lot to make me lose my temper."

"I do know. Look, get it over with. Call them, roll over them when they start on the kids thing, tell them about the job, get off the phone. Once they actually hear what you said, which might be an hour later, they'll call you back to congratulate you. Then if they start on the kids thing again you can hang up on them."

Sandesh was laughing. "Is that what you do? I mean, they know about Paige's thing, right? That it's not because she's afraid of losing her figure or something like that?"

"Oh yes, they know." The brothers shared a commiserating look. "Can you imagine if we'd stayed in the same town?"

"God help us." They were both laughing when Tasha and Paige came back out.

Sandesh called his parents the next morning, hoping to get their voice mail at home, but ended up talking to his mother. The conversation went much as his brother had predicted. He hung up a minute or two later than he'd have liked to, and immediately went to work on clearing the office email in-box. He wasn't expecting to hear from Tanith at all that day, and wouldn't have a piano lesson since Tomás was also at the recording studio, so it was New Job Prep Time. His office profile now had a time tracker, and he used it to enforce breaks. By four o'clock, not only had he gotten up to speed on current issues, he'd scheduled a partnership meeting and a staff meeting for the sixteenth. The goal was to develop a plan to deal with some staffing deficits, for presentation to the partners and the staff. If things went the way he wanted, he might be able to get some interviews set up for the twentieth. *You're going to be as busy as a one-legged man in an ass-kicking contest*, he thought. *Again*. He shut down and went for a walk. Tasha was unlocking the door as he returned. "Hey beautiful," he said, kissing her hello. "Guess what I ordered today."

"Hmmm … a slipcover?"

"Good guess. I had this crazy idea." They were through the door. He pushed it closed and flipped the deadbolt.

"What's that?" She was laughing. He had her pressed up against the wall and she hadn't even put down her tote bag.

"Something like, it's hot out, let's go for full nudity. I got us cold food for dinner."

"Sounds good," she said breathlessly. "What are we drinking with that?"

"Angry Orchard." He took the tote bag out of her hand and set it down, pulled her top off, and kissed her again. "But not yet."

The next day Sandesh dutifully put an hour into law-firm business before calling Lesley and Yoshi to check on the status of costumes and lighting. Finally he called Tanith, to find out about the recording session. "So how'd it go?"

"These guys are killing me, they're so good. I got some great video, too. We all went to Marco's for dinner and some more music happened. Anyway, for next week Valerie's already got the processed tracks ready for our newsreel and funeral scenes, the *a cappella* crowd recordings, and she's prioritizing the track for the men's cabaret routine. Jesus fucking Christ it's *next week*." She sounded slightly panicked.

He didn't give her time to hyperventilate. "Then for week two it's the other crowd recording, and two more of the cast album recordings to get ready. And week three, one more cast album version. So she really doesn't have much to process. I'll check in with her Sunday."

Tanith blew out a breath. "What am I forgetting?"

"Yoshi says he's ready to go. Lesley is picking up jewelry from Lucy on Sunday. She says Lucy says the chandeliers are also ready, Nick will bring them with his stuff. Tomás and I are meeting the piano delivery at the theater Sunday noon. He will make sure the piano tuner does it right." *Pause for laugh*, he thought. "Your loading-in crew is scheduled for one p.m. Sunday. Reza is going to supervise that. He and Yoshi are point for getting the electronics set up, including lights, and those scrim things for the projections. Nick will be there with the props and set furnishings at four. Lesley and Maria are loading in costume at five, then getting the dressing rooms ready. Reza and I will stay as long as we need to, and I will send you a report before we leave. Andy is bitching nonstop because he can't be there." Tanith made a sound of amused recognition. "You've heard from him too, huh. Their security detail said hellz to the no. Anyway, on Monday Valerie and Yoshi will report in with you at seven a.m. Camera crew at eight with all that gear. The wardrobe crew, guild interns and me, also at eight. Cast due to report at nine for wardrobe. Camera-ready musicians due at ten for wiring and tuning." Sandesh checked his chart. "And that's it."

Tanith was silent for a minute. "I'm thinking back to my rinky-dink little play," she said eventually. "We had literally one U-Haul truck full of shit. My heart wants to be there all day Sunday, my head tells me I should stay the fuck away."

"You're paying these people for a reason," he said. "Let Reza and me handle it on Sunday. You can text me a million times if you want."

"I'm not paying you."

"Are you kidding me? I'm getting film school in a box. Did you see the blocking video for the women's cabaret routine?"

"That kicked ass. I mean, considering it was in that brutally ugly stairwell. At the Bradbury, it's going to kick mega ass." She sighed. "Okay. I know we're as ready as we're going to get. My problem is I have two and a half days to live through before we start and I don't have a job to do."

"Sure you do. Update the Kickstarter project page. I mean, unless this invisible man of yours is around. If he's there then he might have a suggestion for a way to spend the time."

Tanith laughed. "He got home at four in the morning. In a few hours he might have a suggestion. I will try not to text you a million times on Sunday. See you Monday."

"Bye." Sandesh disconnected. He could sympathize with Tanith's at-a-standstill position, but he had hours of law-office work to get through before he could call himself ready to ditch it again for a full week.

"You look like a man with a question," Tasha said while they were cleaning up after dinner. "What's up? Anything squirrelly with the movie shoot?"

"No, I think we're in good shape there, though I'm guessing I will be very late getting home on Sunday. Maybe I should sleep at the theater."

She laughed. "Do not do that. That place is spooky as shit. Besides, you said that guy Reza knows what he's doing."

"Well, he's worked on movies before, so at least he knows more than me. Whatever, no, it's this real-world job of mine. I've set up a partnership meeting on the sixteenth, the guys from San Francisco are going to be here for it. Thank God Janice is helping with the arrangements because of course we don't have anybody else to do that. So I'm second-guessing this proposal."

"The one about shutting down the NorCal office? Why?"

"It's such a huge thing. I figured if I was ever going to get it on the table, I needed to throw it in my terms and conditions. But it's like I kind of didn't expect it to get this far." He finished drying the dishes and leaned back against the counter while she put them away.

She turned back to him after wiping the counter. "Thought they'd blow it out of the water? I thought it made sense. I mean, once you told me how much the overhead is."

"Yeah. It's crazy money. And what pissed me off about it was all the people they never hired? The only reason we needed them was to do the office stuff. Someone to open the door, answer the phones, stock the break room, and do the filing. The lawyers mostly did their own document creation, and if they needed admin or research or secretarial, they just borrowed some from down here. So we're renting all this fantastically expensive space for furniture, basically, and a copy machine, and a file room."

"I remember last December, that night." She stopped for a second, remembering how much had happened since then. "That was quite a night. Anyway, that IT guy up there was driving you up the wall."

"He's *such* a pain in the ass. He thinks he should be running everything."

"You can't wait to fire him, can you." She was grinning at him. He laughed, leaning down to kiss her. "Look," she said, "you sold James on the plan. He's a smart guy. I'm sure when those NorCal guys get a look at the upgrades they can have, and the zero commute time they'll have, they won't even care about not having a swanky office."

"Those offices are not even that swanky. Two of them are triangular, it gave me a headache to sit in there, and the other two have a view of the side of another building. The only natural light is what bounces off other skyscrapers. I hate it. At least from our offices here, you can see the sky."

"You have a window office now, don't you? Have you seen it yet?"

"I know which one it is. I'll have to get in early on the sixteenth to get situated." He rubbed his hands over his face. "I need to hire four people as fast as possible. I know there were tons of rejected resumés, but I couldn't find them on the system. Maybe they're in Darlene's office somewhere."

"Your office?"

"No, I asked for a different one. That one's probably been hexed." Tasha laughed again, tugging him along out of the kitchen to the bedroom. "I should do some more work."

"No, you shouldn't," she said. "You're tired. I'm tired too, it was a busy day today. Let's go to sleep early and then walk somewhere for breakfast." She reached up to run a hand through his hair. "This stuff really does grow fast."

"At least I can shave again." Sandesh flopped down on the bed, stretched out on his back, and sighed. "Okay. Sleep, fool around, walk, breakfast, check in with Theo, yoga, fool around. A perfect Saturday."

Tasha leaned down to kiss him. "I'm going to wash up. I love you."

"Love you too." Sandesh closed his eyes, *just for a minute*, he thought. When Tasha came back in he was sound asleep.

The first week of principal photography really was film school in a box. Sandesh couldn't believe how many jobs were being handled by such a small crew. Tanith's executive producer Andy had turned in job descriptions for the guild interns, based on his observations while (as he put it) bored to sobs waiting for something to happen on the set of the TV show he worked on. Sandesh was supervising all those people, doing laps around the theater to get feedback from the camera crew, and shadowing Tanith. Thanks to a walkie-talkie app that all the crew had, she didn't have to run around much herself. Reza was on top of the grips. Lesley and Maria sent up photo texts from the dressing room, and everyone else was in the main auditorium.

When staging was complete on the first day and Tanith said "Action" for the first time, Sandesh just stood still and watched. The first scene to be shot was

Carlos Gardel singing to an audience of aristocrats in a Buenos Aires ballroom. They had live music, six dancers, and six extras. Gardel, played by Victor Garcia, walked on to the set where the dancers and extras waited. His old and new collaborators, longtime manager José Razzano and new lyricist and screenwriter Alfredo Le Pera, were right behind him. There was hardly any pause before Gardel took his position and the musicians began to play the introduction to his song.

A rehearsal tape of the song had been loaded to the production's Dropbox. It was nothing like the fully-produced realization Sandesh saw now. The song itself was thrilling, but the interactions of the performers blew him away. When Tanith said "Cut" he had to do a little re-set, looking at his chart to see where he needed to be. Then she said "We'll run it again." He rounded up the other interns and sent them scurrying, then looked over at Tanith. He couldn't tell how she felt about it. She might have been doing a second take simply because she could. They only had three scenes to shoot that day.

By the end of the day, Sandesh thought 'only' was a grossly inaccurate word. He was exhausted, and the other interns looked like road kill. "And imagine," Tanith said, looking at his face and reading it correctly, "all we really had to do was swap out some props and wardrobe."

"My God," he said devoutly, and she laughed.

He had two days to sorta-kinda recover from week one of filming. Tanith kicked him out of the theater at four on Friday. Instead of going straight home he went to Dmitri's studio to meet Tasha for some tango practice. The big outdoor mobs were on the schedule for the weekend of July twenty-first; they needed to spend some time on the dance floor.

"It's sure better with both arms," he said when they'd been at it for a half hour. "What do you think?"

"All I can say is I love it. I have no idea what we look like, but I love it." Now that Sandesh could complete the dance frame, Tasha had her left hand up on his shoulder, fingertips just brushing his neck. "Your hair is getting long again."

"I know, I need to get it cut this weekend. Think I should shave?" He hadn't bothered that week; getting to the filming location on time had been a higher priority.

"Nope." He looked down at her, smiling a question. She said, "You're getting it cut like you had it for Cicada, right? With some beard, you're going to look like the Indian Alan Rickman. You'll walk into that partnership meeting and they'll be like, oh shit." He laughed.

"Due to the firm's legacy of greed," he said, riffing on the line from 'Die Hard,' "it is about to be taught a lesson. Think it'll fly?"

"You got that new suit. It looks amazing on you. Just stand up straight and look down your nose at them and take them to school, honey." Tasha grinned, listening to him giggle. "Theo sent you something. Or Matthew sent it, I got this package at the office. They've been going to some of the Native American reservations and there was this class. Theo made things for us."

"He is so adorable." Sandesh stopped dancing. "I'm going to ask Rosa to video us for a few minutes.

I want to see what this looks like. I want to look respectable when we do this thing."

"You saw some dances this week, right? They did the big cabaret number with all the guys. And the duel, that dance fight with Victor and Andy, wasn't that this week?"

"That was today. That was rough. Everybody was fucked up after that, I was like -" he mimed sobbing. "I don't even know them that well. But yeah, those two, and a ton of social-style stuff. Everybody's so good."

"Don't be getting all competitive. Those are all professionals, or next best thing."

"I know. But you know me, when I learn something I want to be good at it." He kissed her, then went to find the studio manager. A minute later she came back with him and he handed over his phone. Everyone in the studio's side room seemed to be practicing tango, so he cued up another track and then went to dance with Tasha again.

They didn't look at the video until they got home. Sandesh had been on duty at the theater since eight in the morning, Tasha had put in a full day, and they were both hungry. Tasha called in a food order before she started home and it was delivered a few minutes after they both got up to the apartment. "Some days this is the best thing about L.A.," she said. "You can always get food."

Sandesh laughed, opening packages. "God this smells good, too. You know I was thinking I'm going to have to learn to make chocolate cream pie for Theo, now that Callender's is closed. That was so out of nowhere."

"I know. That was my go-to for a lot of years. Now that I've got a rich boyfriend I'm ordering from Spare

Tire." Tasha chose a bottle of wine to open, smiling because he was laughing again.

"Yeah, about that. I was thinking, does Matthew ever say anything about child support? Because maybe he doesn't need to pay so much now." He was still setting the table. When he looked up, Tasha was staring at him. "What? Too soon?"

She brought a couple of glasses of wine to the table and sat down. "Let's say I wasn't expecting that. Let's let that go for a little longer."

"December?" He smiled at her.

*If I can wait that long to let you propose*, Tasha thought, but said, "Sure. Oh!" She got up and went over to her tote bag, pulling out a small package wrapped in brown paper, with a rubber band around it. She set it on the table, then sat down again. "I peeked, so the tape's broken."

Sandesh had a sip of wine, then unwrapped the package. Inside were two surprisingly finished-looking pieces of jewelry, bracelets made with waxed black cord knotted like macramé around beads. One had pink stone beads, the other had greenish-blue turquoise. "I'm assuming that the green one is for me? Oh, here's a note. That kid, I swear." He turned over the note. Matthew had written on the back: PIX SOON. "Did he send you pictures?"

"Yes he did. I'll show you after we're done here. This trip was the best idea, they're really bonding." After dinner, Tasha pulled up the latest photos from the trip. Sandesh leaned close, a replenished glass of wine in one hand and the other arm around her shoulders. When she'd scrolled through all the pictures, she turned her head and kissed his cheek. "What are you doing for Tanith this weekend?"

“Not much of anything. Staying home. I have to get ready for Monday at the office. Get my head straight.”

“Still planning to go in on Friday too?”

“Oh yeah. There’s so much to get done. I’ve been, like, rehearsing this opening statement.” He laughed under his breath. “I know we were kind of kidding around at the studio, but I need to take control of the situation right out of the gate or it’ll never work.”

“Did you write it down?” Tasha sat back a little so she could see his face. He seemed relaxed, but she had a feeling there were some nerves working. This was such a huge step.

“Sure did.”

“Want to run it through for me? I’ll bet you’re sexy when you’re laying down the law.”

“Well, when you put it like that,” he said, and kissed her again. “But first let’s look at the video Rosa took at the studio.” He reached over to his messenger bag, on the seat of the chair next to him, and pulled out his phone. It was Tasha’s turn to lean close. Sandesh started the video and they watched it through. He turned his head to look at her. “That didn’t suck!”

“No it did not. Feel better now?”

“God, yes. I mean, okay, it’s not what I’ve been seeing all week, but it didn’t look clueless. We looked like we know what we’re doing.” He knew he sounded relieved. There wasn’t much time remaining to get competent, and since he was actually working for Tanith he felt like he had to represent.

“You’re a good dancer,” she said. “And you’re smart, and you pay attention. Let’s plan to go back to the studio next Friday and then we'll be all warmed up for the things on Saturday and Sunday. Get James and Silvia there, too, we can go out to dinner after. You're going to be down at the Bradbury for my cabaret routine, right?"

"Would I miss that? Of course I'll be there." He stood up and started clearing the table. "You sure you want to hear this speech of mine?"

"I absolutely do."

Sandesh got to the office at eight on Monday morning. The partnership meeting wasn't scheduled till eleven o'clock, but he wanted to get a handle on his in-box. He also wanted to check in with James if possible. When he walked in, the receptionist squealed. "Sandy!! Oh my God you look like a movie star!" She clapped a hand over her mouth. "Oops."

He was wearing his new navy suit, a crisp white shirt, and a tie chosen by Tasha, with Theo's bracelet on his right wrist. He knew he looked good. "Hi Nicole, how've you been?"

"Oh fine, nothing much new since May. We all heard what happened. You're okay now?"

"Almost a hundred percent, thanks. I'll be back here full-time next month. Gotta go get warmed up now. It's good to see you," he said, smiling, and turned to go to his new office. He'd been there for fifteen minutes and had barely gotten acquainted with his furniture and equipment (including a Varidesk Pro, per request) when there was a tap on his open door. He looked up to see James' assistant. "Hey Janice. Nice to see you. Want to step in for a minute?"

"No, I know you have a million emails to read, I only wanted to say hi. It's good to have you back. I'll see you at the staff meeting this afternoon. Let me know if you need me to handle anything for you. And by the way, you'd better close the door because there are about forty people who are going to drop in if you don't." She turned to go, then stuck her head back in and said, "You do look like a movie star." He was laughing when she left, pulling the door closed behind her.

Sandesh picked up his phone and dialed James. Not too surprisingly, his friend answered. "Hi James. Anything I should know before we go into the colosseum?"

"Just that the SF people are all here and the mood is trepidatious. Everything as requested in your office, I trust?"

"Yes, I'm all set up here, just checking the in-box for fires. A little nervous, I'll be honest."

"It's a big day. Keep telling yourself, you're the best man for the job."

"James, I was the *only* man for the job." He smiled, listening to the laugh. "See you in a bit." He disconnected and went back to the in-box. There were all the predictable action items for a first-day-back, plus the predictable backlog of requests to sign off on department formalities. He cleared all that by ten, then took a break. He told Nicole, "Back in fifteen," as he went past her again, heading down to the plaza. He knew if he didn't actually get out of the office, he'd start looking at email again.

When he got back upstairs he turned toward Janice, starting a walk around the entire suite. Before the partnership meeting started, he wanted to get the lay of the land. He had to wave and keep walking as people called greetings, saying "See you this afternoon" to all the staffers. He'd never get all the way around if he stopped. He made mental notes about which stations looked idle, which appeared overloaded, and which seemed simply to be a mess. He cut through the warren of connected spaces containing the file room, copy room, and server room, then went back out to finish the tour. Not much had changed since May aside from the now-vacant office previously housing Darlene, and the vacant bay opposite, where Jessica had been stationed. The other vacancies were, he hoped, soon to be filled.

At a quarter to eleven he went to the bathroom, then back to his office for his new leather-clad notebook and a couple of pens. He took a few minutes for some deep breathing before heading to the conference room.

He was the first one there, but James and Carver weren't far behind. Sandesh remained standing as all of the partners gradually filed in and took seats. Everyone greeted him, though most seemed not to know what to call him. He waited until everyone was present and then, still standing, went straight into his opening statement. It was as brief as he could make it, considering he had to cover the current state of the firm, his proposal regarding San Francisco, and a few comments in support of that. Then he took questions for twenty minutes.

"All right," he said at last. "I think we've covered the main points, except for one. Members of the management committee are aware that this office has experienced staff turnover that is significantly higher than industry average. The firm's retention is not strong, and its reputation with recruiters is not good. There is some work to be done there, and it's work that you have to do. This afternoon I'll be meeting with the staff and we will talk about where they perceive the problems to lie. Every assistant will be invited to request reassignment. I will review any such requests, discuss them with the attorneys involved, and then move or hire assistants as needed. If there are any of you with whom no one wants to work, Mr. Levine and I will meet with you to discuss your options. Same for associates."

There was a bit of an outburst. Sandesh and James expected that. Neither of them said anything until the furor died down. Carver had his hand over his eyes. He knew this was coming; it had been in Sandesh's negotiation letter. He was foreseeing an entire afternoon spent in fruitless speculation and complaint. Then Sandesh said, "Please do not take up Mr. Nguyen's time with this issue. He is the managing partner, but he is not the point person on this. That's me. I'll be available, though I won't be in the office again this week until Friday." Carver glanced up and Sandesh made a gesture toward him. "You need to not waste Carver's time." *There, that's blunt enough.* Use of Carver's first name also signaled that he considered himself their peer, not their subordinate. He knew there would be some fuss about that. He almost looked forward to it. "Any questions?"

There were, of course. He didn't get out of there until almost one o'clock. The staff meeting was scheduled for three o'clock, with everyone advised that the attorneys should consider themselves solo for the rest of the day. Sandesh knew there was going to be a lot of conversation once the staffers started talking. And he knew if he were in his office for the next hour, he'd be swarmed. Fortunately, he and

James had arranged a lunch out with Janice. They went back to their respective offices to check for fires, then met in the elevator lobby. James didn't say anything, but he looked amused. Janice was grinning. "What's so funny?" Sandesh said after they got on an elevator.

"James told me what you said about reassignments. You know what you're going to hear this afternoon, don't you?"

"I have a slight idea." He'd been with the firm long enough to see a lot of people come and go. There was one partner's desk in particular that was like a desert island: nothing stayed alive there for long. Two others, and two associates, had significant problems that might be corrigible; this one guy was simply beyond fixing. "Jeez, I'm starving."

"Did you eat breakfast?" Janice was inclined to mother-hen him a bit.

Sandesh kind of liked it. "I did, I swear, but I've been burning calories. I had to change my shirt after that meeting, it felt like running a marathon." James was laughing out loud as they exited the elevator.

Before he left for the day, Sandesh texted Tasha to report in: *I survived*

She picked right up. *Outrage and mayhem on a scale of 1 to 10*

*8.5*

*LOL did the Bond Villain look work for you?*

*It totally did!! I told Theo I wore his bracelet. Also we went to Craft for lunch and spent a lot of the firm's money*

*Good for you. Home at a normal hour?*

*Staying late would set a bad precedent, out of here momentarily. Love you sweetheart, thanks for all your support*

*I love you too XOX*

## Chapter 9
July 2018

The next three days' filming were very different. They were on location, with no sets, no extras, and only the movie's co-stars as musicians. At the end of the day Thursday, Sandesh told Tasha that the dialogue scenes had been a master-class in acting. "They were all off-script, doing these scenes where they're rehearsing the play, so they're in character but doing other characters as those characters and what the fuck." She laughed. "And then there were two songs, and three dances," he said. "I'm seeing these guys do all this stuff and then looking at what's on TV going, is that all you can do, or are you in a box? I mean, I wonder how deep it actually goes. How many TV or movie actors could sing or dance if someone gave them the right vehicle."

"More than you'd think," she said. "I mean, they're not all great, but even Arnold Schwarzenegger's had a dance scene. That's my favorite movie of his, 'True Lies.' You've seen that, right?"

"No, and now I feel like I need to. A good one to watch before Theo gets back?"

"Definitely. I'll find it for us. So what's on the schedule for tomorrow?"

He sighed. "Fighting with a couple of partners, beating up a couple of associates, putting out fires, doing a couple of phone interviews. I'm going to be one tired puppy when I get to the studio, but I don't want to skip that. James and Silvia are definitely going to be there. And then it's down to the Bradbury bright and early on Saturday."

"Better make sure you get a good night's sleep." She made him sit down on the couch and stood behind him, stretching his arm out, testing his hand function. "You really are almost a hundred percent now, huh. Glad we got that little keyboard?" It was not so little, a tabletop digital piano with eighty-eight weighted keys.

"My playing skills are not yet improving, but everything else is, so I'll call that a win. Once we're done with this movie, I'll get back with Tomás for some more lessons. Anything new at your office?"

"Nope. It's been quiet this summer, not too many events. I'm catching up on my reading there at the front desk." She gave him a sideways look while she massaged his arm. "I wonder sometimes if I should be more ambitious. Try to get off reception. But it's so second-nature now, and I like being able to just forget about it when I'm not there."

"I remember those days." Sandesh had worked a reception desk too, early in his career. "For a while there I remember asking myself why I ever wanted a promotion."

Tasha laughed. "I'll bet you did! I thought the same thing, why did he even want that job, once they started running you ragged. But now you're the actual boss."

"And it's still blowing my mind. You know, if you wanted to get off the front desk I'm sure you could. I don't think it's lack of ambition. You've been *busy*. Having a kid is no joke."

"Well, you have a point. I'm so used to it now, and he's so easy now, I forget what it was like for a while there." She patted him. "But it is a lot easier now. So maybe I should start revving a little."

"What's the latest from Annette?"

"The team is going to be back at Cicada in September. Could we go see them again?"

"Absolutely we could. And once I've really settled into this position, we can take a look at things. With me and Matthew both on call, you could do a lot more with dancing if you wanted to. Of course, I'm hoping you'll want to dance with me from time to time." He was gazing up at her with those dreamy eyes that Tasha couldn't resist. She leaned over to kiss him. "Come over here." She went around the front of the couch and he tugged her down onto his lap, holding her close. "That night at Cicada I thought, she wants to perform again. And I was right, wasn't I?"

"Yes you were," she said. "And then all kinds of things happened. We're in a movie. It's the craziest thing."

"So tell me. This guy of Tanith's. Lieutenant Palacio. You met him when you did her play, right?"

This was an unexpected tangent. "Yeah, sure. He and his team interviewed everybody, a bunch of times, because stuff kept happening. He was a detective then. When did he get promoted?"

"Couple of years ago, there's a picture from the ceremony at their apartment. I haven't met him yet, he's the invisible man, so I'm curious. Tanith is complicated. What's he like?"

"Smart," she said. "And he's got a sense of humor. You'll get along. He's almost as good-looking as Victor. Not as good-looking as you," she added loyally. "And you're taller." Sandesh laughed. "Well, Tanith is little, so it's fine for her."

"Stop it," he said, giggling. "Oh man I just realized it's going to be seven straight days of filming after tomorrow. And I have to go over to Chrome on Sunday, before the Grand Park thing, to make sure the set is done. I'm not going to be much good to you."

"Then I'd better get some use out of you tonight, hadn't I?" She kissed him again. "Do not skip your PT next week," she warned. "Tanith's just going to have to do without you for a few hours."

"Yeah, I know. I won't. Let's do some therapy right now." He tipped them over on the couch.

Tasha got a text from Sandesh the next morning: *Call me at lunch OMG LOL.* She thought, *this is just like old times*, and could hardly wait. She went outside to the plaza on her break and called. He picked up immediately. "Okay sugar. I've been laughing since I got your text. Why am I laughing?"

"I channeled Andy today. He's this adorable guy in real life, right. His actor character in the movie is kind of serious, not a dick but very actor-y, like what's my process, what's my motivation, how are we playing this scene. Fussy, almost. Academic. Anyway, but his historical character is a real prick. Arrogant asshole, and –" he had to stop because he was laughing.

She was too. "Are you telling me you were an arrogant asshole today?"

"We had this meeting, me and James, with this one partner. You've heard about him. Desert Island Guy."

"Oh *him*, yeah. Did you fire him?"

"Equivalent. Invited him to leave. Nobody wants to work with him. He's cost the firm thousands in placement fees, plus he hasn't brought in any new business for quite a while, and his client retention is slipping. So James delivers the news, and then he starts to unload on *me*, because of course it's my fault with this socialist scheme of letting the assistants choose their assignments, and I went full Hans Gruber on his ass. It was *awesome*." They were both laughing again. "It was all, I'm going to count to three, there will not be a four. Oh my God. When that dude finally gave up and went flouncing back to his office James just looked at me and shook his head, I could tell he was about to lose it. He had to leave, he couldn't even say anything." Sandesh was wheezing.

"Oh lord," Tasha said eventually. "I haven't heard you laugh like that since, wow, last summer. Are you and James going to crack up when you see each other tomorrow?"

"Shit, I hope not. I have to be professional or Tanith will be so disappointed."

"Either that or work up a Eurotrash accent and just let it rip with that line. Maybe after we wrap. She won't care then, right?"

"No, as long as the logs get done she doesn't care what I do." He took a deep breath and blew it out. Tasha giggled again. "Stop. Oh my God. I swear I'm going to be laughing at that for the next six months. I have to get something to eat and get back up there, those other two partners have probably heard, and they're probably already packing their shit."

"Are you firing more of them?"

“No, but we’re doing an intervention with them and the two problem associates. Oh but I did fire somebody else. Guess who.”

“San Francisco IT shithead?”

“You know it. Love you honey, see you tonight.”

“Love you too.” Tasha disconnected, giggled some more, and then went to get her own lunch. Before she went back up to the office she texted him again: *That was just like old times except I got to hear you say you love me*

*And I got to say it XOX*

Sandesh wrapped up for the day feeling tired but satisfied. He’d done everything he needed to do, half of the staff assignments were locked, he had temporary coverage negotiated on all the other desks and a couple of temps coming in the next week. Janice had requested official assignment to him and James. The other two lawyers on her desk weren’t too happy about it, but he needed someone experienced and she’d been helping cover operations since May. The minute Sandesh was back in the office he’d be doing interviews for permanent staff to fill in the holes. All the resumes he couldn’t find on the system were discovered in an unlabeled file at Jessica’s old desk; he was taking them home to review.

Janice met up with him at the elevator bank. He frowned at her as they got into an open car. “Haven’t you been here since eight? You should have gone home an hour ago.”

“It was kind of a busy day. I don’t mind a little overtime now and again. I’m meeting Susan over at

Rock Sugar. So James said you took care of business today."

"I had to move fast. Won't be in at all next week. You can reach me on my cell, though. Any concerns?"

"Not yet. Can I ask how it went with Sherlyn?" One of the assistants was on probation, for the state of her desk and general inefficiency.

"She's not too happy. But that desk was a health hazard, and her workflow was rock bottom. And I know people with kids feel like they need to keep their cell phones on, hell, I do myself. But on in case of emergency is way different from on to play games."

"Well, that's what I thought. Darlene never addressed it. She'd remind people about policies, but then she never enforced anything."

"We'll have another staff meeting in a couple of weeks and by then there should be a better sense of where we're at. I want people to feel good about working here, but they've still got to deliver for the legal staff."

"I know. You'll get it done." They'd arrived at the lobby level. Janice got off with a wave, and Sandesh continued down to the garage. He wondered how long it would be before he wouldn't be nervous about it. *Maybe I should talk to that therapist after all.* He'd almost forgotten about it. He'd been so busy, ever since that boot camp. He wasn't having any of the post-traumatic shit that might have been expected. On the other hand, maybe that was because he'd been so busy, and learning so much new stuff. Maybe his brain was so thoroughly occupied that it was boxing things up. Maybe monsters would start climbing out of those boxes once things settled down. *After we wrap*, he promised himself.

Up in the office suite, James was in Carver's office. "So that was an interesting day," he said. Carver's expression was eloquent. "You got some feedback, I'm guessing. I hope they didn't take up too much of your time."

"It was only Sean. He was breathing fire when he came up here, wanting me to intervene with the management committee. I told him you and Sandesh had our full support. So he huffed and puffed for a while, tried to get me to say he could stay on. I kept looking at my watch and refusing to engage, like you told me to. Where'd you learn that tactic, anyway?"

"Settlement conferences. Seems like every time, somebody wants to argue the case instead of do what we're there to do. Anyway, so he went away, and I heard he left at three. If he comes in Monday I'll talk to him about transitioning out. Nothing from the other four?"

"Got an email from Dan that was close to an apology. Said he hadn't considered the effect on the firm, blah blah, was sorry to lose Janice and would try to do better with his next assistant. You've done great work on all this." He tried to gauge James' reaction. "And you have a hell of a poker face."

"Settlement conferences," James said again. Carver laughed. "It's been quite the roller coaster. But I hope we're over the worst of it now. Silvia's pregnant."

"Congratulations. Anyway. You probably know when we voted you in, I was a little skeptical. You were really young. But I'm not sure we could have survived all this without you, so thanks."

"Glad I could be of service. Give my regards to Margie."

"Likewise."

James was texting Silvia on his way down the hall to his office: *Just got a tongue bath from the boss*

She texted right back: *Ewww LOL coming home to take a shower?*

*Coming home to kiss my wife. Good day?*

*If you call trying not to puke for half an hour and then fighting with the Franchise Tax Board for a client for three hours good*

*Oh damn. Can I bring something home for you? How's the tummy now? OK for tango?*

*The tummy wants tres leches from Frida but otherwise fine for tango*

*Then I'll be a little bit late. See you soon though. Love you XOX*

*Love you too XOX*

Sandesh finally got to meet Lieutenant Palacio on Sunday night. He showed up at Grand Park with three other off-duty cops to help Tanith clear the area for their shoot. They exchanged a few words after Tanith wrapped the scene, and then all the cops went away with her for dinner. Sandesh went over to Tasha, who'd been waiting for him to double-check the equipment inventory, say good night to the camera crew, finish the logs, and send the other interns home. "Are the guild interns doing a pretty good job for you?" she asked.

"Yeah, thanks to Andy and his who-does-what plan, everybody has their own daily to-do list. All I do is micromanage, so Tanith doesn't have to. In the home stretch now. I'm going to miss this when we're done." He reviewed his list one more time. "Okay, that's it. Did you park at Disney Hall?"

"Yeah. Walk me over there?"

"Definitely. It was fun dancing with you tonight." He bent to kiss her. "I hope we show up on film."

"You're hard to miss, you foxy thing." She patted his ass.

"Kelli said she likes my hair better long."

"I like it both ways. It goes great with the suit this way." Tasha thought for a second. "You know, I remember seeing her and Vince perform a few years back, before he started doing ballroom. He was kind of shaggy then himself." They crossed the street and waited for the next light. "I heard from Theo today. They're up in Oregon. Going to Crater Lake tomorrow."

"Lucky little snot." Tasha laughed. Sandesh was smiling. "We'll have to take our own trip like that sometime, before he gets to that avoid-the-adults age. Is that still a thing? Lochan and I never really had that."

"I don't know. All of my friends have kids Theo's age or younger. We're all going to be surprised, I guess." The light changed again and they crossed the street to Disney Hall. "This building, I swear. When I first saw it I thought, you must be joking. Now I love it."

"Me too. The way it changes with the light."

Tasha stopped him when they got to the corner. “Stand still so I can take a picture with that building behind you. You’re so good-looking.” He took her phone and got a picture of her. She was laughing when he took a selfie of both of them. “So, everything ready over at Chrome? I was about to text Terry while we were waiting for our area to be cleared, and then the cops showed up.”

“It’s ready. Mr. Warner brought over a truck yesterday with all the pre-finished panels, they locked them together and then started on the bar. Today they finished dressing the bar and Mr. Hanover came in with all the props. He brought this gorgeous old upright piano. Completely different sound from the baby grand we had at the Million Dollar, or the one Marco has. Tomás was totally crooning over this one.” They were heading down into the garage. Sandesh knew Tasha was watching him. “I have to confess I still get skeeved out in underground garages.”

Tasha glanced up at him. “Not too surprising. It’s only been a couple of months. And you never had time to go talk to that counselor. You’re going to start next month, right?”

“Yeah, I already made the first appointment.” They got down to Tasha’s car. “I’m on this level too.”

“I’ll drive you around to yours, then. Hop in.” Sandesh was tired enough, and skeeved-out enough, to comply. Tasha drove him to the far side of the level. He leaned over to kiss her. She put a hand on his face, brushing his cheekbone with her thumb. “You’re amazing, you know. I haven’t told you for a while, but I’m really glad you kissed me last December.” He smiled and kissed her again. “Mmm. Best get out of here or I’m going to put this thing in park and then who knows what might happen." He laughed and let her go, got out of the car, opened his and then waved. She waited till his door was closed and seatbelt fastened before she waved and drove away.

Sandesh had been at Chrome for three hours the next day when he got a text from James: *When you get a minute ping me back*

Since he actually had a minute, he wrote back immediately: *What's up? Problem?*

*Sean's on a rampage. Nothing you need to do, a few of us had a powwow and decided to invoke the termination clause. LAPD escort en route. He'll be out by the end of the day, Dan volunteered to do the client contacts for transition and Janice volunteered to help. TG he wasn't equity*

*For real. Thanks for handling, ping me back if I can contribute or if I need to get in this week. I'll send Dan a note too*

*OK btw Silvia says thank Tanith for the mob scenes, those were fun*

*You guys looked great, hope she's feeling better soon*

*Yeah me too. Gotta run TTYL*

Sandesh put away his phone after sending a quick thank-you to Dan. Tanith was between scenes, waiting for a new setup, and watching him. "Everything okay?"

"The most poisonous pill at my office is leaving today. Everything's great. What's next?"

"Hang back and watch, we're about to run scene forty-one." Their one female co-star, Vicky Russo, was on stage warming up for her solo dance. She was wearing the same white halter-top pantsuit she'd worn for one of her scenes the previous week. There was no set, just a projection of gray stone walls on the fabric panels boxing in the stage. A second later a spotlight came on. "That's too warm, Yoshi," Tanith said into her phone. "We need the violet in there." There was no audible reply, but the light changed to blue-white and then edged into something like twilight. Vicky still glowed, but now she looked like a dream. *Or a ghost*, Sandesh thought. "Perfect," Tanith said. "Make a note for when we do scene forty." Then she checked in with her camera crew, the stage managers, and her sound person. "Ready to roll, Vicky?" Sandesh looked around to make sure the guild interns were locked down. They were all lined up at the back of the set, well behind the cameras, with empty hands. They'd all been good about not using their phones on set after the first day.

Vicky straightened up and said, "Let's do it."

"Okay everybody. Scene forty-one, take one. Cameras. Smoke machines. Cue music. Action."

"So then there was another dance, and I was still recovering from the solo, plus Victor's song that we started with, it's a killer. The way they lit that, it totally looked like old black and white film. And then there was this fat dialogue scene that they did twice. I mean she took everything twice, but with the songs and dances I'll admit I kind of zone out and just enjoy things. Oh, and James texted to tell me they had to give Sean the actual boot today because he was over the line."

"Jeez," said Tasha, when Sandesh finally ran down. "Quite an exciting day, in other words. I'm glad you weren't at the office for that."

"Me too," he said, with feeling. "It's a big relief. He could have taken weeks to get his transition done. Four days left. Tomorrow we've got the scenes with all those other actors. Three of them are from the play."

"Oh yeah? Wow, Tanith's really making the most of that, isn't she. Who?"

"Dexter Parker and Tony Rogers, and Marco's wife Cameron. She had a break in this other thing she's doing this summer. I'm sorry, I've been jabbering about this nonstop since I got home." He gave her an apologetic smile and addressed his dinner.

"I wish I could've been there too," Tasha admitted. "I'm sure I'm going to like the movie, but I'd love to see it from the inside. It's kind of coming together in your head, isn't it? Now that it's so close to being done."

He swallowed a mouthful, took a sip of wine, and nodded. "That must be it. So, any news from Crater Lake?"

"Look at this selfie." Tasha pulled up a photo and turned her phone around. Sandesh laughed. The picture showed Theo and Matthew with their heads together, posed as if they were about to fall backward into the lake. "Isn't that great?"

"Yeah, it is. When are they heading back?" That hadn't been decided when the trip began.

"Not till the end of the month. Matthew took all the paid leave he had, and maybe some unpaid. I almost asked him if everything was okay. I mean, I think he'd tell me if there was something I ought to know." She looked doubtful.

"I'm sure he would." Sandesh nudged her shoulder with his. "He probably felt like this might not come around again for a while, and why not make it big. I might do the same thing when we plan our honeymoon."

She laughed. "Oh you might, huh? Just slipping that in there?"

"Well, you know. Don't want you to forget I think about these things."

"I think about them too," she said, smile fading. She put her hand on his. "You're doing everything right. Don't ever doubt that. I just want to give it a little more time, let things normalize a little. This summer hasn't been normal."

He turned his hand so he could hold hers. "No, it hasn't. I get it. What does Terry say?"

"He's glad you moved in. He's going to do a Labor Day party over at their house, invite all my girls, Ricky and Luis, Lochan and Paige. But till then, once the movie wraps, we can work on finding our normal." They gazed at each other for a moment. "Now let's clean this up. I got 'True Lies' for us."

The last day of principal photography was supposed to be a light day; there were no extras, no costume changes, not even any musicians aside from Tomás. Tanith did her usual two takes of each scene, for insurance, even though they looked perfect (to Sandesh) the first time. She was conferring with her camera crew, and Sandesh was eyeballing the general state of things – the guild interns had the air of being imminently sprung from jail – when he noticed Andy over by the bar, looking at his phone. There was a stream of low-pitched but sincere profanity. Victor was trying not to laugh, though he also looked annoyed. Sandesh went over and said, "Everything all right?"

"No. The triplex next to us just went on the market again, and it's vacant. That means some developer's going to knock it down and put up a six-unit pile of ugly. Or some money launderer will knock it down and put up a six-unit pile of ugly. God *damn* it. Could we buy it?" Andy was looking at Victor.

"Yeah, we could. You want to be a landlord?"

"We're already landlords. The thought of that cute little thing getting razed for some econobox makes me sick."

"Not to mention we'd be living next to a worksite for however long," Victor said. "The security guys would absolutely lose their shit." They stared at each other for a few seconds.

Sandesh impulsively said, "I'd rent from you. I might be able to fill the other two units, too." Then he thought *are you insane*, but he didn't retract it. The building next to Andy and Victor's was about the same vintage, but in the 'storybook' style. A one-story front unit was connected to a two-story duplex, offset so that both of the arched, stone-framed entry doors on the ground level were visible from the street. The front had a short tower, the back a taller one, both with conical roofs. It was on a large lot. Sandesh had loved it at first sight when they arrived in the neighborhood for filming.

Andy and Victor were now both staring at him. "Each unit is two-bedroom, one and a half bath," said Andy.

"Perfect," he said recklessly. "Do you want me to get some votes from my people before you make an offer?"

Victor said, "No. We'll get it rolling. Call your people. We'll talk." He and Andy conferred in low voices for a minute. Then Andy sent a text, or email, to whoever had sent him the listing notification. Sandesh, feeling a bit lightheaded, sent three texts in quick succession. The first was to Tasha: *Sweetie can I interest you in a fairytale cottage right next to Andy & Victor? Hope so because I already told them I want to live there, really sorry, total filter fail. RSVP ASAP XOX* The next was to his brother: *Lo would you and Paige move to a triplex with me and Tasha? E of La Cienega So of Olympic celebrity adjacent.* Finally, well aware that this was in the column most people would label 'loco,' he sent one to Matthew: *Hey Matthew, friends of friends are buying a triplex, LACMA end of Mid City. I lost my head, going to do my best to convince Tasha to move, any interest in renting there?* Then he muted his phone and shoved it into his pocket, because Tanith was back in action.

First she gathered all the guild interns together, thanked them for their work, and cut them loose. Then she had a short conference with the five male co-stars. Sandesh knew that Vicky was on her way over to Chrome; a journalist was coming to do an on-set interview with Tanith and the cast. He had some paperwork to do, compiling the various logs that the guild interns had been keeping and then noting down the file numbers for that day's completed takes. He was giving the movie work ninety percent of his attention while the other fraction of his brain thought about the Sleeping Beauty triplex.

Tanith had Tomás do a piano number on camera for the Kickstarter project page before Vicky and the journalist arrived. The interview took an hour, plus the whole cast did a version of one of the movie's dance numbers. Finally Tanith thanked her cast and crew, said

"The Ghost of Carlos Gardel, amigos. That's a wrap" with an expression of disbelief, and sent everybody except her director of photography and Sandesh home. Andy and Victor gave Sandesh a silent 'call us' gesture on their way out.

He nodded to them, and then looked at Tanith. "What else do you need from me, boss?"

"Like I know?" She plopped down on one of the cabaret chairs in the set. "Reza, what did I forget."

The DP sat down beside her and said, "Nothing. You got it all. Now it's up to me and Tina. When do you think you can hand it over?" Tanith had to go through the footage and identify every shot, of every scene, that she wanted assembled for the rough cut. Then she had to do the same with every piece of music.

She was rubbing her forehead, thinking. After a minute she said, "I have to go back to work Monday, damn it. Won't be able to get through everything till, probably, the end of the week." She looked up at Reza, and then at Sandesh. "You guys are back at work next week too, huh? Thanks for giving me July."

"I wouldn't have missed it," Sandesh said. "An incredible education. If you decide to do another one, call me."

Reza said, "Me, too. And Tina will call you about that other thing."

"Get out," Tanith said. "That was not fair."

"The art wants what it wants." He stood up, offering a hand. Tanith shook it from her chair. "We'll look forward to getting your outline." He shook hands with Sandesh and left.

Terry must have been watching on the security monitor. When Tanith and Sandesh exited the set and stepped into the unused portion of the downstairs lounge, he was there. "All done? Y'all happy?"

"I think I'm happy," said Tanith. "I'm too brain-fried to be sure. Our guys are coming tomorrow to break all this down and put it back the way they found it. Let me know if we fucked anything up."

"Why'd you think we scheduled you *before* re-painting? Go on now. See you soon, Sandesh."

"Bye Terry, thanks for all your help." Sandesh picked up his messenger bag, helped Tanith collect her gear, and walked her up the stairs. "What was Reza talking about?"

"Tina threw me an idea. She wants me to write a script for a graphic novel. And it's going to be fucking perfect for adaptation. I was like Noooooo." Sandesh laughed. Tanith was shaking her head. "I told Sid and he was all, great, now you can write that movie for five women. I almost strangled him."

Sandesh waited until he was in his car to check his phone. There was a text from Lochan: *Yes call me later*. A text from Matthew: *If Tasha approves*. And finally a text from Tasha: *CALL ME*.

Tasha had glanced at Sandesh's message when it came in, then looked again, thinking *what the hell?* They hadn't talked about moving at all. They'd barely started living together. She liked her apartment. They had their whole routine worked out.

On the other hand, Sandesh had driven her past the location. Andy and Victor's place was stunning. The triplex next door was on the shabby side, but it was really cute. It was in the same district for Theo's school, and a manageable walk to the museums and the park. Their work commute would hardly change at all. She had to wonder, though, what Sandesh had in mind for the other two units. They couldn't possibly afford to rent all three, not even on his new salary. Neighbors were a crapshoot at the best of times, and she didn't know Andy and Victor beyond 'hello.' They might have their own ideas about tenants. Plus, ugh, she and Sandesh had executed a new lease. They couldn't move before next June, not without hefty penalties. *Quit speculating till you talk to him.* She sent back a text, and then tried to put it out of her mind. It was wrap day, and who knew when he might get free.

It was a little after five when he called. She was ready to go, only hanging around because she wanted to have at least the first part of this conversation as soon as possible. "Hey baby. So, what in the world?"

"That triplex just went on the market. Andy got something from the broker who handled their place. He was having a fit because the building is vacant, a buyer would probably just scrape it off and build something with more units. They've got pretty heavy security, you know, because of the parts they play on that TV show. Their team wouldn't be happy about having an active work site next door for months. Probably more like two years."

"And they would hate it themselves, I get it. So they're buying it?"

"I think so, yeah. Pretty sure they told their broker to write up an offer today. I know it's out of nowhere, and there's a lot to talk about, and maybe I shouldn't have, but I pinged Lo and Matthew."

Tasha took a second. Lochan had come to her mind, too, but she'd hadn't considered Matthew. "You mean about renting the other two units?" He didn't say anything. She had a feeling he was really nervous. "Did you hear back from them?"

"Lochan said yes and Matthew said if you approve." Definitely nervous. "And of course this is all contingent on whether Andy and Victor even get the place, plus a lot of other shit."

"Okay. Obviously this is not at the *planning* stage, it's a what-if. My answer on the what-if is why not. It's the right neighborhood and the place is cute. We both like Lochan and Paige, we both get along with Matthew. Theo would love it. So let's see what happens, and then deal with it."

"Great," he said with audible relief. "Thanks. Are you heading out?"

"Yeah, I was only waiting to talk to you. See you in a bit. Love you baby."

"I love you too." Sandesh took the time for just one more thing, a text to Andy: *Three tenants if you want them.*

They didn't talk about it more that night. Tasha didn't want to mention it to Terry or Anya yet. But she wanted to get an outside opinion on whether they were crazy, so she texted Annette: *How insane is a person who considers moving into a triplex next to her ex?*

Annette must have been at home too. Her reply came back fast: *Well if it were me and MY ex the answer would be very insane. But you don't have fantasies about burning Matthew's house down with him inside it, do you?*

*Bahaha no I don't*

*Sherry told me you had a large rage for a little while*

*Oh lord Sherry saw me at my absolute worst. Maria too*

*How'd she do on the movie thing?*

*I think it went really well. Sandesh said Tanith and Lesley were super happy with her. I'm going to catch up with her next week. You know they had Dexter for a day this week*

*No really?! What for?*

*Historical scenes at a milonga, they needed dancers who could talk*

*LOL I thought they had all those dance extras*

*Yeah but those people were in a bunch of scenes. Sandesh said if they were doing lines too they would have been too noticeable*

*Yeah I guess*

*Oh shit I'm seeing 'Sandesh said' twice now*

*LMAO don't worry about it I know you still have a brain*

*Thanks for that. Anyway we're going to come see y'all at Cicada in September. Maybe by then I'll know about this triplex craziness. Are you free Sunday? Want to get together?*

*Tell you what, I have 2-4 booked at this studio down on Pico. How about I start teaching you to tap?*

*Girl! For real?*

*For real for real*

*That sounds like fun*

*Then go get yourself some tap shoes.*

Tasha read the text exchange again after they signed off, still grinning when she turned to Sandesh. "Honey, I'm going to start making some noise this weekend."

## Chapter 10
August 2018

James noticed that even when Sandesh wasn't in the office, the overall vibe was much more positive. Possibly that was because Sean and his toxic bullshit were gone. Or it might have to do with the warm, fuzzy feeling of being heard. If the team could manage to sustain that, the firm might be able to repair some of the damage before too many people found out how close they'd been to the edge.

He was in the office early on Monday, working with one of the real-estate experts on the least-expensive way to get out of their San Francisco lease. That took most of the hour before nine o'clock. He and Janice both got an interoffice IM at nine: *Mr. Prasad is here if you need him.* That was a thing Sandesh had asked Nicole to do. James wondered whose idea it was to be so formal. Maybe it was because of the haircut, or the suits. James knew from experience what a difference that could make. Silvia hadn't made that an explicit requirement, but he still wasn't sure he would have won her if he hadn't dealt with his untailored wardrobe and the unibrow.

He looked at the administrative to-do list. There wasn't much on it this week, and nothing he needed to address prior to feedback from Sandesh. It was possible that for the first time in months, he might get through the workweek without some emergency.

By Friday of that week, James was completely caught up with his actual work for the first time since May. He wandered out to Janice's desk a little before noon. She looked up at him and laughed. “You look so confused.”

“I *am* confused. I forgot what it’s like to not have my hair on fire. Am I actually getting all my calls and emails?”

She laughed again. “Yes you are. I’ve been fielding the easy stuff for you, like you asked me to. You want me to keep doing that?”

“Hell yeah. What’s new from our friend on the other side of reception?”

“He’s got the e-suite and mailbox organized for San Francisco. The legal staff up there are doing an equipment inventory to send to our IT head here. Once that’s final, they’ll order whatever other bits everyone needs for the home office setups and then schedule return of the leased equipment. Four to six week timeline for completing the transition there. Mr. Prasad has also interviewed six candidates. Parenthetically, it would have taken Darlene two months to do that. Anyway, we’re having another staff meeting this afternoon, starts at four this time. You got that notification on Outlook, right? Good. Oh, and he’s doing a compensation review.”

“Meaning he’s going through to see if anybody else didn’t get a raise when they should have. I’m assuming that will include you.” He leaned on the counter of her desk. He’d recommended raises each of the last three years and had no idea if they’d gone through.

“I hope so,” she said. “Susan wants to go to New York for the chocolate show.”

“Do not mention a chocolate show around *my* wife. She’s hungry these days. So is everybody calling him Mr. Prasad now?”

"It started as a joke, I think. He said that in the first meeting, call me Mr. Prasad, because everyone was looking at him like, who are you. He was gone all that time and now he seems so different, and it's all such a huge change, that I think it just stuck. I mean, he doesn't look like a Sandy now."

"No, he doesn't. He did have kind of a major life event this year." Janice grimaced. "Once everybody's used to it, I expect we'll hear 'Sandesh' more often. Well, speaking of hungry, I think I'm going to walk home for lunch. Ping me if anything crazy happens."

"Give my regards to Silvia."

James nodded and headed out, feeling cheerful. He hadn't really wanted to leave the firm, even though things had been grim there for a while. His own practice was on a solid footing, the location was great, and with a baby on the way the less other change in their lives, the better. Silvia was hoping to get out on the road in September as usual, but promised if she wasn't feeling well that she'd skip it this season. The wineries she represented had been with her so long, one harvest without face time wouldn't torpedo the relationship. And she now had a bilingual part-time assistant, based in San Luis Obispo, who might be able to make the site visits for her. When he got home, James asked her about that. "Have you spoken to Camilo yet?"

Silvia looked up from her laptop. She was sitting on the couch, with Food Network playing at low volume on the TV. "Yeah, I called him yesterday afternoon. Thinking about the winery visits?"

"Well, with any luck you'll be over the morning sickness soon. But just in case. Or maybe this is a good time to officially delegate some of that. What's he doing the rest of the time?"

"He's working at a restaurant in Pismo." She set aside the laptop. "I was thinking about that, too. I've been at this for ten years now and it's been good, but with a little kid my business model might not work. In the office, sure. Local meetings, sure. But all the travel, probably no."

"You've worked with him for two years now. No issues?"

"No issues. At first it was a little weird because he's used to working with women bosses in the restaurant scene but he wasn't used to scheduling his own time, making and keeping appointments. Stuff like that. Once I gave him a checklist and we had a chance to do a couple winery tours together, let him learn the script, he was on it."

They gazed at each other for a minute, then James said, "I really love you."

"I love you too." Silvia smiled. "I know your mom is going to be all over the child care. But at the moment, and maybe it's just pregnancy hormones, I'm feeling like let's take advantage of that for vacations. For the business, let's delegate. If Camilo can do it," she qualified.

He leaned down and kissed her. "Let's find out how much he needs to make, and see what we can do."

*I am nervous about this*, Sandesh thought as he waited in the counselor's reception area. He wasn't sure why. It was talk therapy, not electroshock. He'd never had any problem talking. He tried not to look at the person coming out of the office, speaking to the receptionist, going away. He hoped that person was ignoring him, too.

"Mr. Prasad?"

"Right here."

"You can come in." He went in. She closed the door behind him. "Hi. I'm Dr. LaSalle. You can call me Robyn."

"Uh, hi, Robyn. How does this work?"

"We're here to talk. Have a seat."

It wasn't a couch. It was an upholstered wing chair with a high back, high enough even for someone his height. He realized it provided a feeling of shelter. It was positioned so that he could see the door and the window. "This is a great chair. I was afraid I'd have to lie on a couch."

"The whole sitting behind somebody's head thing doesn't really work for me. And lying on a couch is a very vulnerable position for the client."

*Not 'patient,'* he thought. *Interesting*. "Where do I start?"

"First let's review the events that brought you here." That took up a third of their time. Sandesh was starting to relax. Then Robyn said, "Now tell me why you waited two months."

"Well, I was busy. I had physical therapy, and I had a lot of shit to do about my job, and then I started assisting on this movie. But mostly I didn't feel like I had a problem."

"And now you feel you do?"

"Now I've had some time to think about it and I think I *might* have a problem." They talked about symptoms. He didn't have many. "No, really. I get skeeved out in parking decks. That's about it."

"Tell me about the actual attack."

He shifted, uncomfortable. Did a little conscious breathing. "I almost don't feel like it *was* an attack. It was almost an accident." Robyn didn't say anything, but her expression was skeptical. "Okay. She confronted me. She was not in her right mind. She had a knife in her hand, a very sharp knife. She didn't show up there with a table knife, or even a kitchen knife from her drawer at home. I don't know where you would go to get a knife like that. I guess it speaks to intention. Yes, okay, it was an attack."

"What kind of knife was it?"

"I think it's called a Buck knife. Like a hunting knife." He hadn't seen one since he lived in South Carolina.

"And what action led to your injury?"

"Security guy said something. I think it was, is everything okay over there. I said no. Kind of loud. Jessica turned around to see who was there, and she turned her whole body, and the knife came down and my arm was in the way." He realized how ridiculous that sounded. He thought through it. "Why was my arm in the way? It was bent," he said, remembering. "My hand was moving. I was starting to move at the same time she was. My hand was down by my side, with my car keys, and then when the security guy said that I think I meant to push her back. Because someone else was there, you know? I've been through so many trainings about how you do not ever touch a female co-worker. But he saw her, he knew she had that knife, he wouldn't even have been there if the surveillance camera hadn't picked up what was happening." It was flowing now, his thoughts and actions from those few fraught minutes coming clear.

He'd honestly never tried to reconstruct it. "And I'm right-handed, and the knife was on my left side, so maybe I thought I can shove her out of the way and get some more distance, and then that guy would be there to manage things."

Robyn gave him a minute. When he didn't say anything else she nodded and made a note. "Do you think that's why you were thinking of this as an accident?"

"Yeah, maybe so. Also of course you never want to think, gee, somebody was trying to kill me. I didn't think that. I still don't. I think she was not in her right mind." Then he contradicted himself, because he remembered something else. "Except no. I thought I was about to die. I thought of Tasha. My girlfriend. Wow, I forgot all this shit."

"You lost a lot of blood, you were anesthetized, you were traumatized, and then you blocked it out. This is very common, Sandesh. Also a valid coping mechanism. Do you think talking about this more will be helpful?"

"Yes," he said.

On the way home he was going back over the whole thing, amazed at how incomplete his recollection had been. He was so glad Tasha was going to be there waiting for him. He wanted a hug. Then he remembered Theo was due home that day too. Pulled over to send a text: *Hi sweetie heading home. Should I stop and get pie?*

*LOL that would be great, I forgot. Love you!*

*Love you too XOX*

Over the course of that week Sandesh received a series of brief texts from Andy, starting with *Offer in*, followed by several that said *waiting* (with various embellishments ranging from 'still' to 'FFS' to '#%@$&!'), then *negotiating*. On Friday night he got the one he was hoping for: *Call me*. He was sitting on the couch with Tasha and Theo, working on his laptop while they watched a DVD about the Grand Canyon. Tasha looked over at him when the text pinged in. "It's Andy," he said. "He wants me to call. I'll go in the bedroom."

"Okay honey." She looked almost as excited as he was. They'd driven by the triplex again on Sunday, unable to resist talking about what they could do with the yard. If the unsightly front driveway and parking pad could be removed, and if they could put up a fence, and so many other 'ifs.' The lot was big enough to add parking for six cars across the back, accessible from the alley.

He took the phone into the bedroom and dialed. Andy picked up right away. "Sandesh."

"Andy. What's the word?"

"The word is we got it. I want to strangle their fucking broker, but we got it."

"Imagine I'm saying woo-hoo really loud right now." Andy laughed. Sandesh was grinning. "I totally want to jump up and down. What can I do?"

"Want to bring Tasha over tomorrow and see it? We can talk about what needs to get done. Which is a lot, by the way. Do any of you need to move soon?"

"No, we're good. Lo and Paige are on month-to-month, so is Matthew, and our lease runs to June."

"That sounds about right. Seriously, it's a lot, but at least it's not one harsh word from falling down like this place was. Closing's in a month but that's basically a formality, we already have a set of keys. So can you come over?"

"Pretty sure. Just a second." He walked out to the living room. Theo was absorbed in the movie; Tasha was looking over at Sandesh. He said, "Do you have anything tomorrow?"

"No."

"Want to go see the Sleeping Beauty? Andy has the keys."

Tasha squealed. "Yes! Can we bring Theo?"

He said into the phone, "Can we bring our boy? He's seven."

"Sure," Andy said. "Anytime after ten."

"Great. We'll be there after breakfast. Thanks, Andy."

"See you tomorrow." Andy disconnected and Sandesh perched on the arm of the couch, still looking at Tasha. She glanced at Theo, got up, and went with Sandesh into the kitchen. He seized her and hugged her. They giggled together for a minute before he kissed her.

"I'm so excited," she said softly. "I don't even know why. I've lived here for five years and I thought I liked it."

Sandesh laughed under his breath. "It's a good apartment. I don't know, I just loved that building right off the bat and being next door to those guys is going to be fun. He says there's a lot of work to do. That might mean we can do some stuff to our personal taste."

"I hardly even know what that is." They both snickered, brainstorming for a few minutes before conceding they had no clue. "Are you going to tell the others?"

"Yeah. I don't want them to come with us tomorrow, though, I feel like this is *our* place. Sick, right? Anyway, they'll be able to see inside soon." He'd been texting back and forth with them all week too, and knew they'd done drive-bys already. Paige had texted *OMG squeee!!!* "I'll go talk to them now." He kissed her again and went back to the bedroom. Called Matthew first, got voice mail, and left a message. "Hey Matthew, good news. Andy and Victor got the triplex. They say there's a lot of work to do. We'll be able to get inside soon and start making plans. Really excited over here. Once Theo figures it out he's going to be thrilled. Talk to you soon." Then he called Lochan, who picked up. "Guess what?"

"Did your friends get the triplex?" Lochan sounded excited too.

"Yes they did." He laughed at the muted *woo-hoo* on the other end. "That's what I said. We'll be able to get inside soon, so I'll let you know about that. Andy says there's a lot of work to do, we might be able to personalize things a little."

"Paige would love that. You know she's addicted to HGTV and DIY. She's done stuff around here our landlord doesn't even know about."

"Maybe she could run the reno for us. Tasha and I were just saying we have no idea what our personal style is. And she says those two words are completely foreign to Matthew." Lochan laughed. "We're super excited. Probably looking at nine months to move-in. Anyway, I'll keep you posted, and we'll see you on Labor Day if not before."

"Thanks, looking forward to it." Lochan disconnected, and Sandesh went back to his laptop, where he closed the email program and started cruising HGTV.

The next day they pulled into the driveway at the triplex not long after ten, and sat there looking at it for a minute until Theo said, "Why are we here?"

Tasha stifled a laugh. "We're going to move here next year, honey. You'll still get to go to the same school."

"It looks old." He sounded disapproving.

Sandesh said, "It is old. The building we're in now went up in the sixties, this one is thirty years older than that. It's going to get all fixed up for us, though. There are three apartments here, instead of eighteen like in our building now."

"Who else lives here?"

"Well, you know Sandesh has a brother," Tasha said. "You haven't met him yet because you were on your trip with Daddy. Anyway, he and his wife and their little girl are going to live here. And Daddy's going to live here." She'd turned around to watch his face. It took a second to sink in.

"You mean we'll all be here together?"

"Yup."

"That's so weird." Tasha saw Sandesh bite his lip, trying not to laugh. Theo added, "But it's cool. Really cool. Can we go inside?"

"Sure can. Sandesh is letting our future landlord know we're here." He wasn't, actually, but he pulled out his phone and did that. They all got out of the car and wandered around for a few minutes until Andy came over, trailed at a distance by his on-site security guy.

Andy said, "Don't mind Adrian. He's contractually obligated to keep an eye on me. Hi Tasha." Andy shook her hand, shook Sandesh's, and then looked at Theo. "You must be Theo. I'm Andy." He offered a hand and Theo gravely shook it. "Want to go inside?"

"Nice to meet you. Yes please," Theo said. Tasha looked at him standing between Sandesh and Andy, realizing with a sort of shock that Theo was four feet tall now. His new summer jeans were already showing some ankle. *He's not going to be my little boy much longer*, she thought. When she glanced over at Sandesh, she thought he was thinking the same thing. He nodded and held out his hand. She took it and they followed Andy into the front unit. Adrian didn't go in with them.

"I know that's weird," Andy said, shrugging. "I work on a TV show, Theo, and there are people who don't like my character. So my bosses make sure there's someone watching out for me."

"Why don't they like your character? Are you mean?"

Tasha fielded the question. "Andy is not mean, and his character isn't either. He plays a bartender. But his bartender is married to a policeman, and some people don't think two men should be married."

"That's dumb. Who cares. It smells kind of funky in here." He went a little ahead of them, exploring.

Tasha raised her eyebrows at Andy. He gave her a thank-you smile and said, "There's a lot of cleanup to do here. This carpet's gotta go. And check out this kitchen."

The layout of the front unit was unsurprising, and the rooms weren't large. There was charm to spare, though. The living room had a coved ceiling, a picture window facing the street, and an archway into the kitchen-dining space. All the other windows were old metal-framed casements. "These are cute," said Andy, "but hideously inefficient. We'll replace them with better ones."

It seemed he had already given a great deal of thought to renovation. As they went through he mentioned refinishing the original wood floors, adding soundproofing in the bedrooms, re-wiring, updating the plumbing, and replacing the entire kitchen. "I'm not sure which of you will want this unit, of course, but all of them will get ceiling fans in the bedrooms. We're looking into adding central heat and air. These gas things in the wall, I don't like them, especially with kids in the house."

Sandesh and Tasha looked at each other but didn't say anything. Everything he was saying was great. They were both a tiny bit nervous about what the rent would ultimately be. No one had even mentioned money yet.

The tour continued into the ground-floor unit in back, which was nearly identical to the front except that the floor plan was reversed, so the living-room picture window was on the back wall. Then they went up the stairs that ran between the front and back units, across the open passageway to the entry door in the tower, and into the second-story apartment.

"Well, wow," said Tasha. "What happened here?" It looked as though someone, at some point, had simply gutted the place. There was a ramshackle kitchen, one and a half bathrooms that looked to be original 1930s, and the rest was open space.

Andy said, "I do not know, and the seller's broker couldn't account for it. It was listed as another two-bedroom. Obviously someone had a problem with walls. We have no idea what we'll find when we rip up this carpet. I'm guessing the whole floor will need to be re-done." He shrugged. "Good opportunity to sound-proof it."

"Dad would love this," said Theo. "He doesn't like walls."

Tasha and Sandesh glanced at each other, absorbing this now-obvious revelation. She said, "That's true. What do you think he'd say about the bathrooms?"

"He wouldn't care. His girlfriend might not like them." He studied the kitchen. "She definitely won't like that." All the adults laughed.

"That shows good sense," Andy said. "So, you want to go and see the back yard? It's not much to look at, but that's just as well because once the workers come in they're going to tear it up."

"I'm approaching brain overload," Tasha confessed. "Did you get an inspection?"

"No, we didn't ask for one. We had a pretty good idea this would need a complete overhaul. I mean, you can tell from the bald spots that the roof needs to be re-shingled. We'll get that done as soon as the HVAC situation is dealt with. Have you seen that house over in Beverly Hills with the art shingles?" Tasha knew the one he meant. He caught her eye. "You know the one. Copper cat on the ridge? Yeah, that one. We're going to do something similar here. Might as well make the most of it, since we have to look at it." She was not about to say 'you shouldn't spend that much money,' but she couldn't help hearing *ka-ching* over and over again.

Andy might have read her mind. "Let's go over to my place. Have a beverage, Theo can meet Molly, and we can talk numbers a little."

Sandesh said "Eeek," so Tasha wouldn't have to. Andy laughed.

Theo said, "Who's Molly?"

"Molly is our dog. Do you like dogs?"

"I met a few on vacation. They're okay."

"Then let's go."

Tasha was relieved to see that Molly was a well-behaved dog. She approached Theo with her fluffy blonde tail wagging, sat down nearby, and waited for him to do something. Matthew had evidently given him some guidance on dogs, because he held out the back of his hand for Molly to sniff. She licked it. "Eww," he said, laughing. "Can I pet her?"

"Of course." Andy watched. Molly had a history of instant romances with new visitors. This one was no exception. After a minute, all the adults went back to his kitchen for coffee. Then, seeing that Theo was now on the floor rolling a ball for Molly to fetch, they all sat down at the table. "You're probably thinking the rent is going to be insanely high and what have you gotten yourselves into. Well, don't worry about it. We bought the building because we wanted to control the outcome, not because we need to make a profit. Once the renovation is budgeted and we have an idea what the total cost is going to be, we can talk again, but I can guarantee you we won't be asking more than three thousand."

"That's insanely *low*," Tasha said after a moment. "That's almost a thousand under market."

"Well, look at it from our point of view. We don't have kids. My parents are set for life. Victor's dad is well-off. We make a ridiculous amount of money." He shrugged. "Having neighbors we like and something attractive to look at is worth something to us." He raised his eyebrows and made a 'see all this' gesture. "Already paid for. Victor's meeting with people right now about another movie for next year. We're good." Then he frowned, like *uh-oh*, and said, "We are going to like these other people, right?"

Sandesh laughed. "I think so. My brother and his wife are super mellow, and you'll never know Matthew is even there."

"Fine, then. After closing, let's get them all over here. Then I'll get the ball rolling with our contractor."

Sandesh didn't hear from Andy again for a couple of weeks, and didn't really have a good excuse to call, so he put away his excitement about the Sleeping Beauty and concentrated on work. By the last week of August the firm's exit from the San Francisco office was almost complete. Their Bay Area attorneys were completely set up to work from home. "This is amazing," he told Tasha on a lunchtime phone call. "I never hear about San Francisco anymore. The assistants here do what they need, the work gets done, their shit gets filed, their hours get in, their bills go out. Carver et al are still grumbling about the cost of breaking the lease, but once that works through the system they'll be all, why did we ever need that office."

Tasha snickered. "I couldn't believe it when I saw what the monthly nut was. Have you got all your new people set up?"

"Mostly hired, not quite all in yet. Still looking for an HR assistant. As you can imagine I am being very choosy about that one. I filled in the LAA desks from some of those rejected resumes. You should have seen the notes Darlene had on some of them." There had been a couple dozen applications for Legal Administrative Assistant vacancies over the past year. Darlene hadn't hired anyone.

Tasha had already heard quite a bit about the stupefying inaction of Sandesh's predecessor. "Typical objections?"

"No college degree, not enough experience, wrong field of experience, blah blah. But then she'd bring somebody in for interview with a bazillion years of perfect experience, the attorneys would be like yeah baby, and she'd say oh, nope, too expensive. It's like, make up your mind. Either you want someone inexpensive who you can train, or you want someone who can sit down and do the job as soon as they have a password." He sounded exasperated. Tasha had heard this song before. She didn't say so, but he added, "I'm sorry. I know you've heard me bitch about this for years."

"I don't mind. So which way did you go?"

"I went with hire cheap and train them. Two of them are already on, two of them start in two weeks. We only had one person here who I wouldn't trust with a trainee."

"Still on probation?"

"Yeah. I don't know if she's going to cut it. She hasn't been acting like someone who wants to keep the job. I have to talk to her again."

Tasha had seen that sort of thing many times; a receptionist got a bird's-eye view of an office. "Well, she probably won't admit that she's looking to leave. I never would. I was always, oh yes things are fine, sure go ahead and give me that stuff too. And then it was thanks for the learning experience, peace, I'm out." Sandesh laughed. Tasha hadn't changed jobs that many times, but when she had it had been for the exact same reason he had wanted off a reception desk himself.

"So what's on the schedule tonight?"

"Nothing unusual," she said. "Any word from Andy?"

"Nope. It's almost Labor Day, so I'm just going to hang back. We can all go see the place next month. I keep seeing him and Victor on E or TMZ or whatever, I know they're busy till after the Emmys. Nothing from Tanith either and I *really* want to pester her." Tasha laughed. "Heroic effort of restraint here. Anyway, I know you have to get back up there. Thanks for taking my call." He was smiling.

She could hear it in his voice. It made her smile too. "Oh please. Love you baby."

"Love you too." He set down the phone and glanced at his in-box; nothing hot had landed. He swiveled around to look out the window for a minute. *I like having a window.* The falconer was flying his hawks out in the plaza, scaring away the pigeons. Then he had a sense that someone was at the door, and turned around again. "Hey Janice. Did I forget something?"

"You never forget anything. James wanted to know if you need anything from him before he heads out for vacation, and I thought I'd walk down here and ask because I need to get off my ass once in a while."

"Let me know if you want one of these things," he said, waving at the Varidesk. "I dig it the most. Anyway no, I think he's free to fly the coop with Silvia. Are they going up to Paso?"

"Yes they are. Should he bring back some wine for you? Or rather, what kind of wine should he bring back for you?"

Sandesh gave that some thought. "We are heading into champagne season," he suggested. "Anybody up there do sparkling wines?"

"If anyone would know, it'll be Silvia. Alternate?"

"Rosé. Tasha loves it. Tell him thanks very much, and thank *you* very much for being the messenger. He brings back wine for you, too, right?"

"Yes he does," Janice said. "Why do you think I asked to keep him on my desk?" She turned around and left. Laughing under his breath, he got ready to go outside for a break. It was still hard to remember he could leave his office whenever he wanted.

Sandesh had his lunch out on the plaza, watching the falconer do his thing. Then he did a couple of laps up and around the mini park, thinking about the job and almost not believing that it was already under control. He kept looking back at his own Gantt charts, not trusting all the bars of blue-for-finished. Maybe he truly had been ready for this. *Or maybe it was all that overtime*, he thought. He'd been working from home a lot. Now that he was a key employee, he wouldn't get time and a half for it, but it wouldn't be forever. Not this time around.

When he got back upstairs, he swung by the Problem Desk to check in. It looked a lot better today. He complimented Sherlyn and asked if she had everything she needed. He'd decided to use her as a floater – an in-house temp – till all the new assistants were on-boarded. Once everyone was settled in, they'd do another round of assignment review to see if everyone was still happy where they'd landed. It sounded as though Sherlyn liked floating more than she'd liked being stuck with the same people all the time. If the improvement continued, they could talk about making the assignment permanent. A floater had to be adaptable, even-tempered, resourceful, and patient. He was a bit surprised that this seemed to be working out. Maybe she'd simply been bored.

Then it was time for one of his unscheduled sweeps, roaming through the office to eyeball various workspaces, listen to vocal tones (in a lot of people, stress showed up first in the voice), and make sure the office services people weren't loafing. They typically had a lot of downtime, but he'd given them specific instructions to be proactive and go looking for certain types of fill-in work. Anybody who actually did was going to have a chance at promotion. Anybody who didn't would keep washing coffee cups.

That thought sent him into the break room, which was spotless. *Good job, guys*, he thought, and made himself a cup of tea. He took it back to his office and sent a compliment to the service center.

Tasha spent most of the afternoon, when not answering phones or handling her little bit of administrative-assistant work, thinking about the new confidence in Sandesh's voice. He'd been good at every job he'd done, the whole time she'd known him. He wouldn't have gotten this huge promotion – even though that office was desperate – if his history hadn't supported it. She had the idea that if he hadn't gone to the new role fresh off a long break, the transition might have been harder. When she thought about trying to step sideways, off the reception desk and into an LAA desk, all she could think was that everyone would have such fixed ideas about her. It might be easier to make that change by moving to a new firm. If she actually wanted to do it at all. *Still undecided*, she thought, *and that's okay*. They were in good shape financially. She had fun stuff to do – she was having a blast dancing with Annette – and maybe it was okay to do fun stuff for a while. The thought was in her mind most of the time now, but maybe she could wait to decide on it until after they were moved.

That other thing she needed to decide on was a much higher priority. Although there wasn't much question of what the decision would be. It was really only a question of whether she wanted to make him wait till December.

Sandesh took some work home, arriving back at the apartment an hour before Tasha that day. He was at the kitchen table with his laptop, still in his suit, when she came through the door with Theo. He was in professional mode, concentrating, and she had a moment to study him before he looked up. His automatic smile faded when he saw her expression. "Is everything okay?"

She hesitated for a second before nodding and saying, "Of course."

Theo didn't notice anything was off. He said tiredly, "Hi Sandesh," and went past, heading for his room.

"Hi buddy," Sandesh said to Theo's back. "I'm guessing he's got a ton of homework."

"Already. It's unbelievable." Tasha set down her tote bag and leaned on the wall. "You looked like a different person just then." She watched him as he stood up, took the two steps over to her, and went in for a kiss. "You still look gorgeous," she assured him, patting his chest. He laughed under his breath, shaking his head. "No, you do. You're so in charge these days. It's as if you went from an adorable tiger cub to a full-grown man-eater since last winter."

Sandesh wasn't at all sure that was good. "Damn, really? Is it the suit?" She snickered. "The haircut? What?"

"It's everything. The suit, the haircut, the job. Working on the movie. Almost dying." She met his gaze. They didn't talk about that very often. He'd been going to the counselor every week since the movie wrapped, but he and Tasha hadn't discussed what he might be saying there.

He wanted to deny it, to say oh it wasn't that bad. Unfortunately he couldn't honestly say that. Whatever details he hadn't told her directly, she could have looked up herself. Could have looked up how little time it took for a person to bleed to death. "You're right," he said after a minute. "It did change me. I hope not too much."

He looked anxious now. Tasha hated that. "Honey, we're *supposed* to change. That's what growing up actually is. Have you talked to your counselor about our relationship? Our history?"

It was such a tangent that Sandesh took a couple of seconds to catch up. "A little bit. Robyn knows that I met you a long time ago, that we had a friendship before things changed."

"Has she seen a picture of you, from like a year ago?"

He didn't know where this was going. He leaned against the kitchen counter, crossed his arms, then opened them up again because he didn't mean to be resistant. He set the heels of his hands on the counter, feeling very exposed. "No. Do you think she should?"

"I think it might help her understand that the world sees you differently now. You know most people only see the outside." She reached out, because he seemed so troubled. He took hold of her hand. "You intentionally created a new image for yourself. You knew it would be beneficial with this whole job situation. But you actually did it way before that. She might be able to help you unpack why." Something about his expression made her add, "If you don't already know. Now I kind of think you do."

He glanced away, then back at her. *Those eyes*, she thought. As beautiful as ever, with more going on behind them than she'd ever imagined. "Vince recommended the dance suit. I thought, at the time, it was so I would look right when I took you out dancing. And then we had that date at Cicada. We never did something like that before. I got the haircut because I wanted to look different. I wanted *not* to look like Sandy, the funny guy."

"You *are* funny," she said. "You're quick-witted, and you always see what's ridiculous about a situation. Even when you're pissed off, you're funny with it. You never get all ranty and grouchy and mean."

He was still holding her hand. "I cultivated that. I was like, how do I turn this shitshow of a job into something that will make her laugh. Because for a long time there I thought that was my best play, to be entertaining. I thought that was how I was most likely going to stay on your list of ways to spend your time."

"Oh, honey," she said softly, thinking *you were right*. How very blind she had been.

"And the way you looked at me changed," he said. She knew it was true. "You saw me differently that night. You saw a grown-up. You told me you loved me that night. If a suit and a haircut could do that with you, it had to make a difference at the office too. So yeah, I play it up. I'm Mr. Prasad there now, not Sandy. I have authority, I'm using it, and it's changing things for a lot of people. It still freaks me out on a daily basis. People are out of work because of me. It's a lot of responsibility," he finished in a rush. She closed the distance, putting her arms around him, leaning against him. He wrapped his arms around her back and rested his cheek against her hair.

"What's for dinner?" Tasha turned her head; Theo was standing by the table, looking as though he thought there ought to be food on it.

"Are you hungry, baby? Sorry, Sandesh and I were talking and we lost track of time. Let's see what we've got." She tipped her head up for a kiss, then let go of her man and turned to the refrigerator. "What are we taking over to Terry's on Monday?"

Sandesh picked up the cue. "I thought I'd make that smoked-duck salad and a couple of chocolate cream pies."

Theo said, "Yeah!" Tasha laughed. Sandesh went to shut down his laptop, and then to change out of his suit. *Don't do that again*, he thought, feeling like he'd dodged a bullet. *Be who she expects*. But after dinner, after they watched an episode of Planet Earth with Theo, he went back into the kitchen for a glass of water and saw a fresh red line through IN DECEMBER on that faded sticky note.

Under it she'd printed TONIGHT.

## Chapter 11
September 2018

Sandesh forgot all about hydrating. He stood there for a minute, getting his breathing under control and blinking away tears. She must have changed the note right after they'd finished cleaning up. She would know he had seen it. There was nothing else on the refrigerator except Theo's schedule. He went back out and passed through into the bedroom.

Tasha watched him go through, avoiding her eye. She heard a drawer open and close. *Oh no you did not already have a ring*, she thought, almost laughing. Sandesh would know she'd like a ring. He knew everything. She said, "Theo, honey, why don't you go back through your homework and see if there's anything you need help with so we can get that done before your bedtime."

"Okay," he said reluctantly. He hopped off the couch and kissed her cheek before heading to his room. She stayed on the couch, waiting.

Sandesh came out of the bedroom and went straight to her. Went down on his knees in front of her, gazing at her. Took her hand and put something in it, keeping his hand over whatever it was. He said, very softly, "I love you so much. So completely. Will you marry me?"

She leaned forward, closing her other hand over his. "I love you more than anything on earth except that boy in there. All of you. As you were, and are, and will be. Yes, I will marry you." He moved in and touched his lips to hers. For a moment it was as light as that very first kiss. Then his mouth opened, and hers, and only the sound of Theo's footsteps parted them. Sandesh sat back on his heels, eyes hot and breath short.

Theo said, "Could you look at this one thing, Mom?"

"Sure, honey."

"What's that?"

Tasha looked at the box in her hand. "I don't know yet." She opened it and saw a crimson-enameled gold band with a floral design made of thin gold wire, with what looked like diamonds and emeralds set in the flower petals and leaves across the top. Her eyebrows went up and she looked at Sandesh. He was smiling. "This is something special," Tasha told Theo. "This is my engagement ring."

"Are you getting married?" Theo watched as Sandesh took the ring from the box and slid it onto Tasha's finger. "That's cool."

"Yes it is. Let's look at this thing of yours." Theo sat on the couch and put his workbook on her lap. Tasha looked at Sandesh again; he was stifling laughter. She made a 'what can you do' face and he stood up, leaning in to kiss each of them on the cheek, then went back to the kitchen for that glass of water. He took the sticky note off the refrigerator, but he didn't throw it away.

Terry and Anya both noticed the ring immediately on Labor Day. So did Lochan and Paige. Theo helpfully announced "They're getting married!" to what seemed like the whole world. They were the main topic of conversation for the first half hour of the party. Anya's partner Ricky and his husband Luis were there, showing off their own rings. Terry's boss Tyrone and his wife Indira were also there. They'd spent two months of the summer in India, and had a few things to say about the ring design. After a while, mercifully, the subject changed to Ricky and Anya's upcoming performance.

Later, when the focus shifted to food, Tasha leaned against Sandesh and said, "I didn't think about how everyone always wants to know your plans." He laughed silently. "We haven't even talked about plans. I was like, uh, well, dunno yet." He laughed out loud. "What do you want to do?"

"I have no idea. I'm still not over the fact that it's going to happen at all." He regarded her for a moment, smiling. "Tanith and Sid are getting married at the Million Dollar."

"Are they really?! That spooky old place! Well, it's where they met, I guess. And they probably have a lot of people coming."

"Yeah, I think so. He's been on the force a long time, she said they were expecting like a hundred cops. It'll be the safest place to be in L.A. that day, for sure."

"You and I met in a law office. That's a hard no." Sandesh laughed again. Tasha thought about it for a minute. "Maybe we should do what Terry and Anya did. But what would your parents think? Are they going to want something traditional?"

"Maybe. Probably. I don't much care." Sandesh's parents were still not reconciled to the relationship. He hadn't yet told them about the engagement. "Las Vegas would be fine with me. Anything you want is fine with me. All I want is to marry you."

"That's what Terry said about Anya, I hear. I'll think about it." She kissed his cheek. "Let's go see what thoughts Lo and Paige have about the Sleeping Beauty." It turned out Paige had a lot of thoughts, but was stymied without floor plans and measurements. "We'll get over there soon," Tasha promised. "All of us."

Two days later Sandesh was getting ready for work when he checked his phone and saw a text from Paige. *OMG Sandesh your pals from the movie were shot at last night Victor was hurt have you heard anything??* He hadn't; Theo had crashed early, and he and Tasha had taken advantage of that to go to bed (if not to sleep) early themselves. He immediately fired up the laptop and went online to check for news. There was so much of it, and it was so disturbing, that he sent an email to Janice to say he'd be working from home till the afternoon. He checked his mailbox, disposed of a few hot items, and then made coffee. He was reading the news again, a steaming cup by his hand, when Tasha came out from the bedroom, dressed for work. "What's up, baby? You're usually farther along by this time."

"I'm not going in this morning. Andy and Victor were attacked last night. Victor was shot." It came out sounding flat.

"Oh my God! He wasn't … ?" Tasha leaned over to look at the screen. The headline didn't say 'killed,' or anything like it. She felt a wash of relief.

"It sounds like he's going to be all right but still, Jesus. I sent Andy a text, you know, hope you're okay and let me know if I can help in any way. Maybe he'll talk to the press later. There's bound to be a mob outside the hospital, with the Emmys coming up this weekend."

"The producers are probably having conniptions." She stroked her hand through his hair, then checked the time. "I have to get Theo moving. Call me later and tell me what you hear, okay?" She had Internet access at her desk, but she knew if she opened it up on that story she'd be glued to it all day.

"I will." Sandesh usually packed Theo's lunch while Tasha made sure the boy was clean and dressed, then did the backpack thing. He stood up to do his part. After they were out the door, he took a quick shower, dressed - more casually than his new usual - for work, and then went back to the laptop. There was more email to deal with, and a couple of VOIP messages. He had a minimized window open to the live stream for Pop Quiz, because he'd caught a bottom-of-the-screen crawl saying 'stay tuned for live update at eleven.'

He was reviewing another resume for an HR assistant candidate when his alarm beeped. He switched over to Pop Quiz and turned up the volume. The reporter he knew was on screen. "Hi, I'm Sherry Martinez for Pop Quiz. This summer I was honored to be invited to the set of 'The Ghost of Carlos Gardel,' where I spoke with co-stars Victor Garcia and Andy Martin of L.A. Vice, and their colleagues, about their new movie with director Tanith Salazar. Today I'm here to bring you Mr. Martin's statement on a shooting last night at his Los Angeles home." She turned to face a doorway, which Sandesh assumed to be at the hospital. A standing mic was already in place. The camera looked past her, going wide to take in the impressive number of reporters waiting on the sidewalk and in the parking lot. A moment later Andy came through the door, with one of his security guys on his right and a hospital representative on his left. The Pop Quiz camera zoomed in as people started yelling questions.

Andy came to the mic, looking thin in scrubs, and said, "Shut up, please." He stood there tensely, with his graying dark hair in disarray, eyes deeply shadowed, unshaven. "I'm serious. No questions or I'm going right back inside." Maybe because he was usually so accommodating with the press, the reporters hushed up fast. "Thank you. My husband, Victor Garcia, was shot last night, a little after nine p.m., outside our home. Shot in the back, protecting me. His right shoulder blade was broken and there is an exit wound the size of my hand. I am told he will fully recover, given sufficient rest and appropriate therapy. He is awake, alert, and walking. We don't know yet if he will be able to attend next week's awards. Two members of our employer's security team were with us last night and apprehended the shooter. I am not going to give you those names. Any questions on that end of things should be directed to the LAPD, good luck with that. As for me, I have some epic bruises but am otherwise fine. You can direct your questions about Victor to our manager. I'm not giving you that name, either. Victor is receiving the best of care and I'm going back to him now. Thanks." He turned around and went inside with the other two.

*God Almighty*, Sandesh thought, not even noticing what happened next on the stream. He had chills. Couldn't quite control his breath. He knew Andy well enough to know that the best description for his affect was 'towering rage.' The calm voice and precise diction were simply his professionalism at work. *That's too close, too fucking close.* He sent an email to his counselor to see if she could squeeze him in that day instead of tomorrow. Then he emailed Janice again to say that on second thought he'd be working from home all day, but to call him in an emergency. Finally he emailed Tasha with a link to the Pop Quiz coverage and a note: *working from home all day unless I can see my counselor, this is fucking me up a little.*

After a while he went back to Pop Quiz and saw that Sherry had done a follow-up with the hospital's statement on Victor's injury. She flashed a still photo – clearly a selfie – of Andy in a blood-drenched shirt, sitting in an ambulance next to Victor, who looked pale (and also bloody) on a stretcher but was giving a left-handed thumbs-up. Sherry linked to her on-set interview from the last day of filming. Sandesh watched the whole thing again. By the end of the co-stars' six-way dance, he felt calmer. When Robyn wrote back regretting she couldn't fit him in, he confirmed his regular appointment the next day, and went for a walk. After he got home again he sent another text to Andy: *Saw your statement and follow-up, can't believe you gave Sherry that selfie. Hope Vicky brought you some clothes. Abrazos.* He was guessing about the clothes. He couldn't imagine that Andy's neighbors wouldn't be all over the support side of things.

A reply came in this time. *Thx for msgs we are doing all right and yes I have my own clothes now. Raquel having fits about the selfie. Told her Victor wanted to make sure Emmy viewers know this wasn't fake news*

*OMG Andy you're both nuts*

*This surprises you? I'll ping you when Victor is home. TTFN*

*Thx Andy our love to you both.* Sandesh figured there were a lot of different kinds of love. The respect he felt for Andy and Victor surely qualified under one of those categories. Then he saw there was a new message from Tasha.

*Hi baby that is some scary shit, hope you're doing better. Want Poquito Más for dinner? Extra guac?* It was so prosaic that it made Sandesh smile. He wrote back with thanks, confirmed he was steady, and went back to the work in-box.

Sandesh and Tasha had set their DVR for The Late Late Show, because they knew Andy and Victor had been scheduled to appear, planning to watch it after dinner. They did carpool karaoke, singing along to 'Beauty School Dropout' and 'Delilah.' There were news teasers about the shooting during the commercial breaks. "I can't even believe this," Tasha said. "After you sent that link, I went down the rabbit hole. Good thing I only had bills to send out."

"I can't believe they still do that by mail," Sandesh said, diverted. "What a waste."

"I know! I always think, do the clients want paper bills, or is this just some kind of holdover from the old days?"

"Nostalgic billing." Sandesh stood up. "I'm getting another drink. You want something?" They'd had beer with their burritos, and usually he only had one. He was still having what he could only call flashbacks. Needed to take the edge off.

"Some decaf and Bailey's, I think." Tasha went with him into the kitchen and fixed herself some instant coffee, mixing in a healthy dose of liqueur. Sandesh poured himself a shot of Kraken rum. "Theo's got another hellacious night of homework, I'd better go check in with him. You should try to get to sleep if you can."

"I know," he said.

She studied his face. "And I know you hate to medicate, other than nature's way." He laughed a little. "But I've got those OTC sleep aids. Maybe it's time to make an exception. Did you stretch today?"

"I did. I went for a walk. I watched some dancing. I don't know why I'm so shaken up."

"Because it's too close," she said, echoing his own thought. "Too soon, and too similar. Nobody on the movie even knows, do they?"

"I don't think so. Except for James and Silvia."

"You need to remember you're not in this alone." She put her hands on his face, stared into his eyes, and kissed him. Then without letting go of him she said, "Go take a knockout pill, please."

"Yes ma'am." He kissed her, smiling, and went to the bedroom. She watched him go, thinking, *trying to be a tough guy. Men.*

Talking to his counselor Robyn the next day, Sandesh finally admitted he was angry. "I've been waiting for that," she said. "Where'd you find it?"

"A friend of mine got shot. Victor Garcia." She nodded; she'd seen the news. "I worked with him on that movie this summer. He's going to be all right, thank God."

"Was it a stalker situation?"

"I don't know, but it really tripped me. I had almost like flashbacks. Stayed home, tried to deal with things.

But, obviously." He shrugged. The reason he'd asked to move his session up was clear.

"So what made you realize you were angry?"

"Seeing Andy give his statement. Andy Martin. He's the most incredibly sweet guy. If you've ever seen their show, he's a lot like his character in that. He did some work on this movie that was mind-blowing. He had to do these scenes where he was angry with Victor. Like, murderously angry. And they really love each other," he said, in case she didn't know. "I would swear they never fight. If one of them wants something, the other one is like, okay, how can I help you get that. So I saw him do that. Then yesterday it was there again but it was real." He glanced at her again, to ensure she understood. "And I recognized it. I realized I've had these flashes when I'm like *God damn you* because when this thing happened to me I had so much to lose, and I came so close to losing it. For *nothing*."

"And you've been suppressing?"

He made a face like 'maybe?' "Well, to the extent that I'm religious, which is not very far, I'm a Buddhist. For me it's about sitting with the feeling and accepting it and letting it go. I thought I was letting it go," he clarified. "Because I didn't lose anything, except some blood and some time. My life has changed, but entirely for the better. In a way, what happened was good for me. So it seemed unhealthy to indulge that rage. To sit and say, you know what, how dare you. How fucking dare you, you delusional fucking moron, how dare you stand there with a knife like I've done anything remotely wrong." He knew he was getting loud; his breathing was uneven, and his eyes were wet. "And then yesterday there's Andy, looking like he hadn't slept at all, not wanting to be away from Victor for even a second, and it was how dare you – whoever it was – how dare you, this is the love of my life and I almost lost him and *how fucking dare you.*" He covered his face with his hands and bent forward, crying. Robyn didn't say anything. After a few minutes Sandesh composed himself, taking deep breaths and wiping his face. Robyn handed him the box of Kleenex. "Thanks."

"Thirty is young to have a near-death experience," she said after a few more minutes, when she could tell he was calm. "You haven't been faced with death before, have you?"

"No. I mean, one of my grandfathers died a few years ago, but I never met him. The funeral was in India, my father went by himself. So yeah, I guess this was my Kobayashi Maru." He could tell she got the reference from the quick smile.

"What's your worst fear now?"

"Related to the whole knife incident? I worry about a blood clot. Or rather, I try not to worry about a blood clot. I watch what I eat, I stay hydrated, I stay active, I get massage. The artery wasn't severed. They said if it had been, it might have closed itself up. The top wall was sliced open, along with my tendon and the nerve. I could have lost the arm. But I didn't. It's fine."

"You've been doing the work."

"Well, yeah. I wanted to be … fully functional," he said. She stifled a snort, clearly getting that reference too. *Who knew my therapist was a Star Trek fan*, he thought.

She changed the subject. "Have you had any nightmares?"

"No."

"Any anxiety attacks?"

"No. I still don't like parking garages."

She nodded. "Any suicidal ideation?"

"Fuck no." Robyn laughed out loud. He shrugged an apology. "Sorry, once the F door is open it's hard to close again."

"Don't worry about it. I've heard much worse than that. Well, Mr. Prasad, I'd say you're coping with the situation admirably. I'm glad your friend is going to be okay, and I think you're going to be okay. If you have any more of what you call flashbacks, try to be conscious of when they occur and what any potential triggers might be, so we can talk about them. The odds are against another trigger like you've had this week."

"God, I hope so."

"How is your girlfriend?"

He smiled. "She's my fiancée now. She is perfect."

The following Sunday they tuned in to watch the Emmy awards broadcast. Andy had checked in once Victor was at home, and again to confirm they'd be going to the show. Tasha couldn't believe they were walking the red carpet. "He was shot less than a week ago, what is wrong with him?! I mean, I know all you men want to think you're indestructible, but look at that sling!" The arm sling was clearly necessary; Victor was moving with significant caution. The sling was also rainbow striped - like Andy's bow tie - and covered with color-matched rhinestones. It really showed up in the sun, against Victor's tuxedo. "I mean, look at it." She giggled.

"Look at their security guy. He's about to blow a gasket."

"Probably told them not to do this. Mercy." They watched most of the show with minimal interest, though awards for two others associated with the movie met with approval. They were both waiting for the 'outstanding actor in a supporting role' category. Finally it came along. Tasha was holding Sandesh's hand. Squeezed it between both of hers. "I haven't seen any of those other guys, have you?"

"Nope. Damn, this is kind of suspenseful when you actually want someone specific to win." They both giggled. "Was Matthew going to watch?" Theo was with his father that weekend.

"Who knows. Oh here they go." The presenter was opening the envelope … and reading Victor's name. "Holy shit, oh my God!"

Sandesh kissed Tasha as if he'd won the thing himself and she were the trophy. "Jesus! I'm so glad. There they are." Andy was walking with Victor up to the stage, taking the award, looking at it with an expression of detached interest while Victor – holding Andy's other hand – said a few words, then kissed his husband. Victor plugged Tanith's movie before they left the stage. "I hope they're going straight home."

"I'll bet they are. Victor may be tough, but this is ridiculous." Tasha watched as Sandesh picked up his phone. She knew he was sending a text to congratulate Victor. "Ask him what the hell he was thinking." Sandesh laughed under his breath and added a postscript.

"They probably won't answer till tomorrow. What shall we do now?" He set down the phone. "Want to fantasize about the Sleeping Beauty?"

"I do! But maybe that should wait until the others can see it. I know Paige is going to have a lot of ideas."

"Then maybe we should talk about this wedding thing," he suggested, stretching out his arm so she could snuggle next to him. He kissed her forehead. "Any more thoughts since Monday?"

"With this whole Victor situation I kind of forgot about it," she confessed. "I have to say, I liked Luis and Ricky's wedding. Short, simple, sweet, and casual. Aside from the fact that they were both wearing tuxedos. If we didn't have to do it in a church, that would be even better."

Sandesh was glad to hear that. "Where did you and Matthew get married?"

"At the courthouse. Terry was there, a work friend of Matthew's was there. We all went out to dinner after, and that was that."

"We can do better," he said. "I wonder if Andy would let us do it in their backyard. They've got those piazza lights strung across, and a nice big patio, and that gorgeous pepper tree. It looked really romantic when we were shooting those evening scenes."

"Ooohh," she said. "Did you take any pictures?" She knew he'd taken a few at the various locations, mostly before and after actors were around, and always with permission.

"Yeah, I did," he said, and reached over for his phone. "They were dancing on that patio, too. It's pavers, it's super smooth, but I don't know how Vicky even did that in those three-inch heels." He started flipping through the photos he'd saved.

"I can't imagine a contractor would dare leave those two with an uneven patio, and I think Vicky can dance on anything." She was watching him scanning through photos. "What's that?"

"That is Vicky posing for me after finishing take two of her solo." He put it on screen. "Isn't that lighting spooky?"

"Wow, it is. And that background, there's no scale. You can't get any idea how tall she is. It felt like she *towered* over us in the cabaret thing."

"I loved that routine. I loved the synchronized parts, I loved where you were all weaving in and out up and down the stairs, I loved where Vicky was partnering each of you. Super sexy. Tanith had me watching the other interns to make sure they weren't taking bootleg video."

"We were talking about adapting it for a flat stage," Tasha said, looking at him sideways. "That would be for this month's show at Chrome, 'Milonga.' If we're going to do it, we'd better get our act together."

"Jeez, yeah. You've got a few weeks but the Cabaret people will want to see it, won't they? Why don't you ping the team while I find this damn picture I'm thinking of? I know it's in here somewhere." Tasha went to the kitchen for her phone, coming back with a box of See's chocolates too. Sandesh laughed when she opened it and took a long happy sniff of the aroma. "Got my Scotchmallow?"

"You know it." She handed it to him. "I will always love this company because they let me build my own box." She ate her dark-chocolate buttercream, then started composing a text to the six other women in the cabaret routine. She showed it to Sandesh before sending: *Hey ladies are we doing the Bradbury routine for Milonga? Y/N and if Y where and when to rehearse?*

She received four replies within ten minutes, one of them from a Cabaret principal who assured her that submitting the routine was a technicality and as long as they had it ready by dress rehearsal, it was a guaranteed go. The other two women responded within a half hour. Everyone wanted to do it, and the consensus was to rehearse at Shall We Dance. Vicky wrote *if we do this I'm working on three routines. WTAF one stupid movie and things blow up*

Tasha wrote back right away: *Are the others all for Milonga??*

*No, one with Tomás is but the third thing also with Tomás is for UC in February thank Christ. He came into the studio with this track and seduced me*

*Bahaha what did Sharon say?* Sharon was Vicky's wife.

*Sharon said to remember the celebrity pass only works once. Since I can't actually hand her Lucas I will have to bide my time.* Sharon had a crush on Lucas Gutierrez, another of the movie's (married) co-stars. Vicky had the whole cabaret team in stitches describing her audition dance with Tomás Calderón, and subsequent conversation with Sharon.

Tasha was giggling. *U R so naughty*

*And I've gotta go, we're about to host Emmys party for Mr. Garcia*

*Give him our congratulations and tell him to REST*

*Will do*

"They're throwing a party," Tasha said, half-amused and half-exasperated. "Men!"

"Andy won't let it go too late. Here." Sandesh showed her the photo he'd been looking for. "Could you stand to get married there?"

She studied it for a minute. "I sure could."

"I'll see what I can do. These Hollywood connections have to be good for something." He leaned over to kiss her. "Mmm. You taste like chocolate." He put down the phone and kissed her again.

James dropped by Sandesh's office his first day back from vacation. He tapped on the open door; Sandesh looked up right away and smiled. "Hey there! Welcome back. Did you have a good trip?"

"Great trip. Got some stuff for you," he said. "Silvia went a little overboard, so it's actually at home. I mean, one bottle I would carry over. This is not that. You're going to have to swing by and pick it up." Sandesh was laughing. "Anything exciting happen while we were gone?"

"Not here, thank God." Sandesh pointed at his guest chair with his eyebrows up. "Got a minute?"

"Sure. Janice kept my email so clean I almost didn't even come in today." James stepped in. "Open or closed?"

"Open's fine, this isn't top secret. Friends of ours bought this storybook triplex a little south of where we are now. They're going to fix it up and rent it to me and Tasha, plus my brother and his wife, plus Matthew. We're all so excited we can't stand it. Tasha and I got to see around inside right before, well, actually could you close that for a second?"

James reached over and caught the edge of the door, pushing it closed. “What?”

“It was Victor and Andy.” James knew who he meant, though he hadn’t met them personally. All the extras knew who the stars were. “This triplex is right next to them, and they made the offer basically on wrap day. We went to see it a few weeks ago, the whole gang of us were supposed to go soon, but then Victor got shot.”

“I saw that on the news,” James said. “How are they doing?”

“I haven’t seen them yet but Andy says he’s fine and Victor’s recovering. We couldn’t believe they went to the Emmys, though. That was, like, not even a week after.”

“Well, you went to a tango boot camp a week after your thing.”

“Not quite the same,” Sandesh said, shaking his head. “I mean okay, I lost a lot of blood, but they put it back and sewed me up and I was basically in one piece. Andy said Victor had an exit wound the size of his hand.”

“Damn!” James winced. “I didn’t know that.”

“I guess it was at pretty close range. Guy must be made of unobtainium. Anyway, aside from lots of shopping, how was Paso? Silvia’s feeling okay?”

“She’s doing better. Her assistant there is really stepping up. We went around to most of her accounts, but more to show support for Camilo than to be in charge. You know, we dropped in first to say Hi, told them Camilo would be in after us to take care of business. The plan is to spend a week up in Calaveras and Amador in November, do the same thing. He already did the NorCal wineries. Have you and Tasha ever been out to wine country?"

"No, never. Would she like it?"

"I don't know anybody who doesn't. Beautiful countryside. Great food. Every time we go out it's like being on our honeymoon again."

"Oh yeah? Where did you go?"

"We went to Bordeaux." James was smiling. That had been a very good trip. Then his attention sharpened because he got the idea that was not an idle question. "So, Mr. Prasad. I detect a note of significance."

Sandesh couldn't hide the excitement. "We're getting married. She told me I could ask her, finally. You know originally it was 'ask me in December' and I was like really?! What the fuck." He paused because James was laughing. "That was in May! That's a long time!"

James, still laughing, said, "Congratulations. Have you decided when and where?"

"No, not yet. I haven't even told my parents yet. You're the first here in the office."

"Well, it's great news. I'm sure you'll do it right. You know Silvia's got a lot of connections, if you decide you want to do that wine-country honeymoon she can hook you up."

"We might do that, thanks. Things are so smooth with Matthew now, I know he'd be cool taking Theo for a week."

"You really won a lot of points by letting him go on that trip."

"It wasn't for me to say," Sandesh pointed out. "Tasha's decision. Though she did ask me."

"Of course she did. I guess I'd better get back to my office and see if Janice has left me anything to do."

"Remind her to be thinking about any training she wants to do. Certifications or whatever. Depending on the what, we can work out the how." Sandesh stood up to shake James' hand. "And thanks, again, for all your help with everything. This transition would not have been so smooth without you."

"It was good experience," James said. "Not exactly fun, but good. Ping me when you want to come over and get this heavy-ass carton of wine." He was smiling as he left the office, leaving the door open behind him. Nicole smiled back at him as he passed the reception desk. There was soft piano music playing in the reception area, something classical; that was new. He hadn't noticed it on the way down the hall. *Well, why not*, he thought. *Why the hell not*.

By then, Tasha's team had their rehearsal schedule set, and she was really busy. Sandesh and Matthew traded Theo duty with zero friction, and minimal disruption of the usual routine. Sandesh was finishing up the installation of his last two new LAAs, and had another interview scheduled for a human-resources assistant. "You'll be glad to get out from under payroll, huh," said Janice that morning. "Hope this one works out."

"Me too. It seems like it's taken forever."

"You do realize you've done about five times the amount of work in two months that Darlene did in two years," she said dryly. "You should eat at Craft more often." He laughed. "Seriously, I hope this is the one. Nicole just IM'd, your candidate's here. Go do it."

"Yes ma'am." He went back to his office, double-checked that nothing was on fire in the in-box, and reviewed the candidate's resume one more time. It was one that he was certain would have been instantly rejected by his predecessor. Then he shrugged into his suit jacket and headed for the small conference room. The candidate was sitting alone, looking nervous and out of place, and glanced up anxiously when he entered. "Good morning Ms. Bukhari. I'm Sandesh Prasad." He held out his hand for her to shake. She did so, tentatively, and he sat down, setting his phone on the table.

"Please, call me Fatima," she said softly.

"Did my people offer you a cup of coffee or tea?"

"Yes, they did. I am fine, thank you."

"So I take it you moved to the United States five years ago and were working in your brother's business until late last year. Why did you decide to leave that situation?"

"My brother wanted me to marry his friend. It was not acceptable to me."

"And it's taken some time for you to find a new full-time position. What have you been doing in the interval?"

"I worked with the temporary agency, to become familiar with the office environment in California. This," she indicated her head scarf, "I am told is limiting."

"But you took a chance and applied here." He regarded her for a moment. "You aced the online proficiency tests, by the way. If I quiz you on California labor laws, I expect you'll do fine there."

"I got my degree in England, and have been told I should do it over again here. But my family cannot afford that. You did not require an American college degree. And your name, on the website. Your picture." She was making eye contact now. "There is no one else like you in a hiring position, is there?"

"In the legal community? Probably not. Have other interviewers asked where you see yourself in five years?"

She smiled, as if involuntarily. "All of them."

"What did you tell them?"

"I said, I hope I will have a position here helping you build your business."

"Was that the truth?" He was smiling at her, but didn't give her time to answer. "Because I always said that too and it was never true. I was always thinking, in five years I plan to have *your* job." She almost laughed. "Let me tell you a few things about this office that are not apparent from the website." He told her about the recent staffing changes, the choose-your-own-attorneys policy for the assistants, and a few other atypical things. "We are almost fully staffed. We've trimmed down the infrastructure. By this time next year, we might be in position to add more staff. But for now, the focus is on efficiency, and on building a sustainable culture. Tell me about your ideal workplace."

The conversation continued for nearly half an hour. Sandesh glanced at his phone when Janice pinged him. "My assistant wants to know if she should schedule a lunch. Could you join us?"

"I could," she said, looking cautious.

"Great." He sent a text back to Janice: *Please do schedule lunch you me and Ms Bukhari, add James if available, also please prep offer letter and bring in when ready TYVM.* "Now, let's discuss the salary and benefits for this position." Fatima's eyes went wide. "Because I'd like you to join our team."

After the highly-successful lunch (at Craft), Sandesh went back to his office and sent a text to Tasha: *FINALLY! The HR search is over! Smart courteous persistent and brave, plus BIG BONUS sense of humor. Tell you all about her later, she starts next week, doing a happy dance*

Tasha laughed when she saw it. He'd given her a hint about this candidate. After reviewing over a dozen resumes, and interviewing three other candidates, he'd been hoping this was the one. And now they could both check off that last essential part of his work transition.

## Chapter 12
September 2018

Matthew had Theo the next weekend, so Sandesh and Tasha got together with James and Silvia for dinner. The four of them arranged to meet up at Shall We Dance for a refresher tango lesson after one of Tasha's rehearsals, then walk down to the Italian restaurant on the same block. Silvia looked sadly at the wine list and handed it to James. "I'm the designated driver. For the next year."

"That must have been tough," Tasha said. "Being up there in Paso and you can't even taste anything."

"Torture!"

James was laughing. Sandesh said, "James asked if we'd ever been to wine country and I said no, but then I thought, well I haven't been, but I never asked if Tasha had. Did you?"

"No," she said. "Matthew and I went a few places but it was city places. San Diego, San Francisco, and one time to Seattle but that was for a tech conference for him. Four days. It was cold. And it rained the entire time." She rolled her eyes. "I never left the hotel. Bought this alpaca shawl in the gift shop, wrapped myself in it and read four romance novels. Ate chowder in the bar, in front of the fireplace, with hot bread and butter and many glasses of wine." Silvia was laughing now. "It was good chowder."

"When we go I promise it'll be a vacation," Sandesh said. "I can't promise it won't rain, though."

James said, "I've been to Seattle a few times when it didn't rain. Went to the Space Needle. Seems like a long time ago."

"Once I'm cleared to drink again we can hand the bambino to Ruth and go up there and wallow in chowder and Riesling," Silvia said. "But for now, let's tell this young man what else we want to eat."

After their entrees were well underway Sandesh said, "Tasha, I told James we were engaged. I don't think he knows how long I was after you."

"Oh, he doesn't? Ten years," she said, to James' clear surprise. "We met ten years ago, at this place where we both worked downtown. He was my BFF all that time until last December."

"James was after me for ten years too," said Silvia. "Although there was a significant hiatus. We met in college. I'm glad he's not the only one who sticks."

"Tasha had a lot going on. I was pretending I was happy in the friend zone," Sandesh said, smiling. "I wasn't faithful."

"Neither was I," said James. "Nor was she. We thought we broke up, for a long time. Then I saw her again and had to give it another try."

Silvia patted his hand. "And I'm glad you did. What made the change?" She directed the question at Tasha.

"We were meeting up at the mall there in Century City. He was late as late can be, but when he finally showed up he bent down and kissed me and I went what? Who? Eh?" The others were all laughing. "Then after dinner we went for a walk and he kissed me again."

"I meant to that time," he said. "The first time was an accident. I thought, oh shit, did I just wreck this, is she going to walk out on me. But she stayed."

Tasha was smiling. "I stayed. Once I got my head around it I thought, why the hell did it take you so long to do that."

Silvia said, "There's nothing like a good kiss. I mean, it must have been pretty good."

"Oh, it was good." Tasha glanced at Sandesh; he was blushing, but he had that dreamy expression. "You know when he does something, he does it right." Her tone was suggestive.

"Tasha! Oh my God." He was giggling now.

"You know what, I don't know why I've only now had this thought, but I realized something," said Silvia. "I have the perfect excuse to eat the entire serving of tiramisu by myself."

"Yes you do." James leaned over and kissed her cheek. "And I have the perfect excuse to get a glass of Dolce Far Niente."

"You're going to pay for that," she said after a moment. "Later."

Sandesh said, "Get the bottle. I've heard about that stuff. Sorry, Silvia." She threw her napkin at him. He caught it, laughing.

The whole oddball family was waiting to hear from Andy about a tour of the Sleeping Beauty. Matthew and Lochan were waiting more patiently than Paige. Tasha was happily distracted by her performance prep. When the invitation did arrive, it was for the day of the 'Milonga' dress rehearsal. *Sorry about the overlap*, Andy wrote, *but unavoidable. We'll feed you if you can come after rehearsal.*

Sandesh texted back: *What can we bring? I have several votes of approval for smoked-duck salad*

*Well bring a wheelbarrow full of that then. See you around 15:00?*

Sandesh did a quick round of checking-in, then confirmed: *That works, thanks!*

Tasha was every bit as excited about the triplex tour as she was about her imminent performance. Terry was on duty at Chrome for dress rehearsal, and promised to send her his video of the routine so she could look it over one more time (or a dozen more times) before the following night. Sandesh stayed home with Theo, putting together the salad and making sure the weekend's homework was off to a good start. Tasha got home a little before two. "Hi fellas, let me get changed and we can head over. Everything good here?"

"We're good." Sandesh had the salad ready to go, Theo was at a reasonable stopping point, and he knew he was forgetting something. "Do I need anything besides my phone?"

"I don't think so," Tasha said from the bedroom. "Paige is surely bringing her measuring tape, graph paper, and whatever else." He was standing by the kitchen table, running through his mental to-do list, when she came out. "Still think you're forgetting something? You can always come back. It's not that far."

"Yeah, but that's so inefficient." He shrugged. "Oh well. You look great. Ready to go, Theo?"

"Yeah."

Sandesh was out the door before he remembered. "Hang on!" He passed the giant bowl of salad to Tasha, who was laughing, then bolted back inside and grabbed the bottle of Vina Robles 2012 Segredo that he'd found, wrapped in a note, wedged into the case of wine he picked up from James. "The Chronic was for us but this is for Victor. Whew, that was close," he said to Theo, who rolled his eyes. "Here, will you carry this?" He handed the bottle to Theo, then locked the door and took back the salad. "Let's go."

Andy had told them all to park at the triplex, where there were a few spaces off the alley. His security guy let them in the back gate and they crossed the yard to the patio of the Faux Chateau. "I love that they saved this building," Paige said. She'd found an article on Curbed discussing the post-fire acquisition and renovation. There were no photos of the interior, but Andy had provided before-and-after pictures of front and back. Their engineer had provided details on the work needed to restore the turrets. "And I love that they're saving the Sleeping Beauty. Maybe someday they'll get hold of the one on their other side and fix it up."

"You have some expensive ideas," said Lochan, amused. "I think they'd have to start from scratch over there, even I can tell it's got no style. Look at this tree, Maya! It's fluffy."

Andy opened the back door to greet them. "Hi everybody, I'm Andy. Victor's inside, come on in." Everyone trooped in for a round of introductions.

Victor still had his right arm strapped up, and his expression said he was thoroughly tired of that. Sandesh said, "It's a pain in the whatever, isn't it?"

"Yes it is."

Tasha said, "Victor, we brought you something, courtesy of our friends who just went up to Paso Robles. Theo, honey, give that to Mr. Garcia." Theo handed over the bottle of dessert wine. "I don't know if it's meant to be medicinal, but Silvia said it's delicious and only for you would she give up one from her stash. We're so glad you're on the mend."

Victor smiled, examining the label. "Thank you, and thank your friends. We do like this kind of thing." He set the bottle on the kitchen counter. "Eat first, tour later, right?" That seemed to be the consensus; none of the adults had had lunch yet. Sandesh helped Andy transfer food to the already-set dining table, listening to Victor charming Matthew, Lochan and Paige. *How did I get so lucky*, he thought, and caught Tasha's eye. She seemed to be thinking the same thing.

Victor didn't go with them to the triplex. Andy led the tour, taking the same route as before, and describing the same proposed improvements. Theo had been right about the wide-open top unit: Matthew wanted it, and he didn't care about the bathrooms. "We will make sure they're up to code," said Andy, clearly amused. "And we'll be gutting that kitchen. Do you have any specific ideas?"

Matthew looked over at Tasha as if for help. She said, trying not to laugh, "I was thinking we might appoint Paige as the designer in chief for all three units. I'm good with clothes and nail art, but this is a little bit over my head."

"I have a question though," said Theo. "If Katie is over, there's just this one room." He didn't say what all the adults instantly thought. There was a quick exchange of 'oh shit yeah' glances.

"How about we build you a room, and leave the rest of it open," said Matthew.

"That would be okay."

Paige was clutching her graph notebook. "I'm having a thought," she said, "kind of an expensive thought." She glanced guiltily at Lochan and then at Andy. "Can I have a few minutes?" Andy made a please-be-my-guest gesture. She went over to the kitchen counter and laid the notebook down, plopped her handbag down beside it, and pulled out a tape measure and a drafting pencil. "Tasha, can you note down the measurements for me?"

"I think we'll go downstairs now," Andy said, "and let this happen without an audience. Join us at the house whenever you're ready, ladies." He led the way. Lochan was carrying Maya, Sandesh and Matthew were following.

Theo hung back. "Can I see what they're doing?" Tasha heard him and beckoned him over to her. "I'll be up here, Dad."

"Okay kiddo. Don't let them get too crazy."

The others went back to Andy's house, where Andy's neighbor Sharon was in the backyard with her little girl, two cats, and Molly. She volunteered to watch Maya. Victor looked out the kitchen window and said, "They're squared away for a while. So, what do you think?" He sat down with the others at the dining table.

"Paige literally cannot wait," Lochan said. Everyone laughed. "She's been mainlining HGTV and DIY, worse than ever, since we heard about this."

Andy could relate. He'd gone through that phase after they bought the Faux Chateau. "Realistically, is it enough space?"

"Maya will be our only child. It's fine, and the location is good for my job."

"It's actually better for mine," said Matthew, who still worked downtown. "I've been getting down to

Figueroa from Stoner, up near Santa Monica Boulevard." It was technically a good 'central' Westside location, but nowhere near the closest Metro line.

"Ugh!" Andy said sincerely.

Matthew added, "I could bike to the La Cienega station from here." He heard a tap on the back door and turned around. "There they are." He got up to let Paige and Tasha in, doing a visual check to confirm that Theo had joined Sharon, the other kids, and the pets. "That was fast."

"It's only a sketch," Paige said, but she seemed excited.

"Well, if location is good and size is good, let's talk numbers." Andy went through the same factors he'd discussed with Sandesh and Tasha. Matthew and Lochan had a similar reaction. "Look," Andy said, "after what happened to Victor, half the city thinks we live in the hood."

"Half the *continent*," Victor said. "I get email from my cousins in Jalisco going, are you safe up there." He shook his head. "I mean, this stuff doesn't happen every day, but it did happen."

"I grew up in the hood," said Tasha. "My mother died of an overdose, my brother went to juvie, and I was in foster care for two years of high school. I know what a dangerous neighborhood looks like, and this ain't it."

Sandesh said, "Especially once we're in here. I mean, we are all so ordinary."

"I don't think that's wholly accurate," Andy said, again looking amused, "but we'll go with it. So let's hear from the designer." He looked at Paige expectantly. She handed him the notebook, open to a penciled floor plan. "Oh really!" He handed the notebook across to Victor, whose eyebrows went up on an approving nod. From there it went to Matthew.

He studied it briefly. "Oh wait. Is that, what? Paige, this is *cool*."

"It's open enough for you?"

"Yeah, but Theo's going to go nuts. Or did he see it already, and that's why he was bouncing." He was laughing under his breath as he handed the notebook to Sandesh.

"You're never going to get him out of there," Sandesh said. Paige had moved the second-floor unit's entry door from the corner tower to the street-facing wall. A pocket door and new closet turned the tower into a bedroom for Theo, with a window in place of the entry door. She stole some space from the existing kitchen to make the powder room a full bath, added a closet and laundry area alongside the existing full bath, and sketched a surround for a refrigerator that would include a pantry. The rest of the space remained open. Sandesh smiled at Paige. "Seriously. Lucky little snot." Tasha laughed.

Paige said, "You'd have to add plumbing for the laundry and the new tub, but the kitchen sink and the gas line for the range could stay where they are. It's okay?"

Victor said, "It's great. I would have loved that when I was a kid."

"So, if you want me to, I could sketch some changes for the other two," Paige said tentatively. "Like, the kitchens and bathrooms, and the laundry stuff."

"Have at it," said Andy as Sandesh passed the notebook back to his sister-in-law. "Our friend Mateo is an architectural draftsman, Sharon's dad is a structural engineer. Once we get your floor plans we can have them do the permitting."

"A thing we should also discuss is our schedule," Victor said. "We still don't know what if anything is happening about Tanith's movie. Andy and I may be going out of town for a while in December. By then, stuff should already be happening next door. Vicky and Sharon will be around, but could we ask you, Paige, to be the contact for our contractors?"

"Yes please," she said. "I would love that. I'm studying up on codes and stuff."

Lochan was smiling. "Did you know there's an online Building Code College? She's been on there already, she's almost finished it."

"Smart young lady," Victor said, also smiling. "Are all of you going to 'Milonga' tomorrow? We're going to see if we can sneak in. Tanith lit you up."

"I saw that!" Tasha had received dozens of texts and tags after the on-location rehearsal video of the Bradbury routine showed up on Tanith's Facebook page, with a mention of the upcoming show at Chrome. "Nobody would admit to telling her. I thought it must be Vicky, but she said no. It could have been any of them, I guess." She had a thought. "Wait a minute." She narrowed her eyes at Sandesh.

"You look like Anya right now."

"Was it you?"

"I admit nothing." He was snickering at her 'later for you' face.

There was a little more general conversation before Lochan and Paige said their goodbyes, collecting Maya and heading out. Matthew followed not long after. Victor retired upstairs, leaving

Sandesh and Tasha to clear up the kitchen over Andy's objections. "You need to let people help you," Tasha said. "I'll bet Mr. Garcia is a difficult patient. That red carpet business!" Andy snorted. "I feel you. I had my hands full with this one over the summer."

"Oh yeah, that so-called workplace accident." He clearly suspected there was more to it.

Sandesh answered the unspoken question. "I had a stalker. Co-worker with some bad ideas. She cornered me with a knife in the parking structure. We still don't know if she actually meant to cut me, it could have been an accident." His voice said he didn't really think so.

Tasha definitely didn't think so. "The fact remains that she had a knife and she cut you open with it," Tasha said. "It was pretty bad."

"I went into shock. Forgot all about applying pressure. Stood there watching myself bleed until I couldn't stand up anymore."

Andy was listening with fascinated horror. "How the f-, how the heck did you survive?"

"Building security saw it happen and called up to our office at basically the same time they called 911. One of our guys came down who had done a Red Cross emergency response class. He did the right things till the EMTs got there." Sandesh finished drying their salad bowl. There hadn't been any leftovers. He glanced over at Andy. "I did not fully comprehend how angry I was about it until I saw you giving your statement to the press."

"You could tell, huh."

"Well, I watched you do those scenes. Do you know why it happened?"

"Yes, we know now. It doesn't really help." They stared at each other for a few seconds. Then Andy said, "On a happier note, I couldn't help noticing a rather special ring. Am I to understand that there has been a change of status?"

"He asked me to marry him," Tasha said, smiling. "We're still working out when and where."

"Do it here," he said. "In the backyard. Your friend and mine is ordained and she loves doing weddings for Cabaret-adjacent people. Rory," he added since Sandesh was apparently incapable of speech. "She did ours, right outside that door."

Tasha couldn't believe it. "Andy, I won't lie, we were both like, I wonder if they would let us. But I don't know if we would have had the nerve to ask."

He was smiling at her. "Think about when. Talk to Rory. We're both back working on the show, Victor's got therapy, eventually Tanith is going to throw something at us about this movie. But we'll figure it out."

"Can I hug you? Is that allowed?" Andy laughed and opened his arms. Tasha went in for the hug, kissing his cheek. "You are a national treasure," she said. "I can't wait to be your neighbor." Sandesh jolted himself back into action and said something appreciative, shook Andy's hand, and started organizing their departure.

"Unbelievable," Tasha said after they got home and turned Theo loose for some me time. "Those guys are simply unbelievable." Sandesh laughed. "They're proposing to give us custom-renovated apartments at below-market rent just because they can. Who does that? Nobody, that's who. And then we say oh we're engaged and Andy's like get married here. No wonder

Victor loves him so much. No wonder Tanith wanted to do this movie with them. No wonder you wanted to live next door."

They settled in the living room, Sandesh down on the floor to stretch. "Well, I really did like the building, and it really is a good location for us. But I kind of want to adopt Andy as my west-coast Dad or something. We haven't even had that many private conversations. Hardly any, but I feel like he understands me."

"He's seen you in action, and you've seen him. I'll bet your real Dad has never seen you at work." She regarded him for a moment. "How long has it been since you've seen your folks? It's been a while, right?"

"Almost three years," he said. "I sort-of planned to two years ago but I couldn't get away from the office, and then this past year, there was a lot going on." Tasha made a face that said *understatement*. "It'll be three years at Christmas."

"Have they ever visited you out here?"

"Nope." He glanced over at her. "Maybe I should fly them out here for Christmas. Show them the Sleeping Beauty. Save Lo and Paige a trip back there. We can park them at a hotel so they're out of our hair." Tasha laughed. "Might as well spend some of this stack."

"Might as well," she agreed. "Because I don't really want to travel at Christmas, but I need to meet them. They need to meet me and Theo. And I think they need to see you in your natural habitat." He snickered. "You can take them up to your office and they'll see how people are all Yes Mr. Prasad, No Mr. Prasad, and they'll be like, who is this person? Where's our little boy?" Sandesh was giggling.

He got on his knees and leaned on the front of the couch so she could bend forward and kiss him. "Well I know Victor said they might be out of town in December. But we could see if right around New Years would work for the wedding. Do you think? Then we could keep Mom and Dad out here for that. Give them a week or so to get used to things."

"Do you think they'll accept it?" she said, more seriously. "I'm a little concerned. I don't want to come between you."

"Tasha," he said, "I'll always love and respect them. But my life is with you." She scooted forward so she could hug him. "I'll call them in the morning. Tell them we're getting married, issue the invitation for Christmas. Tell them the wedding might happen then."

"Let me know what they say."

"I will." He tugged her forward and off the couch. She was giggling now. "You need to stretch too, my sexy showgirl."

"Yes Mr. Prasad," she said demurely. "Although how I'm supposed to stretch with you on top of me I'll never know."

"Only for a minute," he said, and kissed her for several minutes. Eventually he rolled off and lay on his back, breathing fast. "I'm so glad we live together, because damn."

She stroked a hand down his body, confirming he was as turned on as she was. "Me too. Hold that thought."

"I'm *always* holding that thought," he assured her. "Jeez, stop that!" He laughed and rolled farther away.

Tasha was having a fit of nerves the next morning as the countdown to performance started. Sandesh was afraid listening to his planned conversation with one or the other of his parents would make it worse. "Should I wait and call them Tuesday, since you're performing again tomorrow?"

"No," she said. "I'm being silly. We know the routine, and it's different enough from the tape Tanith released that if one of us actually screws it up nobody will know. You need to get things squared away with your folks. I'm going to do some crazy nails for the show, that's always a zen thing for me." She pointed to the caddy of lacquer on the kitchen table.

"Okay. I'm going to call from the bedroom, though, in case Theo wants to watch TV. He got all his homework done yesterday."

"Go ahead, baby." He gave her a kiss and went into the bedroom. She sat down to do her manicure and listen to his side of the call.

Sandesh wasn't surprised that his father picked up the phone. Sunday morning was usually a good time to catch him. "Hi Dad, how're things on the East coast?" He listened for a while. "Things are good here, thanks. Lo and Paige and Tasha and I, and Tasha's ex-husband Matthew, we all went to see a triplex yesterday. Some friends of ours bought it and we're all going to move there next summer." That produced a long speech from the senior Mr. Prasad. "Yes, Dad. Yes, we get along with Matthew very well, and Theo's thrilled. Yes, same school. He's a good student. No, actually, I wanted to ask if you and Mom would like to come here for Christmas. I could fly you out, put you up in a hotel." Another pause to listen, then, "Yes, I can afford it. I told you I got a huge raise with this new position. Yeah, huge. Yes, more than that." He stated the number and tried to stifle his laughter at the disbelief on the other end. "Dad, I keep telling you this business is crazy. Yes I know, I would have to have two Ph.Ds, a top security clearance, a bestselling book and a fat research grant to make that in a university. That is one of many reasons why I am not at a university." Sandesh heard Tasha snort out in the kitchen and almost laughed again. "Yes, I probably could stay at this firm for a long time. I might. It depends. No, I'm not interested in moving back to South Carolina, all my friends are here, Tasha's family is here." He had to wait a while after that for an opportunity to speak. "Dad, you remember what I told you when I said I wanted to go to college out here? Still true." There was a long enough pause that Tasha leaned back to look toward the bedroom door; she could see that Sandesh had flopped onto his back on the bed and was shooting the bird at the ceiling with his free hand. She snickered. "Dad. Dad! I love you and Mom very much, but no. Not going back there. My life is here. Actually we're getting married." *Really* long pause. When Sandesh spoke again his tone was harder. "Dad. I have loved Tasha nonstop for basically a decade. She has been, is, and ever shall be the love of my life." Tasha had to set down her tools and take a breath, tipping back her head and blinking. "Yes I absolutely do believe that she loves me too. And Dad, don't even start with that. Theo is the best son anybody could want. I'm very fortunate that Matthew is willing to share him with me." Another pause. Tasha thought, *no wonder he wants to stay three thousand miles away.* "We haven't decided yet, but it might be around the holidays. Like

New Years. Some friends have offered to host it, yeah, family style. Well, if you come out for Christmas you could stay the week and be here for that too. Sure, talk it over with Mom. Obviously we'd love to have you here. Tasha wants to meet you. And Lochan would love to not have to fly back there. Yes, he told me that. Yes Dad. Thanks. I love you too."

Sandesh disconnected, stood up, leaned out of the bedroom and caught Tasha's eye, said "Give me a second" and closed the bedroom door. A moment later Tasha heard him say something (loud but muffled, possibly shouted into the mattress) that sounded an awful lot like "FUCK." She was bent over laughing when he came out of the bedroom. He checked the living room and looked relieved that Theo wasn't out there. "I'm sorry, I just really needed to say that." She flapped a hand at him, still giggling. He leaned over to kiss her cheek. "Hey, I like the design. You've got skills." She was doing her nails to match the engagement ring.

Tasha smiled up at him. "So what did he say, in twenty words or less, because damn."

"They'll talk it over but probably will come out and probably will stay for the wedding if we do it at New Years." He thought for a second. "Twenty-three, sorry."

"I'll bet you're about done talking for the day."

"I'm going to fire up HGTV and zone out for a while." He got himself a glass of water before doing that. Tasha finished her nail art and went to sit on the couch while it cured, watching Sandesh stretch.

After a while she couldn't resist asking, "What did you tell him about college?"

"That I needed a complete change of culture. He and Mom have made a go of it in South Carolina but I did not want to make the compromises they made. Obviously, neither did Lochan."

"I wondered about that. But he went to college back East, right, and then moved out here?"

"Right. He went to Georgia Tech, he got recruited during his senior year. He likes it here too." He smiled up at her. "He'll like it even more once we get into the triplex. Because Paige will be happier. He told me he thought she might want to go back to acting, but when he asked her, she said she was considering getting her contractor's license."

"Oh, that'll be great for her. She's so good at the house stuff." Tasha glanced over the wall clock in the kitchen. "Five hours till showtime."

"When does the sitter get here?"

"Six o'clock. I figured I'm not going to be good for much that last hour before we have to leave, so I scheduled some overlap. Could you take care of dinner for Theo?"

"Sure. I'll get it prepped now." He stood up and headed for the kitchen, then reversed course and came back to kiss her. "Aren't you glad I didn't put that on speaker?"

"Lord yes," she said. "Thank you for that."

They arrived at Chrome right on schedule. As they pulled into the parking lot, flashing their 'Performer' pass to the attendant, Tasha said, "I'm as nervous as a long-tailed cat in a room full of rocking chairs." Sandesh laughed. "I don't even know where I heard that."

"You look fantastic. You're going to be great. I meant to thank Terry for sending you his video."

"I did. I can't stop obsessing about everyone else. Vicky's thing with Tomás is a showstopper, but wait till you see what he's doing with Vince. Then Vince is doing a thing with Kelli, and they've always been so good. I don't feel like I'm in the same class at all."

"Tasha, don't make me turn this car around." He found them a parking place toward the back of the lot.

She laughed, then sighed. "I'm supposed to be concerned with my own stuff and let everything else be what it is. It's been so long since I did anything live on stage." She gave him a sidelong glance. "I wish we could have fooled around before I got dressed."

"So do I. Come on, beautiful. Let's get inside." He walked with her up to the club, flashing his ticket at the door. "This one's in the show."

"I remember," said the doorman. "Break a leg tonight."

"Thanks, Julio." Tasha patted him on the arm as they went past. She had her costume on under a short kimono. Sandesh was carrying her garment bag with a dress to change into after her performance; her tango shoes were tucked into the corners. The seven-woman routine was going to close the first half of the show. Tasha planned to join Sandesh out in the house during intermission so she could watch the second half.

They went downstairs. Sandesh found his table, a bar-height two-top, and handed her the garment bag. "Go get in the mood," he said, leaning down to kiss her. "And have fun."

"Thanks, sweetheart." She looked back over her shoulder and blew him a kiss before going through the stage door.

Sandesh hadn't been seated for more than a few minutes before a server came around. The night's menu included an Argentine-inspired special, chicken with dried fruit and a potato dumpling with tomato-cream sauce. He ordered that, with a glass of Malbec. "Will someone be joining you?" she asked.

"Yes, one of the performers from the first half."

"Okay great." She went off with a smile, and Sandesh studied the table talker listing the show order. There were twelve performances in all, most of them involving people he now knew, at least to say 'hi' to. He recognized quite a few of the song titles, too, thanks to the movie.

Looking around, watching the room fill up, he wondered if Andy and Victor would be able to come. Their security team, and Victor's doctors, would probably have a fit. But one of the loveseats up front – Terry had told him those were always reserved – was still empty. The lights did their five-minute-warning thing just as his food was delivered. He ate, enjoying the food but missing Tasha; it had been quite a while since he'd had dinner alone. He took a moment to appreciate how much his life had changed. Then the lights began to dim. Just before the room went dark he saw two men come through, going to the unoccupied loveseat. *That's them*, he thought, smiling.

What with one thing and another, Sandesh and Tasha hadn't been to a show at Chrome since February. He thoroughly enjoyed it. The six performances in the first half were all completely different interpretations of Argentine tango. When the familiar (to tango enthusiasts) introduction to 'La Cumparsita' began, with the seven women onstage, there was a burst of applause. He wondered how many people there would recognize Victor's voice; since the movie and its cast album hadn't been released yet, maybe only those who were fans – as he was now. The version they'd recorded was nearly four minutes long. Sandesh could have watched, and listened, all night.

The club got very loud very fast during intermission. Sandesh stayed where he was, waiting for Tasha. She joined him within five minutes, greeting him with a kiss. "Hey baby! How did it look from out here?"

"It looked A. May. Zing," he said. "Perfect. How did it feel?"

"It felt great. But I'm so glad it's over. Till tomorrow. Tomorrow won't be so bad." She looked around. "I'm not hungry but man would I like a drink." He laughed and caught the server's eye. She got to their table a minute later and Tasha asked for a glass of the Malbec. Sandesh settled for a Pellegrino.

He leaned close after the server left and said, "Don't look now but the difficult patient is here with his supervisor."

"Oh, they did *not*." She knew they must be up front, but she didn't try to spot them. They'd be better off if nobody really noticed. "Did you look up those dances they did here?"

"Well, yeah. You know I've gotten kind of obsessed with everyone on the project, but especially them."

"How long do you think it'll take Tanith to finish it up?"

"God knows. I get the idea Reza and Tina know what they're doing with editing, but I have only the sketchiest idea how it's actually done, or how much time it usually takes." He watched her sip her wine, looking around the room, tapping her foot to the music. The club was playing tango nuevo tonight. He only even knew what that was because of the movie. "Want to dance? There's a little space here."

She looked back at him, smiling. "You know what, honey, I'd love to dance." He stood up and offered his hand. She set hers in it and slid off her bar stool, settling against him in the close embrace. "I'll always love to dance with you." He turned his head a few degrees, so his cheek rested against her hair. They danced until the lights went down again. Then he kissed her – taking advantage of the darkness – with sufficient thoroughness that she started to giggle before he let her go. The second half of the show was as good as the first, but now all he wanted was to take her home, and to bed. At the end of the closing number, as applause began, he saw Andy and Victor get up again and make their way across the dark room. Andy was on Victor's right, with a hand on his left shoulder blade. A stranger in a suit – it had to be one of their security guys – was waiting at the bottom of the stairs. Andy nodded to him and they all went up.

Tasha was on her feet when Sandesh looked back at her. He stood too, applauding. "What was your favorite number?"

She laughed. "I couldn't possibly pick one. But I know what *you'll* say."

"The one with you in it, yeah. You want to dance a little more?" She shook her head 'no.' "Let's get out of here. Maybe Theo will be asleep when we get home."

"I have to get my dress bag. Hold on."

Sandesh took care of the bill while Tasha went backstage again, which should be a quick errand tonight. He suspected that tomorrow, they'd be much later getting home. According to Terry, there was always an informal cast party on the last night of a show. Before Tasha got back he took a minute to pull out his phone and send a text to Andy: *Saw you at the club, wanted to say Hi but thought you might like to lie low. I guess Mr. G is doing all right. Remind him Tanith sees all*

A reply came in right away: *You better not rat us out*

*Andy your secret is safe with me but there are like 100 people here who know you guys*

*We were NEVER THERE that is FAKE NEWS*

*LOL right!* He saw Tasha coming and put away the phone. "Andy says they were never here."

"Well, of course they weren't, that would have been loco," she said. "Let's go, honey, the mob is about to come out of that green room and then we'll never get away."

Chapter 13
October 2018

They were back at Chrome the following week for a set of torch songs. They found out about it when Tanith sent an email inviting all the cast and crew to a rough-cut screening on October seventh. The vocal performance was scheduled for the preceding Wednesday. Tasha arranged a sitter for Theo again - they'd gotten friendly with a responsible teenager in their building - and they headed back to Hollywood even though they weren't sure who was performing; Tanith's message only said 'friends of ours.' It turned out to be Rosa Ramirez, wife of Tomás Calderón, one of the movie's co-stars (and Sandesh's piano teacher). Not only that, Andy and Victor were performing with her. "Okay really now," Tasha said when she saw the poster outside. "It has literally been one month. That guy is out of his mind."

"Well, he ought to know if he's feeling up to it," Sandesh said, amused. "Andy wouldn't let him do it unless it was manageable. And somebody must have leaked it, because look at this place!" Every table in the main space was occupied, presumably by Andy and Victor's fans, plus Chrome regulars. "There's a spot here at the back, move fast." In the nick of time they found barstools at the counter that ran along the back of the downstairs lounge. More people were coming in, right up to maximum SRO occupancy. "I'm glad they're doing it, actually. I can't wait to see the movie, but this will be a reminder of how good they are."

"I'm so jealous you got to do all that stuff," Tasha said. "I didn't realize it at the time, but when I think about all those songs and dances you got to see, it's like damn. Has it been forever since filming wrapped up?"

"Two months. I have no idea if that's the normal amount of time. I mean, I know Reza and Tina both have jobs, he runs that design company and she's in computer animation. They had to have been working on it nights and weekends."

"It's a good credit for them, though." They were both turned to face the room, which made it easy to spot a passing server. Tasha signaled, and a few minutes later they had drinks. "Isn't it about time to start?"

"Maybe. Oh wait up." Sandesh pointed over to the side of the room. Andy and Victor were coming in, both in tuxedos, with a security guy in front and another in back. Victor did not have his arm in its sling this time. They passed quickly through to the stage door and went back. The security guys took up positions near the stage steps. "They must have gotten stuck in traffic."

"Oh, poor Rosa, she must have been afraid they weren't going to get here!"

"They wouldn't ditch." A few minutes later the lights were dimmed, a last-minute rush of drinks was delivered, and then the lights went down for real and the curtain opened on Tomás' beautiful wife under a spotlight. Tomás was at the piano, the same one they'd had for the movie, off to the side. Sandesh reached for Tasha's hand. They listened with enjoyment to Rosa's first five songs, and then Andy came out. He acknowledged the anticipatory applause with a smile. Then Tomás began to play one of Carlos Gardel's songs, 'El Día Que Me Quieras.' "Oh my

God this song," Sandesh said softly. At the end, he and Tasha stood up to join in the applause. "He is so, so good."

"He really is. I wouldn't have guessed from carpool karaoke." She caught his querying glance. "I mean yes, a good singer, but the *performance.* That was the love song everyone wants to hear, and I don't even speak Spanish."

Sandesh laughed under his breath. The applause was finally tapering off, and the curtain was closed for intermission. Servers were in a mad dash to take and fill more drink orders. "I was thinking of Argentine tango for our wedding dance," he said, after they'd flagged one down. "Are you surprised?"

"Not the least little bit," she said, smiling. "That song?"

"Maybe? I thought I'd ask Vince."

They both got back on their barstools. "Is he here?"

"He could be, it's impossible to see anybody in this mob." Sandesh pulled out his phone and woke it up to send a text: *Hey Vince, Tasha & I are engaged and need a wedding dance. Argentine tango. Should it be the one that Andy just sang?* He set the phone down on the counter, thinking he'd check it when his new drink arrived, but it buzzed almost as soon as it left his hand.

*Call me tomorrow and we'll talk. That's a great song but wedding dance should have personal meaning. Btw congratulations. Where are you?*

*Back counter downstairs, where are you?*

*Front table upstairs, right over your head and not going down into that mosh pit*

Sandesh laughed. The mezzanine seating had a good view of the stage and – according to Terry – was a good bit more genteel. Standing-room admission was only for the downstairs lounge. *Don't blame you, we're like sardines down here. Will call tomorrow thx, give our regards to Kelli.* Vince sent back a thumbs-up. They had enough time to flag down the server again for some water before the lights signaled the resumption of the show.

Andy and Victor opened the second half with a duet version of 'La Vie en Rose' that had Tasha wiping away tears. Then Rosa came back out for five more songs, but it turned out that wasn't the end. After their bows, the guest artists brought her back on and they all did 'La Vie en Rose' again. It was a great way to close the show. "Now I'm jealous of *her*," Tasha said, standing again to applaud. Sandesh stood beside her. "Not only did they join her show, they sang with her! And I don't think she expected that."

"Pretty sure she didn't," Sandesh agreed. "You know, I seem to recall you can sing. Maybe we should see about setting one of these up for you."

She looked alarmed. "Oh lord no. If I was this nervous about doing a group routine, I would pass right out."

"Never say never," he said, smiling.

"And that reminds me, if we're doing Argentine tango for a wedding dance I am going to have to choose my wedding dress very, very carefully. For one thing it cannot be white."

"Why?"

"Because my ass will look like Herbie the Love Bug, that's why." She laughed at his expression. "I know you like it, honey, but this baby got back. Oh look, there they go.  And uh-oh, Victor's looking a little pale."

"I'll bet he forgot he was hurt. He loves to perform. Andy will take care of him." Andy was again shielding Victor's right side, and the security team got them through the crowd without incident. They disappeared up the stairs. A minute later, Rosa and Tomás came out and started working the crowd. "Do you want to hang out, or do you want to go home? Because I was thinking about wedding dances, and that made me think of the wedding night."

"Are you ready?" she said softly, with a mischievous look. She turned toward him and laid her hand on his chest, stroking it down, down, and down while she pressed close and kissed his throat. "Oh yes, you're ready." Sandesh caught her hand, laughing under his breath. "I'm ready too. Let's go, baby."

Sandesh called Vince the next day, as instructed, and gave him the outline of his history with Tasha. He also told Vince the truth about his injury for the first time. Vince said, "That's pretty intense. Do you want your dance to cover this whole story of yours?"

"Is that a thing that is possible?"

"Remember some of what you saw this summer. A dance can say a lot. I have an idea," Vince said. "I'll email you the track, tell me what you think. Now I'm assuming, knowing you, that the basic wedding hug-and-shuffle is not what you want to do."

"Not," Sandesh said firmly. "Tasha can really dance. I want to show her off as much as possible."

"You can also dance, but have you ever learned choreography?"

"Nope."

"Well, listen to the track. If you hate it I'll toss you some alternate suggestions, but we'll need to get you in here pretty soon so I can see how you pick up choreo. When are you doing this thing?"

"End of the year, probably. Maybe even New Year's Day."

"Oh, that's plenty of time." Vince sounded so confident that Sandesh almost believed him. Barely five minutes later he got the email with an attachment labeled 'Un Beso.' *A kiss*, he thought. *One kiss*. The title couldn't be more perfect. He fished his headphones out of his desk drawer and listened. Then he re-started it and listened again, uncharacteristically ignoring the office emails that were rolling in on his second monitor.

It wasn't the usual love song, that was for sure; it started out tense and suspenseful, then went to a slower, more romantic section. He could almost see what a dancer like Vince, or Tomás, or Andy could do with it. The last section brought back the tension from the beginning, with its stronger rhythm and passionate energy. There was only one problem. He took off the headphones and sent a text: *Dude I love the damned thing but six minutes?!*

*Don't be dramatic it's only 5:20*

*ONLY 5:20 are you out of your mind?!*

*LOL yeah I know, sorry, but cutting would ruin it*

*OMFG let me see what Tasha says. She was freaking out over that four-minute La Cumparsita*

*She totally had that*

*I know but Eeek*

*I have a few other options if you guys chicken out*

*Chicken out?! The frickin vows won't even take six minutes!*

*LOL gotta go, let me know*

Sandesh put down his phone, shaking his head, and forwarded the track to Tasha with a note: *This is Vince's first idea for our wedding dance. OMFG.* That was all he could possibly say at the moment. They would have to talk about this one. Then he forwarded the track to James without comment.

Ten minutes later, James came down the hall and leaned on Sandesh's door frame. "What the hell was that?"

"Tanith's choreographer thinks that should be our wedding dance. I'm tripping balls."

James laughed. "Yeah. You know what I did? One minute of marginally competent salsa. It's a wonder Silvia even agreed to go on a honeymoon."

"Well, presumably she knew you were taking her to Bordeaux." Sandesh managed to say this with a straight face.

James gave him a look. "Very true. For the record, my mother says it was the best wedding dance she's ever seen."

"Yeah, because it was *your* wedding dance. I'm trying to imagine my parents' faces if Tasha and I did a five and a half minute production number." He giggled. "It's almost worth doing just for that. What song did you use?"

"Something called 'C'est Ici.' Vince gave us that one, said since we were going to France we should do a French song. He's a great teacher, you know. If he thinks you can do it, you probably can. I mean, there's a reason he gave me one minute." Sandesh snorted. "I will look forward to hearing what you decide to do. In the meantime, I have a brief to write." James rolled his eyes and walked away. Sandesh buckled down to his mailbox.

He got home an hour after Tasha, and she already had dinner ready to go. He set down his messenger bag and went to kiss her. "I about had a heart attack when I saw the time on that track," she said without preamble. "Then I listened to it a bunch of times and I kind of love it."

"I love it too. I was thinking, how about we go in for a private and see how fast I can pick things up? Because I know you can. James said if Vince thinks I can do it, maybe I can. Well, he said probably I can."

"Probably," she agreed. "You're mighty smart. You want to go get Theo?" He kissed her again, and went to do that. After they cleared up from dinner, he sent another text to Vince: *Tasha says let's try it. When?*

*Friday? Kelli and I have a date but she'll forgive me for scheduling a lesson as long as we can have dinner with you guys right after*

*Deal. Dinner's my treat. See you at the studio*

*Hasta.* Sandesh put the phone down again. Theo was at the kitchen table doing homework, looking downtrodden. "They really pile it on, don't they buddy?"

"Yeah."

"If it's not too bad this weekend, you want to go somewhere on Saturday? Your mom and I have another thing to go to Sunday afternoon, but I had this idea." He'd already discussed it with Tasha.

Theo turned around to look at him. "What?"

"I thought we could go down to Long Beach, go to the Aquarium of the Pacific, stay overnight and then have breakfast at the beach before we drop you off at your dad's. How's that sound?"

"You're going out Friday, too, right?" Sandesh nodded. Theo thought about it for a minute. "If I get some of my homework done Friday, I wouldn't have to take any to Long Beach."

"That's true. And I'm sorry we've been out so much lately, it'll settle down after this week. We're going to be getting some more dance lessons, but we can take you with us if you want."

"Okay." Theo turned back to his workbook, looking happier. Sandesh glanced over at Tasha; she was giving him a thumbs-up.

Tasha got on the phone with Anya during her lunch hour on Friday, calling as soon as she was outside the building. They'd prearranged the time so Anya picked up right away. "What's new?"

"Six minutes," Tasha said.

"Six minutes of what? Is that what your boy toy is down to?"

Tasha laughed hard. "No he's still good for a lot more than that, when conditions permit. Vince sent us this track for our wedding dance, and it's six minutes long. Okay, five minutes twenty, but come on."

"Argentine tango?"

"Yeah, it's called 'Un Beso,' do you know it?"

Anya said, "Sure do. They used it in that pro show three years ago. It was this opening number with three couples. Hiro Bossypants gave me a copy of the DVD and told me to watch it and I'm not even sure why because I've only done little bits of Argentine tango with Ricky and who has time with all this shit for our Latin debut."

"How's that going?"

"It's in roughly six weeks and my head is exploding. I can't believe I let him talk me into it." Anya didn't actually sound too bothered by it. "Anyway it's a great track. When do you start work on it?"

"Tonight."

"Still looking at New Years for the wedding?"

"Yeah, we're copy-cattin' you." Tasha heard Anya snort. "That's if it works out," she qualified. "Our hosts have a lot going on all the time."

"True story. Hey, but you know Andy turned in the poster art for 'Vagina Dentata.' The ads just went out today. It's like this kaleidoscope thing but, did you ever see 'Dune'?"

"Uh … no." Tasha had no idea where this was going.

"Terrible sci-fi movie with Kyle MacLachlan. Anyway there are these giant sand worm things, or no! Like the one in 'Return of the Jedi,' basically a penis full of teeth."

"Tell me that is not what's on the poster."

Anya laughed. "No. It's legs, Michelle and Stacey and Paula and Rory, their legs fanned out and repeated in this oval thing down into infinity. It's a trip."

"For a second there I was very afraid. We'll see you at the show, right? You're doing that apache?"

"Yes and yes. This one is, dare I say, romantic. Ricky loves it. Luis loves it. Terry loves it. It is still sick as shit but only if you know the subtext."

"Which is?"

"Well, that I'm going to eat him later." Anya said it like it was obvious. "I have to go. Hirohito is pointing at his imaginary wristwatch. That guy is a fucking tyrant. Talk to you soon." She disconnected. Tasha shook her head, laughing under her breath, and texted Sandesh: *Hey baby I'm told you should see the poster for Underground Cabaret's Halloween show*

*I can do that*, he wrote back immediately. Before she even got to The Stand for her lunch, he sent *YIKES*

*LOL I know!!*

*Well I guess I know what we're doing that weekend*

*That's a start anyway. Anya and I were talking about my boy toy again*

*Giving you ideas?*

*I always have ideas.* Tasha was definitely having ideas. She stepped out of the line of customers because she didn't want anyone looking over her shoulder.

Sandesh had an idea of his own. *You know there's a lock on the door of my office*

*LOL naughty!*

*I dare you*

*All this power has gone to your head*

*Something has, I'm so turned on right now thinking about you in here with me, me in you in front of this window*

She stepped out of the restaurant and looked up at the tower. The windows on his floor were too high up to see inside from ground level. *Can you see me? I'm outside The Stand*

*I see you. Buy you lunch if you do this one little thing for me*

*It wasn't little the last time I checked*

*LOL.* Up in his office, Sandesh was now seriously turned on. If Tasha didn't come up, he was going to have to lock that door anyway until he could calm down. Or something. He couldn't help glancing at his gym bag, with clean towels just waiting to get dirty.

Down on the plaza, Tasha made up her mind. *Tell the front desk*

*You got it.* Sandesh called down to give her name to security so they'd clear her up, then sent an IM to Nicole. He almost couldn't believe he'd suggested it, much less that she was – apparently – in the same reckless mood. On the other hand, the last time - after Rosa's performance - had been the kind of sex you think about afterward. He might have been thinking about it a little too much. His office phone rang; he picked it up. "Hi Nicole."

"Tasha Jefferson here to see you."

"Send her back, please." He would have gone out to meet her except for the state he was in.

"Will do."

He was standing by the desk when Tasha got to his office door. *Oh mercy,* she thought, *that's mine*, because he looked so good. Black jeans, a short-sleeved collared shirt in orchid-colored raw silk, and those hot eyes. "Thanks for the lunch invitation, Mr. Prasad."

He didn't move toward her. "Nice to see you. Step inside and we'll talk about where to go."

She closed the door and flipped the lock. "I wondered why I wore a skirt today instead of jeans. Maybe I was thinking it was because we're going to dance tonight."

"Maybe." Now he moved, taking two steps, reaching out to touch the side of her face, sliding his hand around the back of her neck as he kissed her. Hot, hungry, pressing his body against hers. His mouth moved to her throat and he spoke very low. "Jesus, Tasha, I'm on fire."

She could feel it. "Me too," she said breathlessly. "Touch me." He took her skirt in both hands and tugged it up, moving one hand between her legs. "Oh *Jesus*."

She was wet. "Is that for me?" Sandesh slid his fingers under the fabric of her panties, dipping into her.

"Always." He went to his knees, pulling down the underwear with his free hand and going for her with his mouth. She dug her hands into his hair, legs shaky, leaning against the door and trying not to make a sound. It seemed like no time before she came, biting her lip.

He felt her pulse and stayed with her a moment longer, licking her one more time. "Mmmm," he said, right up against her. She huffed out a breath. He moved away enough to get her underwear all the way off, lifting one foot at a time off the floor. She still had her hands in his hair. They slid down his neck and torso as he stood up. She unbuttoned his shirt and pressed her lips to his chest. He had his hands on her ribs, and he didn't say anything, but she knew what he wanted. She wanted it too, so she stepped past him and bent forward with her hands on the desk. She heard his zipper go down. Then he had one hand on her hip, under her skirt, and she felt him against her. She went to her elbows and he slid inside. She bit her lip again as she heard his breath go out. He moved slowly, not hard and fast as she'd expected, and she was gasping when he surged against her and froze. She heard a muffled sound, felt him come, and turned her head to look back at him. *God almighty*, she thought, throbbing with an aftershock of her own. His head was flung back, eyes closed, lips parted, gloriously abandoned. They held still for a moment longer, then he took a deep breath and opened his eyes. He smiled at her and disengaged. Picked up a towel and wiped himself, then her. "I can't quite believe we did that," he said softly, "but I'm sure glad we did."

"Me too." She found her underwear and stepped into it again, tugging it up, starting to giggle while he put himself in order and rolled up the towel, giving it a drop of orange essential oil before zipping it into his gym bag. "How long did that take?" He went past her to look at the time on his monitor, held up six fingers. "Six minutes?" She laughed out loud, she couldn't help it.

"Are we decent?" They examined each other. "Whew." She could tell he was about to crack up. "I seem to remember I promised you lunch, Ms. Jefferson."

"Yes you did." He unlocked the door. They took one more look to make sure it wasn't too obvious what they'd just done. "I might have to get mine to go," she said.

"I think you already did," he murmured. She put a hand over her mouth to stifle the laugh. "Do you need validation, Ms. Jefferson?" She was still giggling when they passed Nicole.

The rough-cut party started at noon that Sunday, and went till almost five. After seeing everything performed live, Sandesh had a pretty good idea how the movie would come together, but he was still surprised by it. With so much to do at the office, he hadn't sat down with the script to try to visualize it. Coming to it with only the script in mind, Tasha was completely sucked into the framing story of the actors and their play, and the obsession that had them by the throat almost from the beginning. "I always loved how she dumped us right in it," she murmured to Sandesh at the end, while everyone was applauding. "There was none of that back-story exposition crap wasting our time. Just here, here are these guys, they're playing these other guys and their heads are exploding." He laughed. "And oh by the way it's wall to wall beautiful music. I really love how she started with Andy, and how she used him. How'd she even know he had that in him? Nobody's ever going to look at him the same way now."

"Yeah, I thought that too. She said when she started writing this, the only character who wasn't cast in her head was Francisco. She cast Lucas after seeing 'Behind the Strip.' She knew Victor and Marco and Andy all from when she did her play. Vicky did the first-draft read, and her part was written after that. But when Tanith was writing, she'd never seen Tomás act, or heard him sing. I don't know how the hell she did it. Because I can't imagine anyone else in those parts."

"Me neither. Let's go get a drink. I'm not over seeing myself on screen."

"You were fantastic. You looked like a pro." It had been fun trying to find themselves in the dance mobs, but Sandesh couldn't believe what a thrill it was to see his name in the credits as 'line producer.' He hadn't been entirely certain Tanith was serious about that, and wouldn't have minded if she'd been kidding. But he liked the movie a lot; he was proud to be associated with it.

All of the cast and crew remembered him, too. There were as many compliments to him for his work as to Tasha for her dancing. Tanith found them after a while and said, "Well? If I do another one, should I call you?"

"Absolutely," they said together. Tasha added, "Tanith, I know you've got a million people to talk to, but how close was this to your first draft? Sandesh said Vicky's whole part was added after that."

"The first draft of the full screenplay is not too far from this, but the original concept was way different. It would have taken half an hour to get to the first song. I wrote all this back story and exposition crap and when I realized it had to be about the music, all of that went in the trash. Well, it went into a folder labeled 'burying the bodies.' Did you like it?"

"I really did. It's such a great showcase for everybody, and it tells both stories really well. I'm proud I could be in it." Tanith looked gratified as she moved off. Tasha glanced over at Sandesh. "Good job not laughing when she said that about back story."

"I almost did, oh my God." They both giggled. "Let's mingle a little. We might not see some of these people for a long time."

They were at Shall We Dance for their second lesson with Vince when the text came in from Andy. Sandesh had his phone in his hand to take video of Vince demonstrating, with Kelli, his concept for the romantic center section of 'Un Beso.' The text alert buzzed and the name flashed at the bottom of his screen, and he was tempted to click over but he didn't want to risk missing any of the demo. When Vince let go of Kelli she said, "Your phone just said something."

"Yeah, I know." Vince pulled his own phone out of his pocket and read something, eyebrows going up. "Well that didn't take long."

Kelli, reading alongside him, said, "I'm not surprised."

Sandesh and Tasha both said, "What?"

Vince and Kelli both said, "Check your messages."

Sandesh opened the text, holding the phone out so Tasha could see: *Greetings one and all time to get high if you're not already because the movie is SOLD and there will be a premiere event to include all cast and crew. Details to follow, don't call Tanith because I think she's spending the day at the bottom of a bottle. Oh wait that's me*

They were still staring at each other, too stupefied even to giggle, when another text came in: *Sandesh you may have noticed my better half overdid it a little last Wednesday but he is fine and by the way the driveway in front of the triplex is gone. Other permitting underway as we speak. We'll be in touch*

Sandesh had recovered enough to send a reply: *Thanks Andy, congratulations to you and Victor. It was an honor and a privilege to work with you on that project. We are at your service. Didn't know you spotted us last Wednesday*

*Rory pointed you out, she was stage-managing but saw you when she went to get V a shot of tequila*

Sandesh couldn't believe it. *OMG that guy is the worst patient ever*

*HE TOTALLY IS*

*Uh oh our teacher is tapping his foot like get off the phone. Six minute wedding dance, send help*

*LOL can't wait to see it.* Tasha had been following this whole exchange, and said, "It's a good thing we're moving in next door. Andy needs a hand keeping that man of his in line."

"If Vicky and Sharon can't do it, I'm not sure the five of us are going to be enough." Sandesh put his phone away and they got down to business. At the end of the session he stretched out on the floor, flat on his back, and said, "Kill me now." Vince laughed heartlessly.

"You have the whole middle section already!" Kelli said. "You have no idea how well you're doing."

"But I'm hungry," he said plaintively, "and my ankles are like what just happened, and my brain is on fire."

Tasha was sitting beside him, giggling. She patted his chest. "You're really picking it up fast, you know. That's the great thing about choreography, you don't have to actually know how to dance."

"Uh, wait a minute." He frowned at her.

She laughed some more. "Oh honey you know that's not what I meant! I meant all this stuff isn't stuff we would have known to do yet in social dancing, but Vince can teach it to us now, and then we'll know it for when we know what to do with it."

"This part actually would work in a milonga," Kelli said. "What he has in mind for the bookends, not so much. But listen, I'm hungry too. Would it be boring to go to the Italian place again?"

"No," Sandesh said, sitting up. "Take me to your linguine." Vince gave him a hand up, then they both pulled Tasha to her feet.

"Don't forget," Kelli said to Vince, "we owe Esme tiramisu. Like, *all* the tiramisu. She broke a date so we could be here," she told Tasha.

"Oh no! We'd better not do next Friday, then. We owe Theo an uninterrupted weekend, anyway." Tasha looked over at Sandesh, who was changing out of his dance shoes. "Could we do two the weekend after next, honey?"

"Sure," he said. "I'd rather front-load this torture and then have time to practice a lot, than try to pick it up a little bit at a time."

"That's the way we professionals do it," said Vince. "Matrix download, headache, practice, ready to go."

"You should have heard him when he was starting on ballroom with Michelle," Kelli said. "So much whining."

"I did not whine."

"You totally whined." Kelli checked to see if everyone had street shoes on. "And by the way, Sandesh, he had to learn four routines but all four put together was barely six minutes. And he had a year to do it."

"Are you on my side or not?" Vince said, looking betrayed.

Kelli kissed his cheek. "Always on your side, mi corazón. Let's go."

Sandesh and Tasha made plans to go to the Halloween show on a double date with James and Silvia. James had seen the 'Vagina Dentata' ad online and forwarded it to Silvia with no comment, only to receive a text reading *It's about time* in return. Janice heard him laughing in his office. "What's so funny?"

"Are you and Susan going to the Underground Cabaret?"

"Would we miss that show? I hear it's going to be redonkulously freaky."

"I sent the ad to my wife and she said 'it's about time.'" He heard her laugh. "Is every man in this show going to be killed and eaten, or something?"

"It's been a rough couple of years for America, James. I'm surprised they aren't dedicating the show to Elizabeth Warren, Hillary Clinton, and Michelle Obama. Trust me, every man involved is a willing sacrifice."

"I'm glad Silvia's the designated driver," he said, coming out to lean on Janice's counter. "I have a feeling a two-drink minimum is, like, the *bare* minimum."

She laughed. "Susan and I have a bet about the ratio of men to women in the audience."

"Sandesh and I may be the only two there with a Y chromosome who aren't actually employed by the club."

"You might be surprised," she said. "There's a lot of angry gay men in Los Angeles."

"As there should be," he said soberly. "We're going on the second night, meeting up with Sandesh and Tasha, they're going to stay for the wrap party. Are you there that night?"

"No, we're going to the first night. I promise not to tell you anything about it on Monday."

"Thanks. I'm aware there might be spoilers with this one." She snorted and waved him away.

When he got to the office the following Monday, Janice was at her desk pinning up a Vagina Dentata postcard under her counter, where it couldn't be seen from the hallway. "James, no spoilers, but best show ever. And you know that is saying something with this company."

"Okay," he said. "What was the audience like?"

"Passionate. And I heard it's sold out, so you already have tickets, right?"

"Yeah, we sprung for a couple of the loveseats because, you know, pregnant wife. And it would have been rude to sit there with our backs to Sandesh and Tasha."

"Yes it would. You have email. Go get to work."

"Yes ma'am." James had gone for weeks without having any management-type nonsense in his mailbox, but that day there was a message from Carver requesting a meeting concerning associate reviews. For the first time, all of the associates were being evaluated by the full partnership. Each assistant had also been invited to comment on a few key measures of associate performance. This was another of Sandesh's innovations that had caused some anxiety for the management committee. They were all nervous about how it would play out. James sent an acknowledgement and a suggested time that met with approval. He headed down to Carver's office after lunch and tapped on the open door. "Hey. Are we ready?"

"Hi James, yes, come on in. Close the door." Carver was sitting back in his task chair with a stack of written evaluations on the desk in front of him. "So this was interesting."

"What?"

"These notes from the assistants. I was sure it was going to be a landslide of complaints, but there's literally two of those. Most of these notes are compliments. Like, so-and-so never has to be reminded to turn in his timesheets, or always offers to bring coffee. Little stuff like that."

"Quality of life stuff," said James. "I think that's what Sandesh was after. You know his whole deal is efficiency, plus a livable culture. If people are keeping that in mind, that's a good thing. Because you know the assistants don't give a shit about billable hours." Carver snorted. "What are the complaints?"

Carver referred to the evaluations. "Gets snappy when he's busy, and interferes with lunch hour. More quality of life."

"Same associate?"

"No, two different ones." Carver set the papers down again.

"Those should be easily managed. Glad to hear it."

"Me too. Anyway I just wanted to let you know it sounds as though we're on the right track. We won't need any of your time on this, but you're welcome to sit in if you want to."

James thought about it for a minute. He could block out the time, and it might be a good precedent. "Yeah, I'll sit in. Thanks. How's it been for you?"

"Since July?" Carver stared at him for a minute. "Not what I expected. I did not expect us to be in this place at this time. I thought we were still going to be slogging along the way we were in May and June, buried in minutiae. I thought those weekly meetings he demanded were going to eat up so much time. It's been like five minutes. Ten minutes, tops."

"Glad to hear that too." James had the idea that at this point, Sandesh had no major problems remaining to solve. Everything was fine-tuning. His assistant Fatima was now the point person for the support staff, but she and Sandesh were both out on the floor regularly to ensure they each saw – and spoke to – each staffer every week. James knew that Sandesh had also been speaking to the legal staff regularly, doing lunches or coffee breaks, checking in on their view of things.

"We're planning to offer him another raise." Carver smiled. "But if I know him, he'll have an alternate suggestion."

Tasha would have been excited about the Cabaret show just for Anya and Ricky's 'In the Flesh' apache, but it was a full slate of performances by people she knew, or at least recognized. Their new friend Rory was opening with a striptease routine set to 'Get Ur Freak On' by Missy Elliott. Other Cabaret regulars were doing jazz numbers to 'Teeth' by Lady Gaga and 'Ya Mama' by Fatboy Slim. Then there was Sam and Mateo's martial-arts paso doble to Woodkid's 'Run Boy Run,' and an Argentine tango from Shall We Dance owner Dmitri and his Latin expert Hiro set to the Electric String Orchestra's cover of 'Toxic.' The Chrome kitchen's special for the night was a squid-ink risotto with a seared scallop, and the bar special was a pomegranate martini garnished with black-skinned plum. Tasha, Sandesh, and James all ordered the specials. Silvia had to settle for a virgin martini. "Anya didn't tell me they were closing the show," Tasha said, studying the table talker with the full list of a dozen performances.

"Well, if it's anything like that other apache they did, they probably wanted to make sure if they killed each other everyone else would still have a chance to perform." James ate the slice of plum from his martini, then coughed. "Oh *damn* that's been soaked in some kind of firewater, proceed with caution." He sucked down some actual water. "Janice wouldn't give me any hints. Except I know nobody actually died, so."

"I never heard of apache until I met Terry and Anya," Sandesh said. "Then I found that 'Love is Blindness' thing and I thought holy shit."

James said, "Everybody did. I knew a little bit about Anya, because she used to date my buddy Danny. So when I saw it I was also like holy shit, but in a way not surprised."

Tasha was laughing. "I heard about her thing with Danny. That poor guy. I see how she is with Ricky and with Terry, and I can't imagine her being that brutal, but I know it happened."

"It sure did." Silvia knew Danny and his wife Kate pretty well by now, and she'd heard some stories. "If Ricky didn't love her, and if I didn't love Ricky because of Luis, Anya would still be on my shit list." Luis had been Silvia's BFF since high school.

"That Luis is great with Ricky. What does he think of stuff like this?"

Silvia said, “Last I heard was ‘they are both loco,’ and that was at dress rehearsal.”

Then the food was delivered. Sandesh studied the plate for a moment. “This scallop has a whole ’nother aspect in the context of this show.” James also studied his plate. Both women were snickering. “I guess it could have been worse. They could have put two on the plate.” James snorted. “Chop chop, motherfucker.” All four of them cracked up.

“Oh lord,” Tasha said after a minute, “help me not think of that at work tomorrow when I’m trying to answer the phone.”

## Chapter 14
November 2018

Sandesh had requested to be reviewed at the usual time, along with the rest of the staff. His own perception was that the changes made over the summer had begun to settle in and that a new normal was in place. He knew that billable hours for the past three months were up across the board from the previous year's numbers, and that operating expenses were down. Cutting the IT job in San Francisco had almost paid for the cost of breaking that lease. They'd characterized that as a layoff so the guy could claim unemployment benefits, but he'd already found a new job. Sandesh had checked the legal grapevine to find out what had happened with Darlene and Sean. The former had moved to the East Coast and the latter had opened a sole-practitioner office. Rumor had it he was having trouble finding support staff.

The meeting with the management committee was scheduled for the Monday before Thanksgiving week. By that time, they'd spoken to all of the associates, and the whole partnership had met to vote on compensation and promotions. One high-performing associate was being offered partnership, and recruiting would begin for a new associate. Sandesh held another staff meeting to inform them of the changes and to announce the promotion of one of the service center employees to facilities manager. "We're going to start hosting some bar association things next year," he told the staff. "And some business-development things. Our new facilities expert is going to take point on those, working with Mr. Levine. I am going to be recruiting for a docketing specialist, we need to get that off the assistant desks." There was some scattered applause for that. "Now, the volume of work for our two paralegals is starting to get burdensome. If any of you have an interest in getting your paralegal certifications, come and talk to me about tuition assistance. We might structure a couple of positions as paralegal-secretary. Those positions would not have a billing requirement. Something to think about. I would rather enhance some positions from the inside, than hire from outside. Questions?" There always were. Nobody ever seemed to be afraid to ask. Sandesh figured that meant he was doing things right.

When he went into his review, the first thing Carver said was, "Mr. Prasad, you've been with the firm for six years now. At what point did you decide we were worth saving?"

That was not what Sandesh had expected. Fortunately, he'd had a lot of experience in hiding his reactions, so all Carver saw was a blink. Then, "This firm really only had three major problems. I'm sure you're aware that when we made our deal this summer, I had an exit strategy. But you all have dealt with me and with the issues in good faith. You are doing the work that will make this a truly outstanding firm. I believed the potential was here, or I would not have stayed when the last promotion wasn't compensated." He looked around the table. Everyone on the management committee had been in that position at least as long as he'd been with the firm. "And I want to say thank you. Thank you for your willingness to take some big chances. I hope the results speak for themselves."

"Yes, they do." Carver tapped a sheet of paper in front of him. "The committee is prepared to offer you an additional ten percent. Do you have a counter-suggestion?"

"I do," Sandesh said instantly. "Let's spend some of that on a company event, here in the office, a Friday afternoon. Spouses and significant others included. Sometime in January, when everyone's not swamped with holiday stuff and year-end stuff. Maybe the Friday before the Martin Luther King Jr. holiday."

The managing partners all looked around, exchanging glances and nods. The previous year, Darlene had arranged (and Sandesh had executed) an off-site holiday party for firm members only, on a Friday night. Even the attorneys had thought that made for a long day. Carver said, "That appears to meet with approval. Make it so. And how about catering breakfast for the staff on the last business day before Thanksgiving and Christmas."

Sandesh smiled. "Great idea. Oh, and that reminds me, Sherlyn has offered to be on call for November twenty-third and December twenty-fourth. She says her family is taking their vacation from the day after Christmas, so she'll be in town those days if anyone needs help."

"Terrific. I know there are a couple of active cases. Well, is there anything else you'd like to tell us?"

"Yes. I'm getting married New Year's Day and will be out of the office for the rest of that week. But I can be reached in case of an emergency."

"I would expect nothing less, Mr. Prasad. Congratulations."

Sandesh went back to his office and stripped off his suit jacket, hanging it on the back of his door. He went to stand at the window, looking out at the plaza, trying to get his head around everything that had happened in the last eleven months. He picked up his cell phone and sent a text: *Hi beautiful, I just turned down a ten percent raise*

Tasha's answer came back an hour later, during her regular lunch break: *What did you shake them down for instead?*

*LOL on-site fiesta in January, spouses etc included. So everyone will finally get to know what really makes my life worth living, which would be you. I love you*

*I love you too. Have you heard from Tanith about the premiere?*

*No! And you know I didn't nag her about the rough cut but Imma get pestering*

*You do that baby, nobody can pester like you can*

*And speaking of which, we need to practice this weekend. Like, a lot*

*Yes we do. I'll see if Matthew wants to take Theo somewhere. Did I tell you he's coming over for Thanksgiving dinner?*

*Yes you did. I'll make the pies*

*Send me your requirements so I can get to the supermarket before every last fool in L.A. is in there all desperate*

*Yes ma'am. See you at home, love you, XOX*

*XOX*

They had the wedding dance almost ready, with a month still to go. Everything else was in place, too. Because of the movie premiere, Andy and Victor were staying in Los Angeles through December. Rory was on board to officiate, and invitations had gone out.

The senior Prasads had agreed to come out for Christmas and the entire following week. Sandesh couldn't quite believe it, especially the part about that epic dance. Vince took video on the Sunday before Thanksgiving, and even Sandesh thought it looked respectable.

"It's better than respectable," Vince said, "and by the time you do it for real you'll have it cold. Really excellent work, especially considering this is your first experience with choreography. You should know my wife is bound to try to get you to do something with the Cabaret."

"Whatever Tasha wants to do, I will do," Sandesh said. "But you should know I am running and hiding on the inside." Vince laughed and sent them home.

Tasha had gone to the Underground Cabaret's preferred costume guy for a wedding dress she could dance in. It was going to be a knee-length wrap in purple stretch velvet with elaborate Indian-style decorations. Sandesh already had his dance tux underway too. She couldn't decide what to wear for the premiere, though. He was planning to wear his charcoal dance suit for that. *I should wear green again*, she thought, because she wanted him to wear that emerald ring. The flapper dress wasn't quite right. She was standing in the closet on the Saturday after Thanksgiving, looking through all her dresses, thinking she needed to thin out the collection again, when her phone buzzed. She picked it up. "Hey Anya! What's up?"

"Planning what to wear to the premiere. What are you doing?"

"That same thing, and I have no idea. What are *you* doing?"

"I was thinking about that Twenties dress I had on in the picture Andy took at Cicada." It was a sleeveless scoop-neck design in blush chiffon with a dropped waist and car-wash hem, covered with intricate sequin and bead embroidery.

"Oh my lord that dress is so gorgeous. And you wore that in the movie, didn't you?"

"Yeah, for the Paris scene. Guess I should wear that. Okay, problem solved. So what about you?" Anya had already checked in with the others from the cabaret number. Everyone was doing something special; most were going with vintage styles. "Vicky's in her pantsuit from the movie. Michelle's wearing her wedding dress, very Fifties glam. Kelli's getting one that style too. Paula's wearing this Sixties pencil dress Kristine made her for Rory and Dana's wedding. Alison's doing a copy of a Ginger Rogers thing, the two-tone one from Gay Divorcée, but tea-length."

"Oh man, you're all going to look so perfect." Tasha sighed. "Everything I have is either too costume-y or too casual. I mean, movie premiere. I need a serious dress." She didn't exactly want to stand out in the crowd, but she definitely wanted to look like she belonged there. "I wanted to go Twenties, but this flapper dress I have is not up to the red carpet."

"You know Kristine, she made that dress for me in like a week. I mean it took another week for the embellishment, but still. Since they already have your stats I bet she could run one up for you."

"That's … kind of genius. Thanks, Anya, I'm going to give her a call. What's my brother wearing?"

"He's wearing that gray suit he proposed in. It'll go good with my dress. Don't forget shoes."

"Girl, I have *all* the shoes, don't you worry." Anya laughed; Tasha knew she also had all the shoes. "Gotta get this rolling. Give Terry a kiss for me." Anya said she would and they disconnected. Tasha went to find Sandesh's ring and take a picture of it with her phone. Composed an email to Matsumoto Dancewear, attached the picture, and sent it off, hoping they could work a miracle.

Kristine replied a few hours later with a picture of a green fabric that perfectly matched the emerald, printed on the selvage with an Art Deco design in metallic gold. Also attached was a full-color sketch of a dress. The front view showed a sleeveless, body-skimming V-neck with an asymmetrical hem featuring the printed design. The back view revealed a V-cut plunging to the waist, with a fan of gold cord to secure the opening and highlight the bare skin below. The design definitely said "1920s" but would make the most of Tasha's curvaceous figure. *You need a long beaded necklace*, Kristine wrote. *Lariat style. Contact Lucy!*

Tasha wrote back with *Yes please love it and will do!* Then she called Sandesh, who was over at the Sleeping Beauty talking about the renovation with Andy and Paige. He picked up right away. "Everything okay?"

"Everything's fine, Theo is doing this homework I can't even believe they assigned, but I'm told I need a necklace for this premiere. How much can I spend?"

"Whatever it takes. Are you wearing green?"

She laughed "Yes. How did you know?"

"Just hoping. Was thinking back to Cicada."

"That was a big night," she said softly, smiling now. "I'm going to call Lucy. Maybe she'll have something already made up that will work."

He made a *pfft* sound. "Get emeralds." She could tell he was smiling too.

"Big spender. I'll see you later."

"Love you."

"Love you too." She disconnected and went to their shared contacts to look up Lucy's business number, then dialed again.

The call was answered on the second ring. "Rococo, this is Lucy, how can I help you?"

"Hi Lucy, this is Tasha Jefferson from the whole Tanith movie thing."

"Hi Tasha! Let me guess. Premiere, dressing up, jewelry."

"I'm betting you've had a lot of calls about this."

"You could say that. But my helpers here are ready to make you anything we don't already have, it won't take any time. What are you looking for?"

"Emerald green. Doesn't have to be the real thing. Kristine said a lariat, to go with a V-neck Twenties-style dress in emerald green and gold."

"If we *have* the real thing, do you *want* the real thing?"

"Well, Sandesh said so. But he's apt to spoil me."

Lucy laughed. "Tell you what, I'll see what we've got and send you a text with an estimate for the real thing versus imitation. Right?"

"Perfect, thanks. I'll let you get to it." Tasha disconnected again and went to check on her boy. He was flat on his back on his bed, staring at the ceiling. "You okay, baby?" He turned his head with an expression that said a lot about homework assigned over holidays. "Let me take a look." She flipped through the workbook on his desk. "You're almost done! What a hard worker. Tell you what, that's enough for today. You want to go someplace?"

He perked up. "Can we go to the beach?"

"We absolutely can. Get yourself ready." She sent a quick note to Sandesh to let him know where they were going, and then headed out through holiday-shopping traffic to Santa Monica. They didn't start home until after dark. Theo was full of beach food, their sneakers were full of sand, and they both were highly satisfied with the afternoon. Tasha had received Lucy's estimates and (with only a slight tremor) given her the go-ahead for the real emerald version of the necklace. She'd also done a little early holiday shopping of her own, dropping into Penzey's for a custom box of Indian spices for Sandesh. "Was that what you needed, baby?"

"Yes. Thanks Mom."

"You are welcome. It was nice to have an afternoon out like that. I know this year has been kind of crazy. You've had a lot of adjusting to do. Everything okay?"

"It's good. Thanksgiving was good."

"It was, wasn't it? It'll be nice when we're all living in the same place, won't it?"

"I told my friend at school and he said he wishes his parents were friends. We're lucky, aren't we?"

"Yes, honey, we are." *So very lucky*, she thought then, and again when they went into the apartment and saw Sandesh lounging on the couch, television tuned to DIY, looking over at them with those dreamy eyes and that happy smile.

"Hi there," he said. "Have fun at the beach?"

"It was good," Theo said. "I'm full of nachos." He took off his shoes and socks, producing a small sand dune on the kitchen floor, then went and plopped down in front of the TV, doing one of the stretches Sandesh had shown him.

Sandesh leaned over and rumpled his hair. "Then I guess we're on our own for dinner, huh?" He stood up and joined Tasha in the kitchen. "What do you think, Spare Tire?"

"You could convince me." She leaned against him, tipping her head back for a kiss. "Anything I should know about the renovation?"

"HVAC work is permitted and the infrastructure is in. Roofers are coming next week to strip off the old shingles, do whatever repairs are needed, and get the first layer of stuff up so the artsy guy can come and do his thing. That's going to take a while. Reframing in January, the rest of the plumbing and electrical in February. They're not pushing the schedule since they're going to be in and out of town till the beginning of March." Andy and Victor were going out on a promotional tour for the international release of Tanith's movie. "I hear there's already some buzz about it in Argentina."

"Well, there would be, wouldn't there?" Tasha stepped away to get the takeout menu. They took a few minutes to make their choices and call in the order. "I've got my whole premiere look organized. Kristine said I can go get the dress fitted next weekend."

"Can't wait to see it," he said, kissing her again. "I know you'll be beautiful. You always are."

"So are you." She leaned on him again. He wrapped his arms around her. "Why does it feel like we're about to have an anniversary?"

"Well, we kind of are." The premiere was exactly one year from that momentous night at the mall. "But then, we've had a few other significant days. After we're married, we can wrap all of them into that one date."

"That works." They stayed there, hugging, not even talking, until the delivery guy hit the buzzer downstairs. After he'd come and gone Tasha said, "I'd better get these shoes off so I can clean up the sand dune." Sandesh went to find the dustpan.

December 2018

They arrived at the red carpet in a six-door livery SUV with Terry and Anya, Anya's mother Yulia and her stepfather Benjamin. There was a line of shiny black vehicles moving down Broadway in downtown L.A., and theirs was toward the end. Even the guild interns had been invited, and Sandesh had heard that all of them were coming together, with their dates, in a stretch limo. "That looks so dope," he said, leaning out the open window to take a phone picture of the printed marquee wrapped over the Million Dollar Theater's regular marquee. It read THE GHOST OF CARLOS GARDEL with WORLD PREMIERE underneath. "Oh wow, there's all these posters on the barrier, all six of the co-stars, they're like Bogie and Bacall, and there's a mob of press, holy cow."

"Shut up," Anya said, "you're making me nervous."

"*You?* I don't believe it." He closed the window, then turned to smile at her. "None of them will be paying attention to us. Andy and Victor are the last of the stars, once they get inside I'll bet the press will poof."

Tasha thought *They'll be paying attention to you*, because he looked – in her opinion – every bit as good as any of the stars, and possibly better. She said, "Are they out there yet?" Sandesh opened the window again and stuck his head out. They'd advanced a couple of car lengths.

"Oh wait, yup, there they are. They're talking to people, because of course they are." He held up his phone again to take another picture. "Oh my God they're dancing."

"Take video!" said Anya and Tasha together. Sandesh obliged, zooming in as close as he could. Their car wasn't moving, so he kept the recorder on until Andy and Victor stopped dancing, waved to the press, and went inside the theater.

"Okay, they're in. We'll be up there pretty soon. Everybody ready?"

"This is surreal," said Terry. "No other word."

Tasha turned on the seat so she could give him her hand. "I agree. Who would have thought we'd be about to walk down a red carpet? And lookin' *fly* if I do say so myself." Everyone laughed.

"All three of our ladies look incredible," Sandesh said. "We are three lucky guys." Benjamin and Terry agreed. Tasha's dress was made of some kind of lightweight slippery fabric. The emerald-bead lariat necklace ended in a double tassel tipped with gold. She had a matching feathery ornament in her hair, bejeweled gold tango shoes, and a thin line of gold under each eye. Even Theo had been impressed.

Their vehicle came to a full stop and a valet opened each of the back doors on the red-carpet side. Sandesh and Terry stepped out, giving their hands to Tasha and Anya, then making way for Benjamin to slide out and help Yulia. The six of them proceeded up the red carpet, dazzled by camera lights, smiling and waving as instructed. A few people shouted "Tasha!" or "Anya!" They stopped for a few seconds to allow for pictures. Sandesh and Terry stood close, but out of the way. They glanced at each other with amusement. Yulia was laughing with Benjamin behind them.

"Oh my God they knew who we were!" Tasha said when they got inside. It was all she could do not to squeal. Anya was giggling, which was cracking Terry up. "Lord have mercy. Let's go on in." They went down to the front of the auditorium, where there were swag bags on one table and glasses of champagne on another, managing to identify and greet most of the other featured dancers as well as the stars. Vicky was pacing, six feet tall in her white halter-top pantsuit and tango shoes, burning off some nerves. She and Tomás were going to perform before the screening. Sandesh went up and said, "Hi Vicky, ready for your thing?"

"As ready as we'll ever be."

"Do you have any family here tonight?"

"No, my whole family's back in New York. I've been told they're all going to see the thing when it opens over there. Which means the entire theater will be full of my sisters and cousins and aunts."

"I know they'll love it. You're great in it."

"I still can hardly believe I actually *am* in it," she said. "Surreal."

"That's what Terry said. We get to video your thing, right?"

"Oh most definitely. Video, post, tweet, whatever. Blow it up, that's what the boss says."

"Where is she, anyway?"

"Hiding out in the fourth row." Vicky pointed. Sandesh turned to look. Tanith was there beside Lieutenant Palacio. He waved until Tanith noticed and waved back. She looked much more stressed-out than he would have expected. He did a 'what gives' thing and she hunched her shoulders, shaking her head. He laughed. "Yeah, you would think at this point she'd be pretty chill. I'll make sure she gets some more champagne before the Q&A."

"But speaking of champagne," Sandesh said, "we'd better get some and find a seat or two. Do I say 'break a leg' now?"

"You can, but I wish you wouldn't. That is some sick shit. By the way, your date looks spectacular." She grinned at him and went to find her wife. Sandesh went to find his fiancée, who did in fact look spectacular, and they were pointed to a pair of seats. Not too much later, the lights flickered a warning, and then an announcer came on over the PA to introduce Vicky and Tomás. They were, as Sandesh expected, show-stoppingly good, so it was just as well they were the whole show. Then one of the stars of Andy and Victor's TV show came on to introduce the film, and finally it was time.

Not much had been changed from the rough cut; only the titles were noticeably different. Sandesh and Tasha held hands and watched as if it were the first time. He knew he was biased, so he tried to be objective, but he was too close to it. He loved the whole thing, everyone in it, and everyone involved with it. Even those guild interns. "I cannot believe I was lucky enough to fall into this," he said at the end, when he and Tasha were standing, applauding with everyone else. "What an incredible experience."

“I know,” she said. “I would do any damn thing that woman wants me to.” He knew she meant Tanith, and he suddenly flashed back to what Tanith had said in July, about a project for five women. *Don’t say anything*, he thought, smiling to himself. *Not yet*.

There was still the Q&A, which didn’t start until all six co-stars and Tanith had been fortified with drinks and then herded onstage. At the end of that, the stars let themselves be talked into dancing the six-way ‘La Cumparsita,’ taking another set of bows to thunderous applause. And then, at last, it was over. The ticketed audience slowly moved out of the theater, a few lingering to try and have a word – or get a selfie – with one or another of the stars. Then the extras and the crew headed out, per arrangement, followed by the featured dancers, and finally by the director and the stars. The queue of shiny black cars formed up again to take everyone home.

It was quiet in the SUV on the way back to Mid City. They were all going to see each other again soon, at Sandesh and Tasha’s wedding. So when they got to the Miracle Mile, there was an exchange of kisses and handshakes, and then it was into the building, and up to the apartment, still feeling like this might all be a sweet and impossible dream.

But Theo was conked out on the couch and the sitter was watching ‘Ratatouille’ by herself, and that was just as sweet.

New Year’s Day, 2019

Tasha spent the night before the wedding at Terry and Anya’s house. It wasn’t so much a nod to tradition, or superstition, as a concession to nerves. She knew that getting ready for the wedding in the same place at the same time as Sandesh, with Theo right there, was going to be a little much. The whole week had been a little much. The whole *month* had been a little much. They'd had one night off. Matthew had taken Theo on what should have been her weekend, keeping him overnight on the Sunday so she and Sandesh could go on a date, to the Underground Cabaret's holiday show. Aside from that, nothing had been normal.

Between the premiere, practicing that insanely long wedding dance, working with Andy on the relatively minor arrangements needed for the wedding, the regular job, going to get their license, and of course meeting the parents, Tasha had to concede her brain was fried.

Anya had a gig with Ricky on New Year's Eve. Terry was working at Chrome. Tasha had the house to herself, and it was just what she needed. She watched the video from their last practice. Accepted that it was good. Tried on the purple velvet dress again, with the same bejeweled gold shoes she'd worn for the premiere, and that was good too. Her friend Maria was coming to do her hair and makeup the next day, before they all went over to the Faux Chateau. She set everything ready, then got into her PJs, put on some quiet music, took a sleep aid, and spent some time down on the floor stretching. She was in bed before midnight, and asleep long before Terry or Anya got home.

The smell of coffee woke her up. She checked her phone. There was a text from Sandesh: *Missed you last night. Can't wait to see you. I love you*

She took her time composing a reply. *Hi baby. Can you believe it's our wedding day? This whole year has been unbelievable. I watched our practice last night. You look amazing. You ARE amazing. I love you and can't wait to marry you*

His answer came back right away: *Thank you for not walking out on me at CPK*

*Thank you for kissing me*

*I'll never stop kissing you. We'll be a million years old and you'll be like get off me*

*LOL never happen. Did our boy behave last night?*

*He is taking this very seriously. And FYI my parents have already called twice, OMG*

*I thought Lochan was on parent detail*

*HE IS he sucks at it*

After meeting the parents, Tasha had some sympathy for Lochan. They meant well, bless their hearts. *LOL again but honey, I smell coffee, and there are things to do. I will see you soon. I love you*

*I love you too. Make sure Terry drives over, that Anya is a menace*

*LOL XOX.* She put down the phone because she could have kept texting him all day, and that wasn't going to get her ready.

Sandesh knew exactly what Tasha was wearing, he knew approximately when she'd be arriving, and he knew she wanted to do this. He was still flat-out terrified that she would decide this was a bad idea, and that he'd be standing there waiting until a call came saying 'what were we thinking, sorry but no.' He couldn't tell anybody. He couldn't even hint at it. His parents were less than no help – they were still acting like they didn't recognize him - and Lochan was fully occupied running things. He at least had understood, from one look, that his brother's ability to cope was at a historic low. He basically parked Sandesh out of the way and got on with it.

It wasn't until Anya came through the kitchen door saying "Let's get this show on the road" that Sandesh thought it might really be happening. The plan was to have them start for the Faux Chateau after all the guests had arrived. The residences were only ten minutes apart on a holiday. So if Anya was here, everyone else was here, and if anything was wrong she would have come through the door saying "You're fucked." He took a deep breath and tried to relax on the exhale.

Lochan came in after Anya. "Everybody's here. The music's started. Are you ready to come outside?"

Sandesh took another deep breath and said, "Yes." He followed Lochan out, aware that Andy and Victor were behind him. Vicky and Sharon were already outside, along with the amazingly large number of old and new friends they'd managed to squeeze into the backyard. There was a purple carpet runner, thickly scattered with marigold petals, laid from the patio to the back gate. The patio was covered with a wooden dance floor. Tango music was playing.

Everyone in the world was staring at him. He didn't even try to smile, just waved, then looked for Rory. She was standing next to Lochan, looking as though she might crack up. She did a 'what's your problem' thing with her face and hands; Sandesh nearly laughed. Anya, standing beside him, said, "That's better," and patted his back. She none-too-gently steered him into position. Then the music changed to 'Libertango,' the back gate opened, and Tasha came through, looking absolutely stunning, holding Terry's arm. They started up the path to the patio.

To the extent that Tasha was thinking, she was thinking *he is absolutely stunning*. She tried to keep her gaze locked on his, because everyone in the world was standing there staring at her. "This is why brides have veils," she murmured to Terry. "Lord have mercy."

He laid his free hand over hers on his arm. "Almost there." His deep voice was amused, but she knew he understood. When they finally reached the patio, before Terry gave her hand to Sandesh, he leaned in to kiss her cheek and remind her to breathe. She did that, then swallowed, closing her eyes for a second. When she opened them again Sandesh was still there, his beautiful eyes full of such profound love that she almost started crying.

The music faded out and Rory said, "Dearly beloved!" She went into the short version of the Sandesh-and-Tasha story they'd provided, and then extemporized on the essential insanity of working on a movie while blending a family. Tasha sort-of heard it. She sort-of heard the guests laugh at appropriate moments. Then, finally, the important part started. Like almost everyone else she knew, they'd written their own version of the vows. They both had wet eyes after saying "I do."

Then Sandesh had her left hand in both of his, gently removing the engagement ring and replacing it with a gold band set with three sizable diamonds. She looked up at his face, startled. "For you, and me, and Theo," he said softly. He slid the enameled ring back in place and lifted her hand to his lips.

Theo stepped up beside Tasha and carefully put something in her right hand. "Thank you sweetheart," she said. She took Sandesh's left hand and put the plain gold band on his finger. It looked so right there. "May the circle be unbroken."

"Amen," he said.

Rory said, "I think it's time you kissed the bride," and he did.

A few minutes later, they were being congratulated, hugged, and kissed by what seemed like hundreds of people, though it surely wasn't. Tasha could finally appreciate the gorgeous flowers – gold and purple and hot pink – on pedestals at the corners of the patio. Someone put a glass of champagne in her hand. When she turned her head, Sandesh was smiling at her, a glass in his own hand. "We're really married."

She tapped hers to it. "Yes, honey, we really are. Here's to us." They both drank. "I'm inclined to think this is the best wine I've ever had. It might be André for all I know." Sandesh laughed and kissed her again. "When are we doing this dance?"

"Imminently. Need anything before we tell Andy to cue the music?"

"Yes, I'm going to go pee. Hold this." She handed him the champagne glass, listening to him laugh again as she walked away. *That man is going to be fun for the rest of my life.* She passed Victor in the kitchen, and detoured to give him a hug. Sharon was coming through from the other side of the duplex; she got a hug too.

Sandesh's mother Lakshmi was coming out of the bathroom. She put her hands on Tasha's arms and said, "You've made our son so happy. Thank you," and kissed her cheek.

"He's made me happy too. Thank you for being here today," Tasha managed. "We're about to do our dance."

"Oh! I'll tell Agastya, we'll find seats." She patted Tasha's arm before hurrying to the back door.

Tasha went into the bathroom, closed the door and locked it. "Six minutes," she told herself. "That ain't nothing." She giggled, a little hysterically, while she took care of business. Then she checked herself out in the full-length mirror on the back of the door. "Not bad for going on thirty-nine," she decided. She unlocked the door and went out.

Sandesh was there on the patio, saying something to Andy. They both turned to look at Tasha when she stepped outside. Andy raised his eyebrows. "Ready?"

"First I have to say thank you. I love you. You and Victor are wonderful. This whole thing is wonderful." He was blushing a little. She kissed his cheek. "Yes, I'm ready." He nodded and stepped off the patio, signaling someone. She and Sandesh stood there, hand in hand, waiting while people quickly took their seats.

Then Vince stepped up on the patio beside them. "Hi everybody. What you are about to see is entirely my fault. Nobody should have to do this for a wedding dance. These two are going to blow you away. When it's over, I'll tell you a secret." He glanced over at Sandesh, collected a nod of readiness, and stepped down from the patio.

They went to their starting position and Sandesh took Tasha into the close embrace as the music began. The first passage was deceptively simple; then the piano came in and things got dramatic. There was applause. And then the romantic theme began, and Tasha stopped noticing anything but the magic of dancing with Sandesh. When they hit their final position, she was dimly aware that their guests were making a lot of noise. Applause, whistles, and at least one 'woo-hoo.' Sandesh set her back on her feet and kissed her. Otherwise, they didn't move.

"What did you think?" Vince said, inviting another round of applause. "Yeah, me too. Okay, so here's the crazy part. Until about eight months ago, neither of them knew any tango. I would like to be able to take all the credit, but I really can't. Everybody got some more champagne?" He raised his glass. "To Sandesh and Tasha."

The guests all raised their glasses too. "To Sandesh and Tasha!"

"Here's to us, baby," Tasha said, because someone had handed them fresh glasses. "I love you. Even though you waited nine years to kiss me."

"I'm never going to hear the end of that, am I? I love you too," he said, and kissed her again.

THE END

*If you enjoyed A FEW KISSES AGO, please consider leaving a positive rating or review. It really helps! Thanks for reading.*

*Want more?*

*James & Silvia's story is **VINTAGE**, or read the story of Tanith's movie in*

***THE GHOST OF CARLOS GARDEL.***

*Available at Amazon*

*****

About the Author

Alexandra Caluen lives in a small purple house with her husband, a bottle of Laphroaig, a lot of books, and nine pairs of ballroom shoes. She works in patent law and has enough hair for three people.

www.thelastories.com

www.ingramcontent.com/pod-product-compliance
Lightning Source LLC
La Vergne TN
LVHW041112080826
845145LV00007B/1783

*9781733721141*